Without a backward look, a tall, dark-haired stranger jumped in the front seat and put the car in gear as I sat frozen with shock. I didn't know whether to hope he was a simple car thief and would drop me off, with luggage, at the next taxi stand, or an escaping criminal who didn't need a hostage.

"Get down!" the man shouted.

I did. The car swerved around corners to the accompaniment of horns and brakes, and probably shouts, too, though I couldn't hear them over the pounding of my heart.

The horns and screeches died down, and I guessed we had made the backroads, even though we hadn't slowed. That sort of ruled out the simple thief theory. All I could see from my position were treetops and darkening sky.

And then the back windshield exploded. It rained down pieces of glass on me, and the man swore, almost under his breath. Outside, a car passed us and the back side window shattered.

I had given up hope when the man braked the car so hard it spun completely around. "Get out!" he shouted. "Run! Hide!"

CATCH UP ON THE BEST IN CONTEMPORARY FICTION FROM ZEBRA BOOKS!

LOVE AFFAIR (2181, $4.50)
by Syrell Rogovin Leahy
A poignant, supremely romantic story of an innocent young woman with a tragic past on her own in New York, and the seasoned newspaper reporter who vows to protect her from the harsh truths of the big city with his experience—and his love.

ROOMMATES (2156, $4.50)
by Katherine Stone
No one could have prepared Carrie for the monumental changes she would face when she met her new circle of friends at Stanford University. For once their lives intertwined and became woven into the tapestry of the times, they would never be the same.

MARITAL AFFAIRS (2033, $4.50)
by Sharleen Cooper Cohen
Everything the golden couple Liza and Jason Greene touched was charmed—except their marriage. And when Jason's thirst for glory led him to infidelity, Liza struck back in the only way possible.

RICH IS BEST (1924, $4.50)
by Julie Ellis
From Palm Springs to Paris, from Monte Carlo to New York City, wealthy and powerful Diane Carstairs plays a ruthless game, living a life on the edge between danger and decadence. But when caught in a battle for the unobtainable, she gambles with the only thing she owns that she cannot control—her heart.

THE FLOWER GARDEN (1396, $3.95)
by Margaret Pemberton
Born and bred in the opulent world of political high society, Nancy Leigh flees from her politician husband to the exotic island of Madeira. Irresistibly drawn to the arms of Ramon Sanford, the son of her father's deadliest enemy, Nancy is forced to make a dangerous choice between her family's honor and her heart's most fervent desire!

Available wherever paperbacks are sold, or order direct from the Publisher. Send cover price plus 50¢ per copy for mailing and handling to Zebra Books, Dept. 2708, 475 Park Avenue South, New York, N.Y. 10016. Residents of New York, New Jersey and Pennsylvania must include sales tax. DO NOT SEND CASH.

DEADLY IMPULSE

CAROLYN B. MASON

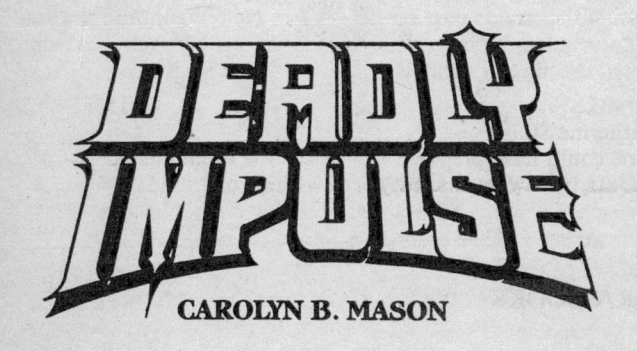

**ZEBRA BOOKS
KENSINGTON PUBLISHING CORP.**

For Dan, Mary and Cathy

ZEBRA BOOKS

are published by

Kensington Publishing Corp.
475 Park Avenue South
New York, NY 10016

Copyright © 1989 by Carolyn B. Mason

All rights reserved. No part of this book may be reproduced in any form or by any means without the prior written consent of the Publisher, excepting brief quotes used in reviews.

First printing: July, 1989

Printed in the United States of America

Chapter 1

Roger accepted his drink from the stewardess and watched her move down the aisle. He leaned back and contemplated his scotch and water with a sigh of contentment. "If you have to travel, fly," he said. "And if you have to fly, fly first class."

I shook my head to blot out the memory. "I hate flying," I muttered.

"Eh? What's that?"

I had startled the man in the airline seat beside me from his reverie, just as he startled me from mine.

"I said, 'I hate to fly.'"

"Ah. Well, at least you're flying first class." He had a lovely English accent that reminded me of Sherlock Holmes.

"Yes, that's what Roger would have said."

"Roger?"

"My husband."

He nodded in contemplation of this. I judged him to be about twenty-seven, a few years younger than myself. We'd sat through most of the ten-hour flight from Houston to London without speaking, though he had made several friendly overtures. I hadn't felt like talking. He was a nice man, good-looking and well-mannered, but I just hadn't felt like talking.

5

"Are you meeting your husband in London?"

Maybe, I thought. Maybe I'll walk through a cold cemetery and meet him one last time. "Roger's dead," I told him. "I'm a widow."

"Oh." He shifted in his seat, finding his position a little uncomfortable. "I'm sorry. I didn't mean to pry."

"It's all right. I don't feel pried upon. It's been two years since Roger died. I like to think I'm getting used to it."

He took a sip of his tea, and I could see him building up to another attempt at polite conversation. "Going to London on holiday?"

"Well, yes, I guess so," I answered. I looked out of the window, down at England, just now appearing underneath the plane. "But maybe . . . I mean . . ." I let out that breath and took another. "I really don't know why I'm here," I said softly, to myself. "I didn't really want to come just now, but . . ."

When I remembered to look across at him again, I saw that he was watching me intently, puzzled concern on his face. Where are your manners, Valerie Douglas, I demanded of myself. Since Roger died I've been in a steady decline, myself answered as the pilot came on the intercom announcing our imminent arrival at Gatwick Airport.

I turned back to the window. Roger and I were married for five years, during which he took care of everything and never made mistakes. Life was easy and ordered in the precise detailed way that appeals to bankers, if not to haphazard types like me. I had loved Roger, though, despite his maddening perfection, and he had loved me despite my approximate housekeeping. When he died, everything he had so carefully plotted out fell apart, and that's why I hated him. Mortality might have been his only flaw, but it was a fatal one.

Overhead, I could see clouds approaching as our plane braked to a stop. Roger had said it was always raining in England, but then he'd been dead for two years, after all. Somehow I had hoped the climate had improved in the interim. Not that it mattered, I assured myself. I had glimpsed the green hills beyond the airport. England was scenic. People came here for vacations, to have a good time. Roger had loved London. I would, too.

"I beg your pardon?" I said to the young man beside me.

"I said, 'Is someone meeting you?' We could share a cab if you'd like."

"No, thank you. I mean, yes, someone will be meeting me. But thank you for the offer."

He seemed reluctant to go. "Well, I hope you enjoy your stay."

"Thank you, I'm sure I will." But of course, I wasn't sure. I would much rather have been at home. Spring is pleasant in Houston.

The man hesitated for a few seconds more and then joined the exodus. Most of the other passengers in my section were grappling with unwieldy bags and boxes stuffed with America's best discount-store technology, and I sat patiently by the window, letting them fight each other for exit space in the aisles. There would be relatives waiting for them: mothers, fathers, children, sisters, brothers, wives and husbands. Perhaps Nicola would be waiting for me, but probably not. It was morning here, and Nickie's working day wouldn't be over until evening.

I had lines to get through when I did get off of the plane, and stamps to get on my virgin passport, and I tried to be cheerful about it all, even though I only understood about half of what was said to me. Roger had prepared me for that, though. He'd said that American and English aren't the same language. Chalk up another one for Roger.

Coming at last into the main lobby with one suitcase in hand and the other rolling behind me on a leash, I was temporarily relieved to find a man holding a placard saying, "Douglas." Then I wondered if I was the right Douglas. The man looked annoyed when I asked him if he was waiting for *Valerie* Douglas, but he admitted he was (I think) and took my bags. Putting the big one in the trunk of his tiny car took a lot more out of him than it would have me, but I didn't offer to help. Roger had told me that England was still pretty chauvinistic.

But Roger had told me *nothing* to prepare me for English driving. The man's main goal seemed to be arriving first at the finish line of each stop light and leaving first after the light changed, as if one or two precious seconds might make the difference between a profitable day and bankruptcy. Even less reassuring was the realization that the other drivers felt exactly the same way. We went through several traffic circles where raw courage seemed to be the entry fee before I decided to just shut my eyes. Relaxing rides through verdant countryside and quaint villages would obviously have to wait.

With my eyes closed while we were moving, the ride was much more pleasant. I had bought a London guidebook before leaving home, and knew at least approximately where we were going, but we seemed to be zigzagging to get there. I dared not mention this to the driver, however, afraid he would take it as an indication that I was in a hurry. I had no desire to find out how English drivers behaved when they were in a hurry.

He must have looked in the rearview mirror and seen my eyes squeezed shut, because he asked me, without any disapproval at all, if I was all right. Well, actually what he said was, "Oy! You all right, madam?"

"Yes! Yes, I'm fine," I said, trying to sound confident.

" 'Ere," he said, "you wanta cuppa?"

Cuppa, cuppa, I pressed my memory, what is—? Had Roger . . . ?

"Tea," he answered. "A cuppa tea."

"No," I said. "I don't drink tea. I mean," I added hastily, not wanting to sound ungrateful for his offer, "actually, I . . ."

"Coca-Cola. That's what you Americans like, innit? That's all right, luv, I'll just pop in to the shop ahead for you. I could do with a pack of fags meself."

I nodded. I had aspirins in my purse, thank God, to fend off an already approaching headache that could only get worse if he started to smoke. And English fags were cigarettes, far less appealing to me, in fact, than American fags. The consumption of more caffeine with the aspirin couldn't hurt, though I was beginning to doubt whether or not it would help my grogginess.

He pulled in and parked in an incredibly small spot several yards past the shop, and I took the opportunity to look around without having to suppress gasps. The shop, "J. Wentworth, Tobacconist," was sandwiched between a real-estate office and a betting shop. On the other side of the street were a pub, The Hawk and Dove, a dry cleaner's and several unmarked entrances that might have been apartments, although I couldn't imagine why anyone would want to live on such a busy street. But Roger had said that England would seem crowded at first.

Certainly there were homes behind the commercial frontage, for I could see small houses and postage-stamp lawns and gardens down tiny sidestreets. This certainly wasn't Nicola's neighborhood, but it was interesting, all the same. The locals seemed happy enough. Two ladies pushing young children in strollers met outside the pub and stopped for a shared smile and small talk, a man lingered outside the real-estate office to read the ads before going into the betting shop, and someone made a mad dash across the street, causing brakes to screech and horns to honk, and me to drop the guidebook I'd been holding.

I bent down to pick it up, and the driver got back in the car. Except that it wasn't the driver I had started to trust with my life and my possessions. This new man was taller, dark-haired, wearing a worn leather jacket and in much more of a hurry. Without a backward look, he put the car in gear and tore off down the street, and I forgot completely about my headache.

I'm not one of those people who think well in emergencies. First of all, it takes me longer to realize that I'm in an emergency, and then it takes a very long time for me to calm down enough to think at all. Meanwhile I just freeze with my mouth hanging open, and that was my exact position when the man looked in the rearview mirror and saw me.

"Bloody hell," he muttered, quite distinctly.

I know a curse when I hear one. I didn't know whether to hope he was a simple car thief and would drop me off, with luggage, at the next taxi stand, or an escaping criminal with an aversion to violence who didn't need a hostage. I kept trying to come up with an explanation that allowed me and my luggage to survive. What would Roger have done and why wasn't the bastard here to do it?

"Get down!" the man shouted.

I did. I squeezed myself into the narrow space between the back seat and the back of the front seat and pretty much held my breath, allowing myself only shallow pants. The car swerved around corners and other cars to the accompaniment of horns and brakes, and probably shouts, too, though I couldn't hear them over the pounding of my heart. We slowed down once or twice, but we didn't completely stop. I wondered if I would have the courage to open the door and run if we did. I wondered if I would make it if I tried. Policemen didn't carry guns in England. Did criminals?

The horns and screeches died down, and I guessed we had made the back roads, even though we hadn't slowed. That sort of ruled out the simple car thief theory. All I could see from my position were treetops and darkening sky.

And then the back windshield exploded. It rained down pieces of glass on me, and the man swore, almost under his breath. Outside, a car passed us and the back side window shattered.

I had given up hope when the man braked the car so hard it spun completely around. "Get out!" he shouted.

"Run! Hide!"

I opened the door, struggled to stand up on two cramped legs, and fell to the ground. The man was yelling something about running again, and I managed to get to my feet and reach a low stone wall in a crouched run. I got over the wall, lost my footing, and rolled down a surprisingly steep slope. But the car sped away, and I was grateful for that.

Lying spread-eagled on my back, bruised and scared and fighting for breath, I was glad to be alive. Blessed peace enveloped me, and I could smell the scent of grass and flowers or weeds, I didn't care which. I looked up at the gray sky and smiled at the drizzle it produced to wash my face. After my fall and tumble, something should have hurt, but I couldn't feel anything except the gentle rain. I closed my eyes, and miraculously, blacked out.

I don't know how long I was unaware. Maybe I just lost track of a moment, or perhaps an hour had passed. I hadn't checked my watch before I lost consciousness, and it seemed like too much effort in the first groggy moments of awakening. I just wanted to get to Nickie's and into a dry bed and sleep. I might have drifted off again, but for the sounds of someone approaching, scrambling for footholds on the slope. Help, at last.

The man's face centered itself in my vision, and my spirits sank as low as my energy. He took one look at me and muttered, "Bloody hell!"

I closed my eyes and waited to die. But the man said gruffly, "Easy, love, I'm not going to hurt you."

I opened my eyes again and tried to blink back tears. He produced a handkerchief and carefully lifted the left side of my jacket. I hadn't noticed until then that it was soaked in blood. He pressed the cloth against the wound while I clenched my teeth to stifle a yelp.

"We've got to get you to a doctor," he said. "Can you stand?"

I doubted it, but the question became academic. He held me up until I found what little balance I retained, and we climbed the slope slowly. The journey seemed endless. I could feel a gun sandwiched between us beneath his jacket, probably still smoking.

Several times I stumbled, and he mostly dragged me, picking me up to carry me over the fence to the car while I tried not to moan. Roger hated moaning. He'd never let me feel sorry for myself in sickness or injury. But then, he'd never let me be injured. The man carefully brushed the pieces of glass off the seat of the car and lowered me onto it. I heard the door close and consciousness slipped away before he started the engine.

Once after that I almost woke up. I remember a brief glance at a white ceiling, and I could hear voices, although I couldn't quite follow the conversation. I tried to raise my head enough to see who was talking, but couldn't get any of my muscles to respond.

Someone must have noticed my stirring. A gentle voice said in my ear, "Just relax, Mrs. Douglas. You're all right now. Everything's going to be fine."

So I was alive. Still. I went back to sleep.

The second time I woke up more or less completely. I was thinking of a line: "Oh, to be in England, now that April's there." On the edge of sleep, I couldn't remember where I'd read it, and when my eyelids finally opened and focused, I found no evidence of spring at all, only the stark white of a hospital ceiling. Roger hadn't had any comments on English hospitals, not having had the experience I had. But a hospital is a hospital. I felt I could handle it even without coaching, until Mr. Bloody Hell came into view.

I made a small helpless moan, the sort of sound one makes at the beginning of a recurring nightmare.

He waved an official ID before my reluctant eyes. "I won't hurt you, Mrs. Douglas," he said. "I'm not as bad as I seem."

It took a moment for this to sink in. "You're not a criminal?"

"No."

"You're a policeman?"

"Yes, sort of."

I thought about that. I wasn't foolish enough to believe that all English policemen wore tall black hats and didn't carry guns; television news and terrorism had seen to that. Nor was I bothered by the lack of uniform. The worn brown leather jacket and corduroy slacks suited his dark hair and gray-blue eyes; Roger's weekend costume had been much the same. But policemen were supposed to announce themselves to innocent bystanders before the shooting began, and they definitely were not supposed to dump injured and scared people by the roadside and then come back to terrorize them again. I watched prime-time television, and this wasn't the way the script was supposed to go.

I eyed him with more than a little mistrust.

"I'm sorry," he said, not specifying exactly for what he was apologizing.

I looked for evidence in his face that he was sincere, but couldn't find any. He'd probably been sent by his boss to apologize to the nice lady and hope she doesn't file charges. If he had asked me next whether or not I would file charges, I wouldn't have had a ready answer.

That wasn't what he asked. He said, "Your medical expenses will be taken care of, of course."

Of course. I asked, "Where am I?"

"In a private hospital on the outskirts of London."

"Am I okay?"

His face softened. "You look better now than when I first saw you."

"Well, I don't *feel* much better. Getting shot hurts."

"I know." There was a half-smile on his face, and the private amusement annoyed me. "You were lucky it was a clean wound, though. You'll be up and about soon."

Up and about where, I wondered. God, what was I doing here, anyway? He stood patiently, as if waiting for me to reveal that, too.

I was tired. Too tired to carry more than my side of the conversation. Surely someone else could answer these questions without quite so much work on my part. I thought of Nicola.

"Where's Nicola?"

"Ms. Hansworth is waiting outside. Shall I send her in?" His face revealed that he approved of Nicola. Men always did.

"Yes."

At the door, he turned. "There are some reporters downstairs."

I thought, God, no. Anything but reporters. Roger hated publicity with a passion. International bankers didn't require publicity; in fact, anonymity was jealously guarded outside of money matters.

15

"Do I have to see them? Couldn't you just send them away?"

I had surprised him. He was reevaluating me. "I could have them removed, but they'd come back. I'm afraid that eventually you'll have to make a statement."

"But not eventually today."

"No, eventually tomorrow would do just as well." Again, he started to leave, but hesitated one more time. "You'll be quite safe here, Mrs. Douglas I don't expect any repercussions."

Repercussions hadn't occurred to me, but now they settled upon my chest, an invisible load.

"Thank you," I said with all the sarcasm I could muster. "That makes me feel a lot better."

Nicola came in looking backward. "I can't believe it!" she gushed with customary enthusiasm. "You've had more excitement in one day in London than I've had in years!"

I had to smile. Nicola at her best put Tallulah Bankhead in the shade. I knew that there was a studious, conservative, intelligent banker under that façade, but it was well hidden. She was beautiful and acted dumb, and that had fooled more than one accountant who thought he knew everything. It had probably fooled Roger once, too, but I had never asked and didn't want to. It gave me pleasure to think that he might have made a mistake.

"Excitement can be painful, Nickie," I reminded her.

"Oh, you poor dear!" She hugged me with her voice and gave me a peck on the cheek, probably depositing a badge of blood red lipstick. "But that man! It was worth it."

"Nickie, you're hopeless."

"Darling, you're crazy! He's the most gorgeous thing I've ever seen! What's his name?"

"I didn't ask."

"And you call me hopeless! Is he coming back?"

"I didn't ask that, either."

She arranged herself on the chair beside the bed and pouted at me. "What am I going to do with you? Val, it's been two years! Life goes on."

"It's good to see you, too."

"Well, you might at least have gotten his number for *me*."

I smiled, finally giving in to being cheered up, and much of her pseudo persona melted away. "Val, what happened? They didn't tell me anything except that you'd been hurt and you were here. I heard one of the nurses say you had been shot."

I nodded. "Shot. Yes, I guess so. But I'm still not sure how it happened. I was just waiting for the cab driver to buy some cigarettes and Mr. Bloody Hell—it seems to be his favorite expression—jumped in the car and floored the accelerator." I gave her a rambling account of the rest of the story, stopping to rest from time to time, which only increased her impatience.

"Who was shooting at you and why?"

"I don't think they were shooting at me. They were shooting at him. Mr. Bloody Hell. I think he was chasing them."

"If he was chasing them how could they shoot out the rear window?"

"I don't know. Maybe there were two sets of them."

"You didn't ask about that, either."

"Well, no. Listen, if you want to know, why don't you call the world's most gorgeous man and ask him? His boss is paying the bill for this place, somebody here should be able to give you a phone number. And while you're at it, talk to the press people downstairs." I remembered Nickie's profession. "Or maybe you could get someone from public relations at the bank to do it."

Nickie patted my hand and grinned wickedly. "Don't worry, dearie. I'll take care of Mr. Bloody Hell *personally*. And I'll satiate the wolves of the press, too. Anything else?"

"My tape player and tapes?"

She got up and opened the doors of the wardrobe across the room. "Here's your luggage." She got the carry-on bag opened easily. "You should learn to lock your bags when you travel, Val. You just never know . . . Here they are. You'll want Mozart, I suppose." She slipped the tape into the player, but before she put the headphones over my ears, she gave me a long, serious look. "You just take it easy and get well. Leave the details to me. I'll take just as good care of you as Roger did."

After she left, I closed my eyes and let Mozart's Sonata in A for flute and guitar fill my head and drive out the lingering confusion. It always reminded me of Roger, and it always relaxed me to sleep when nothing else would.

Nickie was as good as her word, or perhaps even a little better. The next afternoon she came in brandishing a small newspaper. "You made the news!" she announced as if it were a personal coup. It probably was.

I read the four-inch-high headline. " 'BLOWN TO BITS'?"

"No! Oh, that's about some wrecked ship off the

coast. Sinking was cheaper than salvaging, I guess. You're here."

I read the small item on the second page. " 'Tourist Injured in High-Speed Chase.' It sounds like I was run over trying to cross the street."

"The secret of avoiding media harassment," she explained patiently, "is to be so boring that nobody cares."

" 'Government sources say no charges will be filed,' " I mumbled to myself. "*That* sounds like the whole thing was my fault!"

"Who cares?" She was about to launch into a lecture on the value of anonymity when a nurse burst in.

"He's coming!"

"Who?" Nickie and I said in unison.

"Him! Your man."

"*My* man? You mean Mr. Bloody Hell?" She nodded "He isn't mine anymore," I said. "I gave him to Nickie." But no one was listening to me. The nurse had begun to rearrange my sheet and blanket, and Nickie was brushing my long brown hair.

"Fairy princess hair," Roger had called it. Sitting on the edge of the bed to watch me brush it at night had always pleased him.

"Most illustrators favor blond princesses," I had told him once.

"Get Peter to paint a brown-haired one for you in your next fairy tale. He'd do it if you asked him."

"I don't write fairy tales, I just write stories for children," I had explained patiently, not for the first time. "Mostly about animals."

"So, write about a princess with a pet." Then he'd laughed, gathering up my hair in his hands and bending his face to it, breathing in the fragrance of his

19

favorite shampoo.

Over Nickie's shoulder, I saw the door open. The man stopped there, leaning against the doorway, surveying the activity and grinning.

"Well, what do you know?" I said. "Mr. Bloody Hell can smile."

He laughed, freezing my two other guests. "Mr. Bloody Hell can be civil, too, if you'll let him have another go at it." He nodded in the direction of Nickie and the nurse. "If you'll excuse me, ladies, I'd like to talk to Mrs. Douglas alone." I was surprised to see that Nickie closed the door as she was leaving. Did this mean she'd changed her mind about the prey? Had she called him and changed her mind?

I waited for him to begin, determined this time not to work quite so hard at communication. It was odd, in a way, but I didn't really care about the why or the how of what had happened, as long as I was assured it wouldn't happen again. It had happened and I had survived, having permanently lost only my time and my favorite tweed blazer. The time was unimportant; since Roger's death I had more time than I wanted, anyway. And the blazer . . . Nickie knew talented tailors all over the world.

He said, "I do have a name."

"Really?"

"Unless you'd prefer to call me Mr. Bloody Hell." My expression must have been sufficiently pained, for he sat down with a sigh in the chair that Nickie had recently vacated. "Mrs. Douglas, I really am sorry about what happened. If I had known you were in the car, if I'd known you'd been shot — things might have been different."

"Might have been?"

He winced, catching himself too late. "I have a tough job, Mrs. Douglas. Sometimes I get carried away, and sometimes I just get dragged along."

Huskiness has always been my weak spot. Men say that they can't stand to see a woman cry. I can't resist that quality of a man's voice that seems to promise he is telling the honest, heart-wrenching truth. Roger, actually, had never used the husky approach, and probably never learned about its effectiveness with me. Roger announced his position firmly and stuck to it until the desired results were achieved.

I said, "If that is an apology, I accept. Yes, I do want to know your name. Bloody Hell isn't a phrase that can be used easily in polite company."

"Have you been talking about me in polite company?"

Again, quite innocently, I was on the defensive. "The nurses and Nickie won't talk about anything else. Are you a state secret, Mr. Bloody Hell? You failed to mention that at our last meeting."

He shook his head slowly. "I have this feeling that if I could just make a proper start, the rest of this conversation would follow quite smoothly. Perhaps you could help just a little."

Roger used to do that, and I hated it just as much now as I did then. "I did all the work the last time we talked, too. For a policeman, you certainly are a lazy conversationalist." He took the insult well; I liked that. But I was still irritated. "You were going to tell me your name, before you began grilling me on my discretion.

"My name is Ian Chiswick." He pronounced it "chizzick."

"Delighted to meet you. My name is Valerie Douglas. I can produce proof that I am intelligent, if necessary."

He looked at his hands. The fingers were strong and blunt, not unlike the man. "I really have made a poor job of it so far, haven't I? Because I know you're quite bright. That's why I'm here."

"You're here because I'm intelligent?" I said this quite gently, considering my mood.

"I'm here to ask you some questions." His eyes were gray-blue, the color of the darkening clouds that gathered beyond the window behind him.

"So ask," I said, with disciplined politeness.

"Did you happen to see the man I was chasing?"

"You mean the one who ran across the street just before you got into the car? Yes, I saw him. Well, sort of. I didn't see his face, though. I couldn't pick him out of a crowd, if that's what you're asking. Is that what you're asking?" I added, not at all certain the conversation would take a predictable turn if I didn't.

"Yes, I suppose so. Did you notice anything at all about him that was unusual?"

"Like, he walked with a limp? He had a large scar on the back of his head?"

He smiled in spite of himself. "Did he talk to anybody?"

"He was running, Mr. Chiswick. He didn't talk, wave, or even look around. He simply ran. Surely you could find better witnesses. At least someone who saw his face. What about the two mothers talking in front of the pub? Or one of the drivers who almost hit him? Or the man going into the betting shop?"

"Man going into a betting shop," he repeated. "Are

you sure?"

"Positive. I remember he stopped to read the ads in the real-estate office window before going inside the shop. He must have still been in the doorway when your man ran across the street."

Chiswick shook his head. "He wouldn't have seen any more than you." He stopped, took a breath and went on more hesitantly. "You realize that you could file charges, don't you? Against me."

"Could I?"

"Please. It's been a very long day."

He did look tired. In fact, he looked like he hadn't slept for a week. Even I felt better than that. "All right, yes, I realize. My press agent has advised against it. She thinks you're the most handsome man in London. Worthy of worship."

"But you don't."

"I don't find irritation all that attractive. I'm sorry," I added quickly. "That wasn't called for. Actually, I think I might feel differently several years from now. But today, right now, well, I'm not looking for complications. What does this have to do with anything?"

"I was hoping you'd let me buy you dinner, by way of apology."

I was sorely tempted to tell him he could apologize by buying dinner for Nickie, who was more likely to appreciate it, but he was standing hat in hand, so to speak, shaming me into being gracious. I said, "I won't be out of here for a few days yet, and even then Nickie's going to hire a nurse to keep me captive in the apartment. You may have to wait a while. Why don't you talk to her about it?"

"You don't have any definite plans?"

"I won't be leaving town in the near future, Sheriff, if that's what you mean. Hey. *That* was supposed to be *funny*, not sarcastic." I allowed him a gentle smile. "Talk to Nickie. She's the one making definite plans."

He shifted. "Mrs. Douglas . . ."

"You've apologized; I've accepted. Couldn't we just leave it at that until I feel a little better? Right now even the thought of making the trip to Nickie's is too exhausting to contemplate. I really don't want to think about future plans."

He turned to go and then stopped. "Suppose I picked the two of you up and drove you to Ms. Hansworth's?"

I remembered the steady strength that had all but carried me up a steep slope. "Now that I would appreciate."

He nodded to himself, satisfied at last, and left.

But I wasn't satisfied, I realized with some surprise. I wanted to think about future plans. I wanted to think about going back to Houston as soon as possible. But I didn't.

Chapter 2

I was ready early on the afternoon I was to be released. A nurse had come in to help me, combing and braiding my hair in a single braid at the back of my neck with special care, evidently still caught up in the notion that Chiswick and I were fated to be a twosome. I felt as if I were dressing up to go unescorted to a party I wasn't sure I wanted to attend.

But I was going, anyway, I knew. Roger and Nickie were alike in that respect. Both of them knew better than I how to care for me, and Nickie would be no more easily thwarted in her intentions than Roger had been. It was comforting in a way, I thought, that I still had someone to lean on. I sat down in a surprisingly uncomfortable chair by my single window and looked out on a day that was cool and damp. I wasn't alone, after all. I still had Nickie.

She slipped in the door quietly, and cleared her throat, looking radiant in ivory cashmere and subdued brown tweed.

"The heat is on," I observed.

She laughed and pirouetted "Am I gorgeous?"

"Fabulous. He doesn't stand a chance. But how is the bank holding up without you?"

"I took a little vacation. And I brought my beeper."

She patted her handbag. "I'd better start packing. Ian will be here pretty soon."

"Oh. Ian. Very nice. What about my nanny?"

"Your nurse. She's already at the flat, sterilizing it, no doubt. But she's okay. You'll like her. Ian recommended her."

"Ian. Oh, well, I'm sure she'll be okay. Used to nursing criminals like me."

I didn't have much to pack; most of it had never actually been unpacked in the first place. Nickie was finished in only a few minutes. "I've planned a little reception for you tomorrow night," she said. "At the apartment, of course. People from the bank, mostly."

"A reception or a wake?" I asked, fatigued even by the thought. I could have used another day of rest, but Nickie was never one to waste time.

"Vallie. It's a hurdle that has to be taken eventually. You can't hide out for the rest of your life."

"Maybe not, but I'd be willing to bet I could manage two or three more years, with help."

She clucked in admonition. "Well, you're not going to get any help from me."

"Why not? You owe me one for Ian. I gave up blood to find you this guy."

"And I am willing to endure a considerable amount of bitching to find one for you."

"But I don't want one!" I sighed for emphasis, weariness pushing me deeper into the lumpy chair.

"I know. You want the sun to stop coming up and time to end. But what you need—" A soft knock at the door silenced her.

"Come in!" I called.

Chiswick was in top form in jeans and a light blue

26

sweater. He looked pale enough to have cheated death only minutes ago, which I now realized to be his normal color. I idly wondered how a month under Galveston's sun would change him. Would he tan to Roger's deep brown or turn successive shades of gold, as I did? He smiled, first at me and then for Nickie. Careful, I mentally cautioned him, Nickie gets jealous.

"You're right on time," she said with approval.

Oh, Nickie, I thought. You'll never train this one to heel. "I hope the chariot's still warm," I said. "Is it always this cold in the spring?"

Again he smiled. What could he read in my face? "Usually. It's only barely spring. But you won't feel it so much after you've recovered a bit more. Isn't it cold in New York, still?"

"Probably. But I came here from Houston, and it definitely isn't cold in Houston, still. It wasn't cold in Houston at Christmas."

"Packing's all done," announced Nickie, as Chiswick held open the door for the nurse and wheelchair, my escort to the edge of hospital territory.

I don't know what I'd expected in the way of transport, but it wasn't the comfortable, sensible silver car at the hospital's front door. Neither did I expect Chiswick to insist on seating me in the front seat. Nickie stood it well and that, too, was surprising. I'd have expected her to laugh it off, but wind up next to him, anyway. Chiswick got what he wanted easily, with a quiet but confident voice. But how long would that last? I thought to myself. The fireworks from an eventual contest of wills would be spectacular.

I felt like I was sitting on the driver's side, but of course I wasn't. Chiswick slid in beside me and buckled his seat belt. A meaningful glance in my direction persuaded me to buckle mine, too, although the belt passed over my left, potentially painful, shoulder.

Either I was getting used to the English traffic or Chiswick was dawdling for my benefit — probably both, although anything less than Monte Carlo would have paled against my memory of the last ride I'd taken with him. I was able to watch the scenery without gasping.

My fascination wasn't lost on Chiswick. "Is it what you expected?" he asked.

"I don't know. I guess I never gave it much thought," I answered, a little surprised by the question. "I wasn't really expecting anything in particular."

"You never traveled with your husband?"

"No, not outside the U.S."

"Odd," he said, "that he traveled so much and never took you." Nickie shifted in the back seat and Chiswick watched her in the rearview mirror.

"I had my own work." There was a sharpness in my answer, and he didn't pursue the line of questioning further.

I had wanted to come to London with Roger, but he'd always refused. "I won't have time to take you sightseeing," he'd said. "This is a business trip." They were all business trips, and yet when he called he would talk about going to a concert with Nickie, or eating in a quaint restaurant not far from the banks of the Thames. Maybe that was why I'd come, I thought, because I'd always really wanted to come, to see what I'd only heard about.

It wasn't something I wanted to ponder, and I turned my attention back to the passing view. The houses, with their tiny gardens, became smaller and closer together, until they became row houses with window boxes. Any patch of ground not covered by buildings or streets still sprouted green, however, and at varying intervals we passed through neighborhoods of large, tree-obscured houses with brilliant flowers in well-kept beds.

The more crowded it became, the more I worried about the inhabitants, until we entered a large park.

"Richmond Park," Chiswick announced.

The gently rolling green turf stretched before us, crisscrossed by hiking trails, until it disappeared into trees. I turned, as much as was comfortable, to see that the houses behind us were almost shielded from view by trees as well, but they wouldn't have detracted from the beauty of the park, anyway. They were beautiful old houses, from Victorian picture books.

A sign at the entrance we had entered identified it as Robin Hood Gate, and it was easy to imagine that Robin Hood might have spent time there, sitting underneath the huge trees watching the color of the bright green new leaves deepen. Incredibly, deer grazed peacefully on either side of the road, not bothered by the traffic. It was for the deer, I assumed, that the speed limit was so drastically reduced. I thanked them.

"This is incredible," I said, softly. "This park must be over a mile wide."

"About two, actually," Chiswick said. He cocked his head over his shoulder. "And Wimbledon Common, another square mile or so of parkland, is back there."

"So that's how they do it," I murmured.

"How they do what?"

"How they live in such cramped, tiny houses. Be-

29

cause this is here."

He didn't answer, unless he nodded. I wouldn't have seen a nod, because my attention had been captured by the scenery again. There were people walking dogs, throwing sticks to be fetched, couples strolling hand in hand, older men walking with canes, and two mothers pushing baby carriages past a small pond. I felt that we had passed a time barrier at Robin Hood Gate, going back to a simpler, more pleasant era, where it wouldn't be thought lazy to sit on a park bench and watch the seasons pass in ancient, ordered cadence. As we passed the watchers seated on the benches, I envied them, because I had forgotten how to be still, and now at least for a time, I would have to be. But there would be no serenity in it for me, and no peace.

I realized that Chiswick glanced across at me from time to time, but he kept a respectful silence, as if he knew that the park was speaking to me and how badly I wanted to hear it. And if he saw me brush away a quiet tear, he made no comment on that, either.

We had come to the edge of the park, and I turned again for one last look. Would Roger's grave be as green and peaceful? If I paused there for contemplation, would I find an answer for my restlessness?

As soon as we exited the park we were back among the teeming masses. I had expected London to be a collection of diverse neighborhoods and I wasn't disappointed. What surprised me was the lack of shopping areas. "Where do they buy groceries?" I asked him.

He stopped for an elderly woman burdened with large, white plastic bags in a crosswalk and pointed to a small corner store. "Sainsbury's."

"Yes, but where are the supermarkets?"

Nickie groaned in the back seat, but Chiswick only allowed himself a tolerant smile. "There aren't any supermarkets this close in. Shopping for food means a number of stops. The butcher, the greengrocer for vegetables and fruits, the bakery, and Sainsbury's — or something like it. You've lived in New York, haven't you?"

"Well, no, not really," I answered as the store disappeared over my left shoulder. "Roger went there on business lots of times. You remember the apartment, Nickie, the one he owned a share in. I've stayed there overnight, but I never really — What's an 'off-license'?"

"Liquor store," Nickie said. "Ian, where are we going? We'll never get there at this rate."

"We're taking the scenic route," he said.

I smiled, but I didn't look at him. "Look at the mothers with the baby carriages, Nickie. They're everywhere."

"They probably don't have cars, Vallie. There *are* still people in New York who don't have cars, aren't there?"

"Sure." I thought for a moment. "I just don't know any of them." I could imagine her rolling her eyes behind me. I'd never be cosmopolitan. If Roger couldn't remold me, no one could.

London, and probably the rest of England as well, was a navigator's nightmare. Even the straight roads weren't really straight. Chiswick had a hardbound book entitled *London A-Z*, well-used. I riffled through it; the pages looked like the remains of a dish of spaghetti. Every so often the road's name changed, as if each little neighborhood was trying to claim control of the thoroughfare by right of naming.

Highways, as I thought of them, didn't seem to really exist outside of the motorway I had briefly seen on my ride from the airport. Numbered routes turned out to be residential streets, with pedestrians, cyclists, delivery trucks and what I was discovering to be the standard number of drivers in a standard amount of hurry. Street signs seemed to be optional, a considerable handicap in my opinion.

Chiswick said, in answer to my question on the subject, "The street signs were taken down during the war so that when the Germans invaded London, they wouldn't be able to find their way."

"You're kidding."

"I'm not."

"Seriously. World War Two was a long time ago. Even if that did happen, signs should have been replaced long ago. For the sake of the motorist, if nothing else."

Chiswick kept his eyes on the road. "Motorists are numerous enough without encouragement. I say, keep the signs down."

He had a point. The streets were crowded. He had a minimum clearance of inches on both sides of the car, not that it slowed him or the other drivers down in the least. I kept telling myself that this wasn't my car or my problem.

We caught a glimpse of the Thames, then drove alongside of it for a while, until Chiswick said, "Look," and pointed ahead.

"It's Big Ben!" I cried, overcome by typical tourist excitement. The creamy stone tower was rosy in the glow of late afternoon. "It's just like *The Twenty-nine Steps.*" I leaned forward as we came nearer. The traffic and pedestrians seemed largely oblivious of the wonder of it, except for a few fellow tourists searching for the best photographic approach.

"It's the clock tower, to be exact," he said. "Big Ben is the name of the bell in the clock."

"It looks . . . lacy. Can we stay until the bell chimes?"

"No!" Nickie said firmly.

He looked across at me, and I was surprised to see his expression was almost apologetic. His voice, when he spoke, was quieter than Nickie's, and firmer. "You look tired, and it's past teatime. You'll have plenty of opportunities to hear it later."

I rested my head against the back of my seat, wondering if all Englishmen were unfathomable. "I am tired," I admitted. "But I'm not going to drink any tea."

"You won't have to," Nickie promised. "I've laid in a supply of Cokes."

"Cokes?" Chiswick pretended to be offended.

I ignored him, looking back until the clock disappeared from comfortable vision. I could tell we were in Nickie's neighborhood; apartment buildings took up whole blocks (although not usually square blocks) and were imposing, mansionlike brick edifices rising from solid pavement. Nickie's building was dark red brick with white trim. The corner nearest us as we approached promised a bay window set with four floor-to-ceiling windows on each floor, six stories high. Around these windows were white iron railings. I hoped Nickie's apartment was a corner one.

"Like it?" she asked.

"It's beautiful!"

"That corner window on the third floor is my living room."

I couldn't help wondering if Roger had really stayed

in a hotel during his business trips to London. I had never actually called him there. He'd made it plain that I wasn't to try to contact him except in an emergency, and one never arose. He called me, anyway, and picked up his mail at the London office. I had never felt the need to really investigate his whereabouts. Could he have been here, I wondered, and then rebuked myself. Fatigue was making me silly.

Empty parking spaces were a rarity in this neighborhood, so Chiswick let Nickie and I out at the front entrance and disappeared around the corner. Waiting for the elevator, I realized Nickie had been right to insist on shortening our tour.

"Nickie!" I said when she opened her door. "This is lovely!" She had chosen the decor well, mixing antique and modern with the emphasis on comfort. The bay window was home to an overstuffed armchair and a small round table, creating a comfortable nook for reading. There was a large area containing several groupings of sofas or chairs and tables, which in turn gave way to a spacious dining room with a table that could apparently expand to seat eight. I counted eight chairs. Just the thing for intimate dining, darling.

Chiswick came up behind us with the bags. Checking his expression, I decided he'd been here before. Nickie, I knew, was never one to hesitate when she found a man she liked. Chiswick must have passed her initial interview with flying colors. He passed us and led the way to my room.

I liked my room. It was roomy, quiet and across the hall from a bathroom. This filled all of my major requirements. The bedspread on the double bed matched curtains and the walls were papered a coordinating shade of peach. Before the window was a chaise longue and a small round table covered with a cloth that matched the curtains.

My nurse was a pleasant surprise, too. She was shorter than I but looked strong and confident, with curly auburn hair and a delightful smile. She couldn't have been over thirty.

"I'm Felicity Amesbury," she said, extending her hand.

"What a lovely name," I said, testing the bed.

"That's it, dearie," she said. "Why not have a nice nap before dinner? I'll shoo these two out."

"Wait," I stopped Nickie. "You promised a Coke."

Chiswick followed her out. I heard the doorbell ring in the hall while Felicity helped me out of my coat and shoes, and looked up a few seconds later to see Chiswick entering again.

"Package for you," he said.

"For me? Open it for me. I'm a hand short."

He opened it and dropped into my hand a gold cuff link, with the initials R.D. engraved in fancy script. I closed my hand around it and fell back on the bed, transported to another place and time.

"You were wonderful tonight," Roger said. He was standing in front of the sliding glass doors in the bedroom of a New York apartment. The lights of the city sparkled behind him.

I laughed. "I'm wonderful every night."

He leaned over to kiss me, champagne on his lips. "You were more than simply wonderful. You were magnificent. The quintessential hostess."

"You only married me because I can order from menus in French," I teased him.

He took off the cuff link and traced a pattern on my cheek, his kisses in its wake. "Well, that and several thousand other things. Thank you, darling, for the cuff links and this evening. It was a perfect birthday dinner."

There had been a dinner, yes, in a French restaurant, with musicians and champagne and other people. I couldn't quite remember who.

He stood up again and smiled, unbuttoning his shirt and then taking off the cuff link in the left sleeve. He held it up to me in a mock salute and kissed it. "It could all disappear tomorrow, and I would still have you. And you, lovely lady, are worth more than your weight in gold cuff links."

I pulled him back to the bed and my arms.

But it was Chiswick holding me, tensed with concern. "Valerie, what is it? What's wrong?"

I realized that an unaccounted-for minute or so had passed, during which I had probably been glassy-eyed. Felicity was taking my pulse. Up somewhat, probably.

Roger's last birthday, in New York. We had stayed at the New York apartment, a rare occurrence. Why? I couldn't quite remember. The dinner was special, for some other reason than Roger's birthday, but I couldn't remember that, either. And who were the guests? There were too many blanks in the memory. I wasn't usually that absentminded, but I was tired, I told myself.

"Just memories," I said. I opened my fist and looked at the cuff link. "Strange, after all this time to see this again."

"Val?" Nickie halted in the doorway and took in the scenario in a glance. "What's wrong? Should I call the

36

doctor?"

"Look, Nickie." I held out the cuff link. "Someone's sent me Roger's cuff link."

She took it and inspected it carefully. What was she looking for, I wondered. "Sick," she said. "That's sick. Who would do a thing like this?"

"Who *could* do a thing like this? And why wait until now to do it?"

"Would someone please tell me what's going on?" demanded Chiswick.

Nickie gave him the cuff link, and I said, "It's Roger's cuff link. I gave them to him on his last birthday."

"Mmmm . . ." Chiswick, too, was looking for something that I hadn't seen.

"Maybe someone stole it out of his hotel room," I said, "and had a change of heart."

"But how would they know you were here?" Nickie asked.

"Well, I was in the paper."

"But *I* wasn't, Vallie."

"That's right. Okay, who knows I'm here?"

Nickie thought. "Only about twenty or thirty people. The ones I invited to the reception. But I can't imagine any of them burglarizing hotel rooms." She turned to Chiswick. "How did it arrive?"

"Delivery service. I doubt we'll find anything there."

"Well, you could *try*, couldn't you, Sherlock?"

"Yes, I could try." He gave the cuff link back to me. "In the meantime, keep the doors locked."

I objected to that. "I can't believe there's anything sinister about this. Maybe Roger was just having an affair with someone, left the thing in her apartment, and she's returning it. That isn't impossible. It could even be someone connected with the bank." I shook my head at Nickie's protests. "It happens, Nickie."

"Even if it happens, and I find that hard to believe, it's pretty damn tactless."

But Roger could be painfully blunt, too. Wouldn't he have chosen a woman after his own heart? I looked to Chiswick for support.

He nodded, as if he'd understood. "Get some rest," he told me, and to Felicity he added, "Lock the door after we leave." To Nickie, he said, "Come with me. I'll show you London Vice in action."

And though she was reluctant to go, she left with him, and I marveled at the ease with which that had been accomplished. But Roger had handled me much the same way, because I had trusted him. I looked at the cuff link again. Was I wrong to have done so?

Nickie had left the Coke on the table beside my bed, and Felicity offered it to me with pills, which I accepted gratefully. Sleep would be better than remembering. I'd had experience in this area.

Roger had loved those cuff links. He'd probably worn them at the Mozart concert he and Nickie had attended before he was killed. I had assumed they had been found in the plane wreckage and he'd been buried in them. I should have asked Nickie, I told myself. I should have done that two years ago.

But, for the time being, I allowed Felicity to put the cuff link in the nightstand drawer, and demanded my tapes and player. I fell asleep easily, thinking to myself that if this were really serious, it would keep me awake.

I woke up briefly in the early evening to eat half a sandwich at Felicity's insistence and change into pajamas. The room was dark, except for a small bedside lamp, and peaceful. I had no desire to investigate the muted sound of voices that drifted down the hallway; I knew that Nickie's latest conquest was good for the weekend, at least.

Chapter 3

I found Chiswick the next morning in the dining room, sitting at an angle to the table, his stockinged feet resting on the polished mahogany seat of an antique chair. He was dressed in faded jeans and a sweatshirt, reading a paper and nursing a cup of coffee.

It was his coffee I had smelled upon awakening. I drank coffee when public occasion demanded it, but had never learned to like it as much as I liked the smell. It had been a morning smell in the house, and I had made it every day, even when Roger was away, which he was much of the time. If no one came by to drink it, I threw it out just before lunch. Roger never knew. It was just one, I realized, of a number of secrets I had kept from him.

Chiswick appraised me over the top of his paper as I sat down. "Good morning," he said. "You look much better today."

"Thank you. I feel better. Is Nickie gone yet?"

He disappeared again behind the paper. "She left early for the bank."

"That sounds right. Seven days a week, twelve hours a day, by choice." I watched Felicity bring in a tray and set it before me, smiling. I looked at its contents and couldn't share her optimism. Perhaps that was why she left so quickly.

The main course appeared to be a bowl of gray mush. "What is this stuff?" I asked Chiswick.

He leaned over to look at it. "Porridge."

"Three-bear porridge?"

"What?"

"Three-bear porridge. You know, the papa bear and the mama bear and the baby bear."

"Ah." He nodded, as if I had just told him a profound truth. "Three-bear porridge. Yes, I suppose so."

I sampled a spoonful. "Goldilocks ate this out of choice?"

"Maybe *she* wasn't fond of IV needles, either."

"Ah!" I nodded, having just been told a profound truth. "IV needles. Yes, I suppose so." I flooded the bowl with milk and buried the evidence under sugar. "Tony the Tiger, where are you when I need you?"

"Tony who?"

"Tony the Tiger. Frosted Flakes. They're grrrrreat!"

His eyes rolled heavenward as they vanished again behind the newsprint, so I ate quietly and let him read. Roger had always demanded silence during The Ritual of Reading the Paper. I usually kept a paperback stashed somewhere in the kitchen, so that I could read while he read. And after he left for the day, of course, I would read the paper in my own way.

I was halfway through the oatmeal, making slow progress, when Chiswick folded the paper and offered it to me. I shook my head.

"I checked out the delivery service," he said.

"And?"

"The cuff link was dropped off at their office by a tall, blond male in his mid-thirties. Do you know any-

41

one in London who fits that description?"

"Sure." I put my spoon down and pushed the bowl away. "Roger."

"I think we can rule out the supernatural."

"Well, *I* think we can forget about the whole episode. Nickie was right. Sending me the cuff link was pretty damn tactless. But people can be that way, for various reasons. Reasons which I, personally, don't want to know." I pushed back my chair and stood up.

"Do you really think Roger had a lover?"

I picked up the tray with my right hand, balancing carefully. "Ask Nickie," I said on my way to the kitchen.

I thought about it later, as I lounged in a hot bath. I hadn't meant to implicate Nickie as Roger's mistress, although I privately admitted it was a possibility. Nickie had no immediately obvious motive for sending the cuff link, and sending it without an explanation or demand wasn't her style.

I had been truthful in saying I didn't want to know why it had been sent. If an explanation or demand came in the future, I would deal with it then. I wouldn't go looking for trouble.

Nickie came back for lunch, bearing several guidebooks on London she'd purchased at a bookstore close to the office. Chiswick had left, presumably to police the streets and make them safe for luckier tourists than I.

Nickie and I made ourselves comfortable in my room, she on the chaise longue and I in the bed, propped up by pillows. We reviewed and renewed the good old days.

"Do you remember," she asked, "Roger's last promotion in New York?"

"I remember. We had dinner out somewhere, I can't remember the restaurant. But I remember the wine."

"Vouvray."

"Yes, and I ate scallops Provençale. Roger threatened to make me ride in the trunk for eating garlic." We smiled at each other, and then mine faded. "He was so proud of that promotion. And you were, too."

"Yes, I was." She thought for a moment. "Do you remember the waiter? A short, round man with a bald spot?"

"No." I grinned again. "Too much Vouvray, I guess."

She laughed. "We *all* had too much. I'll never know how we made it home!"

I shook my head. "Roger could drink winos under the table and not show it. I never saw him truly drunk."

"I miss him," Nickie said suddenly, a little hoarsely. "Sometimes when I walk down the hall where his office was, I look into the room, as if . . ." She looked away, uncomfortable with the sadness.

"Yes, I know," I said quietly, surprising myself with the steadiness of my own voice. "But he is dead, Nickie." I waited, knowing I shouldn't say what I was going to say, yet unable to stop myself. "He loved you, too."

She looked up sharply, startled, and for a moment I thought she might confess to being Roger's lover. But then she regained control of herself and said, "He was a good friend."

A friend, I thought. I let go of an inward sigh. I hadn't heard what I hadn't wanted to hear, although I couldn't help being troubled by what I had seen. But I had pressed her, and I shouldn't have, I scolded myself.

I owed her too much.

She had been my rock when Roger had died. His death had been an accident, a plane crash on his way from London to Scotland in the company plane. Nickie had been unsuccessful in convincing the bank's officials to let her break the news to me, but she was on the phone to me moments afterward, talking me through the decisions that had to be made immediately.

I decided not to have Roger's body returned to the States. What good was a charred remnant of Roger? The real Roger was gone. I asked her to find a peaceful place for him, which she did, and immediately after she flew to New York to commandeer the memorial service there.

She started me on the long trail of Roger's investments and properties, and advised me constantly. And then, when everything was done, and I had nothing more to occupy my days and my publisher was expecting a manuscript to signal my return to writing children's books, Nickie wrote and asked me to come and visit her in England. Maybe to hear her next words, or to hear everything else except the words that she couldn't bring herself to say.

She didn't say anything at all, and eventually I got up and crossed to the chaise, sitting down beside her and putting my good arm around her shoulders. Life goes on. That's what she'd said at the hospital. Yeah, Nickie, and that's the hell of it.

Nickie had caterers, maids and God knew what else to occupy her afternoon, but I didn't. I read for a while, tried to sleep but couldn't, and waited for the great hurdle, the reception, to present itself. I dressed early and slowly with Felicity's help, and established my domain on a loveseat in the living room.

Chiswick was the first to arrive, about half an hour before the scheduled starting time, letting himself in with his own key. In a white shirt, red tie and black suit, he looked suitably dressed and more. He looked dramatic. Was his appearance artistically planned and created, or did he just get dressed without thinking of the effect, I wondered.

I watched him cross the room and sit down in the chair across from me. He was attractive, with his angular face, gray-blue eyes and hair that threatened to curl if allowed to grow longer, but he wasn't the most handsome man in the world. Nickie was wrong about that. And yet, there was something about him that was hard to resist. A patience with people, perhaps, or the capacity to listen rather than simply hear.

"You're quiet tonight," he observed.

"The first one will be the hardest."

He cocked his head, puzzled. "Sorry?"

"Yes. The first one to say he's sorry will be the hardest. After that, it'll be okay. It'll be hard, but okay."

"What will you say to the first one?"

I stared at him.

"If you plan what to say," he explained patiently, "it'll be easier, when it comes."

I nodded, slowly. "Yes. But what will I say? What did I say two years ago? I can't remember. Two years ago, no one expected me to make sense. But now they will."

"Will they?" he asked. "Or will they be more worried about what you expect *them* to say?"

I closed my eyes and sighed a weight away. "Yes, I

guess they will. What does it matter what I say? I'll say 'thank you' and that will be enough. But, God, I don't want to do this."

Chiswick's voice was gentle, but I felt the interrogation creeping in. "Why did you let Nickie plan this party, then?"

"Because she's right, I can't hide forever. When I accepted her invitation to come, I knew what it would mean, I knew this would happen. It's for the best."

"Why does Nickie have so much power over you?"

Despite the last-minute preparations and scurrying of the caterers and servers, the room was quite still and silent. His eyes never wavered, but he must have known he had gone too far. It must have been obvious to him. I said, "She cares," and got up and left the room. In the hallway I was passed by Nickie. "I'm just going to rest in my room," I told her, before she could ask. "I'm just going to listen to some music before the party starts."

I closed the door behind me. Nickie had been surprised, and Chiswick would be interrogated when she found him, and he deserved that. I didn't owe him any explanations. He was Nickie's man, not mine.

Later, back in my position not too long after the first guests arrived, the first person said he was sorry and I said thank you, and the conversation flowed without Chiswick's assistance. He watched me without actually looking. What was he hoping to see? What was my pain to him?

The party guests proceeded like a receiving line, each individual or couple sitting beside me for a few moments and then surrendering the chair to the next mourner. Most of them expressed their sympathy without mentioning any specific event involving Roger, but the names and faces alone evoked five years of memories.

Mr. and Mrs. Edward Farsleigh: a Christmas party in Houston, maybe four years ago, or five. Ed had been head of something. Trust department, perhaps. He had ended that evening by singing "Londonderry Air" in a rather surprising high clear tenor.

Dennis Penning, once Roger's immediate supervisor, now minus a wife and two children: Roger arriving home late one Friday evening in the early fall. He went straight to the kitchen and poured himself a large measure of whiskey, not even bothering to speak first. I asked him what was wrong, and he said, "I get tired of working with assholes like Penning. Some things are worth killing for, but Penning is just worth killing." That night Roger had had a terrible nightmare, waking up in a cold sweat and searching for his gun; he'd said it was just another Nam flashback.

Barry and Elizabeth Martin, Barry an accountant at Roger's level and Beth a teacher: Roger and I, the godparents of their first child, attending the christening. I remembered the baby's delicate lace gown and the delight in Roger's eyes when the tiny little girl grabbed hold of his finger. Why hadn't I pressed to have children sooner? Why had I let him talk me into waiting? What had we been waiting for? I had wanted a child so much. I realized with shock that I still did. I wanted to read my stories to my own child.

My mouth became unbearably dry and I quickly drank the glass of champagne a waiter offered. "Thank you, thank you," I answered the condolences.

Roger sailing on a bright, hot day in June, laughing

at me as I clung to the side of the catamaran, wearing a lifejacket but not totally trusting it to keep me floating, then slowing down so that I could relax. That evening we ate seafood and drank beer at a small café on the waterfront, hoping the hangover would eclipse the sunburn.

"James Bromley," the man standing before me said. "I was your husband's assistant here in London when . . . when . . ."

I remembered the name. "When Roger died," I finished for him. "Yes, Roger spoke very highly of you when he called." He seemed more disconcerted by this; a nice, soft-spoken Englishman with brown hair and red cheeks waiting for the floor to swallow him up. I patted the space next to me on the sofa. "Won't you sit down?"

He said, in a rush, "If only I hadn't put him on that day's flight . . ."

His face had turned whiter than Chiswick's, and I realized that he was going to faint. I had no wish to go through that, and I felt certain that Bromley didn't, either. I looked around for Felicity in vain; she had probably decided to read in her room rather than spend the evening with increasingly drunken strangers. But Chiswick caught my searching eye and came. He surveyed the situation in one quick glance and put his shoulder into Bromley's stomach just as the younger man collapsed, lifting him easily and moving out of the room before many of the group noticed.

My bedroom was the natural choice. Nickie's bed was buried under coats, and Felicity slept on what was little more than a cot in the study. I turned back the comforter so that Bromley's head would rest on the smooth coolness of the pillowcase. Chiswick retrieved some cushions from the chaise longue and put them under Bromley's feet.

"Now what?" I asked. "Smelling salts?"

Chiswick shook his head. "He'll come 'round in a minute. Who is he?"

"He was Roger's assistant here in London."

I swallowed hard to keep the nausea down. My face must have been pale by this time. Chiswick appeared torn between two invalids. "You want to toss it?"

"Toss it?" I thought, and then realized he meant "throw up." "No," I told him. I looked at Bromley. He couldn't have been more than twenty-three or -four, his face smooth and innocent in apparent sleep. "Jesus," I said. "I should have talked to him a long time ago. He's been tortured by guilt all this time . . . I should have come here to the funeral."

"Why didn't you?"

"I don't know. Cowardice, I guess. Or shock. Everything seemed to take such a lot of energy. Just walking to the kitchen for a glass of water was a tiring journey." I closed my eyes and sighed, caught up again in that horrible fatigue. "The thought of flying to London was more than I could manage." I hadn't meant to give such a personal answer, and when I realized what I'd said, I looked up sharply.

Chiswick was watching Bromley, seeing the first stirring. "You stay with him," he said. "I'll get some tea."

"Tea?" I said, firmly back in the present. "Don't you think a cold drink would be better?"

He shook his head at the strange health practices of Yanks and left. Bromley's eyelids moved, and I sat down on the other side of the bed, with my back to the wall and picked up his hand.

"Unnh," he said.

"Take it easy, Mr. Bromley. Everything's okay."

Pale eyes focused on me and widened in despair.

"It's all right, really," I assured him. "You got us both out of an awkward situation. Mr. Chiswick went to get you some tea."

"Tea."

I was beginning to like James Bromley. We shared a common inability to function well in times of stress. How he had survived Roger, I had no idea, but the man deserved a medal for it. Roger had specifically said he was "a good boy." That must have taken some doing.

He sat up slowly, carefully.

"I'm so sorry, Mrs. Douglas. . . ." His voice quavered.

"I'm the one who should be sorry, Mr. Bromley, and I am. I hadn't thought about the way Roger's death might affect the people who knew him. If I'd known you felt this way, I'd have written, or called, or even come to London much, much sooner. You've endured two years of needless torture for me. Please don't let it continue."

He stared at his nervous hands, but he was able to let out his breath, and very slowly, he began to relax. It would take a long time, I thought, before he would let go of the guilt, but maybe I had provided a start.

I smiled, trying to lighten the mood. "What were you expecting me to be? Roger in a dress?"

The grin was furtive, tentative, but it was there. "No, ma'am, I saw your picture when I packed Mr. Douglas's things to send them home."

Chiswick returned with the tea, which Bromley accepted gratefully.

"Mr. Bromley was my husband's assistant," I told Chiswick, largely for Bromley's benefit. "He packed Roger's things to send to me." I turned back to Bromley. "Thank you. That couldn't have been easy for you."

"No, ma'am." His interest centered in his teacup.

I hesitated, then decided to ask the question that had been at the back of my mind all evening. "Mr. Bromley, I know it isn't a pleasant subject for you, but there's a question I would like to ask. Roger had a very special pair of cuff links, ones that I had given him for his birthday. I know that he took them to London, but I've lost track of them. Do you remember packing them?"

"Cuff links." He thought. "No, I don't remember any cuff links. I don't think he had any formal shirts."

"But he did. I saw him pack it. And he and Nickie went to a concert the night before he died, and Roger would never go to the theater casually dressed."

"Yes, ma'am," he said, "that's true. But there wasn't a black suit, either, don't you remember? One gray, one blue, two browns and some slacks and a couple of sportcoats."

"My God," I marveled. "You really are cut from Roger's cloth. I didn't remember that. Are you sure?"

"Yes, ma'am. I sent a list of the contents with the luggage."

And I, of course, hadn't had the courage to open the box. And if the box had been there in the room with us then, I still wouldn't have been able to open it. I looked away from them both, hoping to find support from Roger's ghost, leaning in some darkened corner of the room, but it wasn't there.

"I hope, Mrs. Douglas, that you don't think I could have taken them," Bromley said.

"Of course not. I was just thinking . . . No, I know you didn't take them." I was just thinking Roger probably didn't go back to the hotel that night. The reason the cuff links, shirt and suit weren't found in the hotel was that Roger had left them somewhere else that night, and the next morning he got dressed in the clothes that he had brought to Nickie's place earlier. Nickie's place, or some other woman's place.

"Valerie?" Chiswick's voice broke a silence that had grown deadly still.

"I'm okay," I said, without turning around. "I'd just like to be alone for a little while."

There was a noise of leaving behind me. I covered my face with my hands. I had been so falsely brave with Nickie. If she'd told me she was Roger's lover, I would have crumbled and dissolved the pieces in tears. I'd never be prepared for this truth. Not tonight and not on the last night of my life, which I was close to wishing tonight was.

My throat tightened until I could barely breathe. I felt a desperate need to just get up and leave, to put on my coat, walk out of Nickie's door and wander in the night, a night unpopulated with memories and pain, a night that granted anonymity.

The touch on my shoulder made me jump. Chiswick was standing before me.

"Please," I said. "Please just leave me alone."

He sat down beside me and put an arm around me. "Nickie sent me back to get the guest of honor. You're missed."

"To hell with Nickie."

"Maybe it wasn't Nickie that kept Roger out that night."

I tried to get up, to move, but his grip tightened.

"Let me go."

"No," he said. "I'm not going to let go, so you might as well stop fighting me. Maybe it wasn't Nickie. Maybe it wasn't another woman."

"Sure. Maybe Roger was a homosexual."

"Use your imagination. There could be dozens of reasons why Roger didn't go back to the hotel that night that have nothing to do with sex. Maybe he had a business meeting, or met a friend for drinks. He was no stranger to London, surely he had personal friends here."

I thought. Farfetched, but I wanted it to be possible. "A couple. Not many."

"But it could have been one of them. It could have happened."

"Maybe."

He was quiet for a moment and then said, "We could find out."

I looked at him to be certain he was serious. He was. "I'm not sure I want to know."

He nodded. "I can understand that. It might not be welcome news. But it might make things easier between you and Nickie."

"Or harder. Anyway, it was two years ago. Who would remember now?"

He gave me an extra squeeze. "You can leave that to me. I'm good at that sort of thing."

"I don't know." I hesitated, still not quite convinced. Better the devil you know, I thought.

"Think about it." He stood up and helped me to my

feet. "Let's get back to the party." As we walked back into the main room, I knew immediately that something was different. Not wrong, exactly, but different. I stopped and searched the crowd for the familiar or absent face, but it wasn't there or it was there. Which?

"What is it?" Chiswick asked.

"Nothing."

"What is it?" More insistently.

"It's . . . I don't know." My eyes rested on a short, heavy man with a large bald spot and a thinning white fringe. He saw my attention and drifted toward us. "But there's something."

The man had threaded his way through the intervening guests. He extended his hand and said, "Ah, Mrs. Douglas, how delightful to meet you at last."

I offered an uncertain hand to be firmly shaken, then inched backward until my back touched Chiswick's chest, unable to understand my own reluctance. "You have the advantage," I said. "I'm afraid I don't remember your name."

"But of course not," he assured me in polished British tones. "We've never been introduced."

"No? But you seem . . ." His eyes were pale blue, shining out of the ruddy complexion of a round little face. A face not remembered yet not forgotten. I shook my head. "There are too many faces tonight. I always depended on Roger to remember names; I'm terrible at it."

"But in this instance, blameless. My name is Michael Mosby."

The name meant nothing to me. "Were you a colleague of Roger's?"

He smiled. "In a manner of speaking, yes. We did a

small amount of business together."

I could feel Chiswick stiffening behind me.

"I wanted to personally offer my condolences," Mosby continued. "Roger was a most amazing man."

"Thank you," I said, unable to dredge up anything more suitable from a frozen brain. I felt like a victim in a horror movie who has just sensed the monster approaching from behind, and has slowly begun to turn. But, of course, I knew who was behind me, although for some unknown reason I wished he weren't. I couldn't let him know . . . whatever it was that I couldn't quite figure out.

Mosby nodded at my sling. "I understand your stay hasn't been as pleasant as one might wish. I hope you won't be cutting your visit short."

"No."

"Then perhaps you will do me the honor of attending a small dinner party later this week in my home."

"Yes." It wasn't what I wanted to say. I never wanted to watch the horror movies, either. But I would always peek through my fingers to see the monster when the victim turned around. Roger refused to take me to scary shows after the first two we saw together. He told me I had a strong streak of masochism. He must have been right. "Of course I'll come."

"Marvelous!" Mosby seemed not to notice the woodenness of my voice. "I've given Nicola the address and time. I shall look forward to seeing you." I nodded. "And now, if you will excuse me, I must be going. I have another call to make this evening. Mine is a business not restricted to the office. Good evening."

He turned and left, waving to Nickie as he opened the apartment door.

But I didn't move. A business not restricted to the office. How many times had Roger given me that explanation, phoned in from a restaurant or bar? Too many. My birthday. The night I fell off a ladder while decorating the Christmas tree, and had to go to the hospital for stitches. Dinner with my brother, the night before Thanksgiving, when I had cooked all day. Two award banquets where I accepted prizes that were important to me.

Even there, in the room filled with talking, laughing people, Roger's ghost lingered to tell me again. Listen, listen. A business not restricted to the office. You know what to do, darling. Go back to the guests and smile and pretend you aren't hurt. It's all part of the business. Not restricted to the office.

"Valerie?" Nickie held my hands between hers, concerned. "Are you all right? Your hands are like ice."

I smiled. "Of course I'm all right. I'm just tired." I pretended to stifle a yawn. "Do you think it would be all right if I went to bed? Say goodbye to the guests for me, okay?"

But long after midnight had passed and the last guest had left, I was still awake in the darkness of my room, trying to catch an elusive memory. The window in my room was open, and although the traffic had died down, I could still hear the night noises. They were city street noises: beeps and engines and an occasional faint conversation. Not the sort of noises I would have heard after midnight at home, even if it were cool enough to leave a window open.

I got out of bed and pulled the curtains back to look outside. It had been drizzling, and the street beneath the streetlamp was slick and shiny. It even smelled like a city street, I thought, but different than Houston. England was foreign, as foreign as the moon.

The moon wasn't visible that night. I had to assume it was there, hidden behind a low cloud cover that made the sky look more gray than black. Even the stars had deserted me.

Or had I deserted them? I sat down on the chaise beneath the window, and then leaned back and closed my eyes. I might have gone to sleep there, had I not realized that someone was talking, not on the street below, but in Nickie's parlor. I crept to the doorway and shamelessly pressed my ear to the crack between the door and jamb, expecting to hear Nickie and Chiswick.

Chiswick's voice was clear enough, but the woman arguing with him was Felicity.

"You're pushing her," Felicity was insisting. "She's too weak."

Chiswick's answer was mild, but firm. "I didn't make up this schedule. Anyway, she *wants* to go to Mosby's. We can't keep her a prisoner here."

"I'm not suggesting a life sentence! Just a little more time to recover." Felicity's voice had risen and then dropped self-consciously.

"Mosby's party is in four days," Chiswick said. "That will be time enough. It'll have to do."

There was a short silence, and then I heard approaching footsteps. I hurried back to bed, but my door didn't open, and after a while I put some Mozart in the tape player and fell asleep cradled by the earphones.

Chapter 4

I had been dreaming about Houston and traffic jams in ninety-plus degree heat. I woke up in London, sweating under too many blankets. It was almost ten o'clock, and the sunlight through my window looked promising. A perfect day for sightseeing.

I was surprised to find Nickie curled up on the sofa with a newspaper until I realized she was reading the Sunday Times. She looked up as I entered the room, and I said only two words: "Buckingham Palace."

It was her turn to be surprised. "So soon? Don't you think you should rest another day?"

"I *have* rested. For three days. If I have to spend another day cooped up in this apartment, I'll go out of my mind."

She folded the newspaper carefully, giving the act far more attention than it required. "I thought we might do something quieter today. I'd planned to take you to see Roger's grave."

The firmness of my reply caught me off guard. "I don't want to see Roger's grave. I want to see Buckingham Palace."

"We *will* see Buckingham Palace," Nickie hastened to assure me. "We'll see everything you want to see. But I just thought—"

"You thought wrong," I cut her off sharply, walking past her through the archway to the dining room.

She followed me, hurt plain in her voice. "Vallie, please. I'm only trying to help."

"I know you are." My irritation melted away as suddenly as it had arisen. "I'm sorry. But I don't want to see Roger's grave. I'm just not ready yet."

"It's been two years, Vallie. You have to go sometime."

"Then a few more days won't matter, will they?" I sat down at the table, but I couldn't yet face the plate that Felicity set before me. "Not today, Nickie," I said finally. "Soon, but not today."

She sighed. "Eat, then," she said. "And get dressed. The guard changes at Buckingham in a little over an hour."

"Can we go by subway?"

Nickie rolled her eyes. "God, you've become a typical tourist. All right, by subway, but the minute you start looking tired . . ."

I had thought that the journey by subway might be just about as interesting as watching the changing of the guard, and I was right. Even on Sunday, the stream of passing people was hectic and varied. After a few painful bumps to my left side, I learned to dodge them (out of vanity, I hadn't worn a sling, because I didn't want to be conspicuous; I wanted to watch others rather than be watched myself), though I noticed that they rarely dodged each other. They simply glanced off of each other like pinballs, muttering a "sorry" that seemed perfunctory rather than sincere.

We bought our tickets at the ticket window because we didn't have the proper amount of change, but

Nickie showed me the vending machines and the list of destinations and price to each. Frequent commuters bought a pass, but Nickie, of course, either drove or took a cab. Traveling by "the tube" was too dirty and too time-consuming.

I had to admit it wasn't sparkling clean, although I enjoyed the advertisements on either side of the escalator (particularly the one for men's underwear) and the movie posters alongside the tracks. It was typical big-city grime, I told her, only nicer. It was, in this case, exotic big-city grime. And it wasn't really all that time-consuming. The train came fairly quickly, the people rushed forward and crammed into the train, sweeping us with them, and at the next stop a portion of them surged out of the train, leaving seats which Nickie and I gratefully took.

We got off at St. James's Park, having been joined along the way by a band of similar-minded tourists, and made a leisurely stroll to the palace, to join a crowd that had evidently gotten up earlier. I didn't mind. I had come to see the pomp, and there it was, marching up the street behind us, now entering the fenced forecourt of the palace, now lining up in impeccable rows.

Once inside the gates, the band began to play, lest the tourists become restless, perhaps.

"Oh, no, Nickie!" I cried.

She whirled, fearing the worst, I suppose. "What?"

"Do you hear that? The band is playing a selection of tunes from *West Side Story*. I came all the way to London to hear British soldiers play 'things will be great in America'!"

Several people around us tittered. Nickie's slight

British accent broadened. "You may be interested to know that *West Side Story* enjoyed a successful run in London, too."

"Yes, ma'am. Sorry, ma'am. I was just expecting something else."

" 'Land of Hope and Glory'?" offered a man in a red ski parka.

"Yes, some Elgar. Thank you. That would have been nice."

Nickie glared at me, so I watched the rest of the affair in silence. Music selection aside, I loved it. The guards had evidently marched from Chelsea Barracks today, but Wellington Barracks was just around the corner. The guard marched from there, my guidebook told me, in bad weather. I felt reassured. Tomorrow, if it rained, I would see a different band, perhaps.

"All right," Nickie said, when the old guard had disappeared down the street. "What next?"

"Trafalgar Square."

"Let us hope there are British pigeons on hand for inspection."

I smiled. "Well, Nelson will be there, anyway, and it isn't a very long walk."

It wasn't, but it felt like it by the time we arrived. Trafalgar Square, however, seemed planned for tourists, particularly out-of-shape tourists. We found a convenient bench facing the fountain and were not disappointed by either the pigeons or the kindly souls feeding them.

I stared up at Nelson atop his pedestal, wondering if the metal face at close inspection was any less stern than the Buckingham guards or any less unreadable than Chiswick's. "My guidebook says he won the battle of Trafalgar," I said to Nickie.

"Yes."

"Who lost?"

"The French."

"What were they fighting about?"

She turned and made a face at me. "Didn't you study any history in school?"

"Of course I did. American history. Want to know who won the Revolution?"

"No!"

I shifted my gaze downward to the bronze lions. "Is it serious, with you and the world's most handsome man?"

She turned her face away and was silent for a long time, so long that I thought I must have offended her. Then she said, "Why? Does it bother you?" She looked at me, not angry, but a little more than simply puzzled. Her face was too tense for the casual tone of her voice.

"No," I hastily assured her, embarrassed now by my nosiness. "But Chiswick . . ." I searched for the words that would convey a tentative and delicate meaning. "He watches me, Nickie. He sees everything, hears everything—even things I don't say." A small child ran past us, scattering the pigeons, squealing with glee. I shook my head, trying to rid myself of an uneasiness I couldn't define. "I'm just being silly, I guess. Seeing things that aren't really there."

Nickie's look was appraising, the tension gone. "I have a remedy for this."

"No, thanks, I'll work it out for myself."

"Ian must know lots of single men."

"Lots of single men with long prison records."

"Well, then what about James Bromley?"

"Too young."

"Valerie . . ."

I stood up. "In my own way, in my own time." But I was thinking never, never. Never again and never so much. "Steak and kidney pie time."

Nickie stood up, too. "I recommend steak pie without the kidney. I know a great place not too far from Oxford Circus. Tube?"

"Not this time." I grinned. "Double-decker bus!"

The bus ride took a bit longer than the subway ride, but the view from the top was fantastic, and I appreciated the chance to rest. I thought about passing up lunch and riding the whole route, but I knew Nickie would get restless long before that.

"Oxford Circus," I said when we got there, "isn't really a circus."

Nickie grabbed my arm and propelled me down the stairs. "You haven't seen it during rush hour. Or during Christmas shopping. Or during the sales."

I stepped down from the bus and looked around. "But why . . ."

"I don't know. Keep walking."

I was content to follow her across Regent Street, though we had to stop on the island in the middle to wait for yet another light to change so we could complete the crossing. But shortly afterward, the streets became suspiciously small, until finally I accused her, "We are walking down alleys. What kind of restaurant fronts onto an alley?"

"These are streets. This is England. It's supposed to be quaint, remember?"

"Yes, but—" We rounded a corner, and found the quaint English street all but blocked with parked cars.

Expensive cars. I looked down at my gray raincoat, wondering if I was sufficiently well dressed. Under the raincoat I was wearing a well-bleached pair of jeans. I had brought them as a point of pride, having worn them in college and then gained too much weight to fit into them after marrying Roger. But now losing weight was easy, and I had a bit of room to spare inside the denim. I should have worn a skirt, I thought. Nickie was wearing pants beneath her raincoat, too, but she would appear well dressed in trash bags.

The sign over the door identified the place as The Guinea Grill, a pub. I was surprised to find it so busy on a Sunday, but Nickie assured me it was a very special pub, purveyor of the very best steak pie in London. With patience and Nickie's practiced eye, we managed to find a table, scarce though they were. I peered around us through the smoky fog, trying to see without seeming to see. I wanted to capture the picture in my mind and hold it until the time was available to put it into words.

"Don't they have a dart board?" I asked.

Nickie pretended not to hear.

I leaned across the table. "How about a bathroom."

"A loo."

"A who?"

"Not who. Loo. It's commonly referred to as a loo."

"Oh. Okay. Where the loo?"

She nodded toward the rear of the pub. "Through there."

I was washing my hands, ready to come out again, when the building was rocked with an explosion. I put a hand out to steady myself and felt the wall shaking. There was a long, agonizing moment while the infor-

64

mation was processed in a brain that didn't want to believe what it knew to be true. Then I remembered Nickie and rushed out of the door.

The smoke was too intense to see all of the room, and several small fires along what used to be the bar were adding to it. I tried to remember where our table had been, and retrace my steps, but I discovered that the customers who had been busily eating and drinking and talking only a few seconds before were now scattered on the floor, moaning and bleeding and probably several other things I didn't want to examine too closely.

"Nickie!" I called out between coughs, but there was no answer. People were starting to get up and out, some of them helping each other. "Nickie!"

My eyes were tearing uncontrollably when I found her. The heavy table had survived the blast upright, but Nickie and her chair had been knocked over by the force of the blast. She was lying on her side, one arm flung out and one beneath her. I moved several short but heavy pieces of wood that had fallen on her and knelt beside her. "Nickie? Nickie?"

I wanted to move her, but remembered the warning of my high school first-aid class: accident victims should not be moved until professional help arrives unless it is absolutely necessary. Was it necessary?

Her eyelids fluttered and then opened. "Val. Run. Get away."

"It'll be okay, Nickie," I promised. "I'll help you."

"No! Val. Listen."

I brushed the dirt and debris from her face, gently. "I'll stay with you, Nickie. Help will be here soon."

"Val. Danger," she gasped. "Go!" She fumbled for her

purse. "Paper. Ian's number. Call him, Val. Get away from here and call Ian."

"Nickie, I can't leave you!"

"Please, Val," she pleaded. "Go! She had gotten her purse open and was digging inside with one hand.

I looked at her face, that lovely face now streaked with dirt and blood. She hadn't been Roger's lover, I told myself. Only a fool could have thought that. I couldn't leave her like this.

"Miss," said a heavily accented voice near my ear. A man was tugging at my coat sleeve. "Let me take you outside, miss. The ambulances are coming. They'll need room to work."

"No!" I said. "Nickie!"

"Go!" she cried, and I took the paper from her hand and let myself be led away without looking back.

Outside the scene was no less chaotic, although considerably more visible. I could hear the sirens of approaching rescue as the walking survivors continued to trickle out of the dark interior of the pub. I inched farther and farther away from the group of injured until I blended in with the surrounding crowd and then worked my way slowly backward until I could turn and walk away unnoticed, the paper crumpled in my hand.

I went back the way we had come out of Bruton Place, but when the tiny street crossed Bruton Street, I turned left instead of right. I needed a place to recover my thoughts, and Oxford Circus wasn't the place. Bruton Street ended at a small fenced park, with grass and trees and peaceful benches. The locals who had recently been there had evidently opted for the excitement of the explosion, for the park was deserted. I walked through an open gate and sat down on a shady bench, shivering; the sun had disappeared behind threatening clouds.

I uncrumpled the paper in my right hand and stared at the seven-digit number. It had been written, in Nickie's hand, I guessed, on a lightweight Rolodex card. There was no name, no instructions, only a number.

I couldn't figure out why Nickie hadn't wanted me to talk to the policemen who would naturally appear at the pub, and that was why I postponed using the phone booth at the far side of the grassy lawn. I had nothing to hide, and I had assumed Nickie had no secrets that would interest the police, since she allowed Chiswick to come and go freely. Where was the danger, and was it mine or Nickie's?

I thought about Chiswick, swearing when he heard about the explosion, as I knew he would. I had accepted him as a policeman; I had even seen his identification, although briefly and not entirely in focus. In fact, thinking about it, I had to admit that all I had really seen was a picture and some print that I hadn't been able to read. It could have been nothing more official than a driver's license, for all I knew.

But Nickie wouldn't have been that trusting, and Nickie had accepted Chiswick as a policeman. Or at least, as a lover. Could Nickie have had other motives in mind besides pleasure? I remembered her long silence at Trafalgar Square.

The gray clouds had begun to produce a fine mist that thickened to a freezing drizzle. I looked at the paper. The anchor in all these circular thoughts was that I trusted Nickie. Whatever her intent might be, whatever manipulations she had put in motion, whatever the outcome of the phone call I would have to make sooner or later, I instinctively trusted her.

After reading the instructions for making a telephone call very carefully, I checked my change. The coin slots specified 2p and 10p, both of which I had. I settled on 10p. Better safe than sorry. I dialed the number and waited, clutching the coin, until a flat, disinterested female voice answered, repeating the number I had dialed. The phone began beeping at me and I pushed the coin into the slot, gaining silence on the line.

"I want to talk to Ian Chiswick," I said, through chattering teeth.

"Mr. Chiswick is out at the moment," the voice answered. "Would you care to leave a message or arrange a meeting?"

"I . . ." I hadn't been prepared for this. What was I supposed to say? "I'll leave a message," I said on impulse.

"Yes," the voice prompted.

"Tell him that Nickie and I were having lunch at a pub, The Guinea something or other, and I went to the bath—" I paused, closing my eyes, trying to concentrate— "the loo and before I came out again there was a loud explosion and when I found Nickie she said to get out of there and call Ian at this number." I stopped for breath, realizing that I was babbling.

But the voice on the other end had become very interested indeed. "Mrs. Douglas?" she asked. "Are you all right?"

"I'm all right. Well, I'm not hurt. I'm cold and my shoulder hurts like hell and I'm hungry, but I'm not hurt."

"Where are you?"

I looked around at the park and the surrounding buildings. There would be a street sign somewhere, if I could just focus on it. But I was cold, so cold I was shaking, and I was not only hungry but weak as well. I realized that I just wasn't up to this. What I really needed was food, and some aspirins from my purse. There had to be a sandwich shop somewhere close by these office buildings.

"Mrs. Douglas? Are you still there?"

"I'm here. But I don't know where I am, not really. Listen, I'm cold and hungry and a few other things too. I'm going to find a sandwich, okay? I'll call you back in a little while."

"Wait!" the voice cried, but I hung up.

I found several sandwich shops, but most of them were closed. There seemed to be sirens everywhere, and I found myself moving away from them, circling around and beyond the park, walking the city streets without really seeing them, searching only for the glow of a lighted café.

I was dangerously tired, panting even at my slow pace when I found the shop. It looked cheerless and dingy, with grayed linoleum and mismatched tables and chairs, but it was open and there were people inside.

I pushed open a glass door that seemed to be made of lead and went inside. The man behind the counter seemed angry to see me. "Yeh?"

For a moment I was confused, in the pub again, thinking I should run.

"What do you want, then?" the man demanded.

"A sandwich." I knew I had spoken too quietly. I

hadn't put enough effort into it. "A sandwich, I repeated, louder.

"What kind of sandwich?" he asked, with mock patience. "Ham and cheese—"

"Yes!" I interrupted him. "Ham and cheese. And a Coke."

He slapped the sandwich and a Pepsi on the counter as if I had asked for something incredibly disgusting, and I paid him and sat down at a table in a barren corner, but within sight of the large glass front window.

The sandwich might just as well have been made of cardboard, for all the trouble I had getting it down. I had to wash almost every bite down with the soda in order to swallow it, and there was no taste to any of it. My lungs still seemed to be filled with smoke, so that everything I ate and breathed seemed to be smoke also.

It was warm inside the café, but I couldn't seem to get warm. My muscles were stiff from the cold and between each bite I sat on my hands, hoping to stop them from shaking.

Roger, Roger, what should I do? I was alone in a strange country and his ghost had deserted me. And Nickie was gone now, too, or as good as gone. I clung to that last image of her face, determined and urgent, alive. But out of my reach.

I had finished the sandwich. People would be expecting me to go. Where?

A noise beside my chair startled me into looking up. It was Chiswick, having crept up on me again. He said, "Valerie."

I didn't know what to say.

"Valerie," he repeated gently, prying my right hand from underneath my leg. "It's time to go."

"I'm s-s-so cold."

"I know you are, love. Come on. You can't hang about waiting for the world to make sense. You'd be here forever. Let's go home." Gently, he caught me beneath the arm and lifted me to my feet, taking more of my weight as my knees threatened to buckle.

"But Nickie said . . ." What was it ? "Dangerous."

"I've taken care of that, too. You'll see. Everything will be all right."

We were walking toward the door, and as we did, we passed a table of two young women. One said, quietly as we passed "Lucky girl."

Lucky?

Chiswick stopped me from turning back. "Let it go, Valerie, let it go." His voice seemed laden with sadness, and responsibility.

We got in the back seat of a car, one I hadn't seen before, with another, younger man driving. "Keep it warm," Chiswick said. "She's freezing."

"I've got a blanket in the boot, sir."

"Get it."

And so there appeared a blanket, woolly and musty, and the car pulled away from the curb. Chiswick took my two hands between his and began to rub them, watching my face, worried.

"Nickie," I whispered.

"She's okay. Nickie's a brick, you know that. A slight concussion. She'll be out in a couple of days and you can see her."

"I want to go to the airport. I want to go home."

Chiswick had produced a small flask and was pouring a drink. "Drink this," he said.

I shook my head.

He lifted the paper cup to my lips. "I wish I could get you home. I really do, Valerie. I wish I could promise that it's all over and there's nothing to worry about. But I can't. I'm going to make you drink this, not because I want to, but because that's what I have to do."

It tasted awful and burned all the way down, but the glow it gave was worth the choking. I drank all of it.

"I have some pictures I want you to look at," Chiswick said. "I want to know if any of them look familiar."

I stared at him. Surely I wasn't the best witness they could find!

"This is important. The face we're looking for is one that might not have been noticed by anyone else. But you might have seen it. You weren't injured in the explosion. Please look."

With hands that were stiff from more than cold now, I turned the pages and looked at the pictures. They were young, most of them, hardly more than children. College students, some even high school students, and some of the pictures might even have been class pictures.

But some of them weren't young, and had no air of fresh innocence. Some of them made my stomach constrict, as though I had known them in a former life, or I would know them in a future one, demon memories and premonitions. Toward the end, I found the face that Chiswick was looking for: the man who had led me out of the pub.

He had a pleasant face, framed by curly, red hair, and in the picture he was smiling, as if at some casual joke, looking straight into the camera, easy and confident. "Who is he?" My voice had come back croaking, but it had returned.

"Are you sure this is the one?"

"I'm sure. Who is he?"

"His name is Brendan Fierlan. Call it in, Enders."

"Yes, sir."

I stared at the picture until Chiswick took the book away. "Who is he?" I asked again.

"He's a thief, a murderer and a traitor," Chiswick said. "The lowest form of human life."

"Who is he?"

"He's a terrorist."

I closed my eyes, squinting as if some force were going to try and open them without my permission. "Is everyone who associates with you in constant mortal danger, or is it just the people I care about?"

There was a long silence before he spoke. "I'm . . . sorry."

I tried to read his face in the failing light and turned away. London had gone gray outside of the window. My impressions of it were fast fading to absolute black. It had been a random bombing of a pub, I tried to tell myself. No traveler to Europe was immune to terrorism. I began to shake again. Nickie was my anchor. I needed her.

"I'll take you back to Nickie's," he said. His voice was quiet, hardly audible.

I nodded, then stopped. "Tomorrow . . ."

"I'm afraid you'll have to stay in London for a while, Valerie, at least until the initial investigation is completed."

"Yes," I said. "But tomorrow is Michael Mosby's dinner party. I have to be there."

"Why?" he asked. "What's special about Michael

Mosby?"

My answer surprised me, too. "I don't know, but . . . but I have to be there, even if I have to go without Nickie. And I really don't want to go without Nickie."

"Then you will be there." The car stopped in front of Nickie's building, and he rested for a moment with his hand on the door handle. "I'll go with you."

His easy acceptance seemed a little too quick, but I was tired. I would be tired tomorrow, too, but I would go to Mosby's.

Chiswick got out and turned to offer me a hand. It was essentially a stranger's hand, but it was warm. Mine wasn't.

Chapter 5

The rain fell in a fine mist, in drops too small to see but enough to keep Chiswick's windshield wipers going. I shivered in the front seat beside him, bundled up like a small child sent off to school in the snow, but chilled by memories and expectations. Nickie was still in the hospital, not having completed her twenty-four-hour hospital stay. I needed her here.

Chiswick hadn't asked me if I wanted to see Roger's grave. He had simply told me we were going. When I had protested, he'd said, "Nickie keeps a pair of Wellies in the pantry. Put them on, it's wet out."

So there was nothing for me to do but find the rubber boots and wear them. Felicity helped me pull them on over my patterned silk stockings and two pairs of heavy socks, the latter at her insistence. I felt ridiculous riding down in the elevator in an evening dress and galoshes, but Chiswick and the two women we passed in the hallway took no notice.

It had been raining the day Roger left for England. He'd called a cab rather than have me drive to the airport. We walked to the door together and he leaned over and kissed me. "I'll be back before you know it," he said, as he always did. "Don't let the mail pile up unopened, and don't forget to have the car serviced on Monday. I've already made the appointment."

"I won't forget," I assured him. "I'll open the mail and pay the bills and throw away the junk mail."

"Good girl." He picked up his suitcase and turned back for one last, quick kiss. "See you soon."

Soon, Roger?

A passing building brought me back to the present. "Look! That was such a beautiful old house. Couldn't we stop for a moment?"

"We can't stop for every nice block of flats you see."

"It wasn't flat. It was two stories."

"Yes, but it was probably divided into flats."

"Flat whats?"

"Apartments."

I was horror-stricken. "Why would anyone want to carve up such a beautiful old house?"

"Because they couldn't afford to keep up the whole house anymore. Old houses take a lot of time and money. The council—the town government—buys the houses, divides them into flats and fixes them up, and then lets them out at reduced rates to people who need them."

"Where does the council get the money for all this? Taxes must be outrageous."

"That's the price we pay for civilization."

I didn't want to get into that argument. Most of what I had seen didn't seem, at the moment, to be all that civilized. I said, "Where do you live?"

"In a flat."

"In a flat where?"

"In a flat in London."

"Okay. Your secret's safe with me." It was a reminder that we weren't really friends. We were policeman and witness. "Is it nice?"

"It's enough," he said. "I'm not there very often."

"What about your family?"

I could tell from his sigh that he didn't approve of this line of questioning, but he answered anyway. "I see them for holidays."

"Oh."

He slowed down and stopped for a mother and child in a crosswalk, not taking his eyes from the road. In profile, his face revealed nothing.

I wanted to ask if he and Nickie were really lovers, but remembering her face in Trafalgar Square, I didn't dare. He would have been good for her in some ways; Nickie wasted time on too many spoiled rich boys who would never be men. But Chiswick gave so little of himself that I couldn't imagine it happening. Maybe underneath the smooth, hard exterior, there was another child, frozen in development not by money, but by something else. He was controlled and he controlled others. I found that comforting in my present situation, but I was still curious. We had successfully traversed a traffic circle and turned down a narrow road overhung with huge trees. He stopped the car in front of a small church. Next to it was a cemetery, marked by an arched wooden gate with daffodils blooming on either side. I forced myself to look at it through the window. It was peaceful, beautiful really, the sort of place that reflected Nickie's elegant taste. There were no ordered squares here, just a casual happening of memorials, interlaced with flowers and trees and serenaded by birds.

Chiswick got out, unfolded a massive umbrella, came around the car and opened my door. I forced my head to turn toward him, my heart suddenly pounding.

"I don't think I can do this," I said, panting.

He leaned against the car and looked over the roof, one hand resting on the painted metal and the other still holding the umbrella. I imagined another sigh, but didn't hear it. His stomach was close enough to my face for me to feel the warmth of his body through his open jacket, and to see the gun secure in its holster beneath his left arm.

"It's your decision," he said, but there was disapproval in his voice.

"No, it isn't. It wasn't."

His voice became gentler. "You've got to do it sometime."

"Why?" I challenged him. "Why do I have to do it at all?"

"What are you really afraid of?"

My mouth had gone dry, and the words came out hoarsely. "It isn't seeing the grave. I can manage that. It's just that . . . It's so unprotected."

He got back in the car. "I remember my first time," he began, talking to me but not looking at me. He did that, I was beginning to realize, when he had something to say that he really didn't want to say. "I had to walk across a street. Not a big, busy street. Just a small village street. There were people watching me, protecting me, and I knew that. I knew they were there, but not exactly where. And I knew that somewhere, there was a man determined to kill me, maybe then and there, maybe later. Crossing that street was the longest, loneliest trip of my life."

"Are there people watching out there?" I asked.

"Yes. Remember Enders, the driver from last night? He's there. He's been out there since early this morning."

"I can't see him."

"I know," he said, patiently. "But he's there. Valerie." He turned to look at me. "There is a strong possibility that Fierlan is out of the country by now. You may not be in any more danger."

"You might never catch him. Is that what you mean? I might have to live with this forever."

He turned away.

"Okay," I said. "Let's go."

The air outside was colder than the car had been, and I was grateful for his helping hand. I was stiff, not too far from rigor mortis myself. I took a deep breath and began to attempt a negotiated compromise with my body. All right, the palms can stay clammy, and I'll feel cold. But give me more strength in the knees. Please, please don't let me fall.

Chiswick knew his way through the churchyard, and probably would have carried me to the marker, if necessary. We stopped before a headstone that said "Roger Allen Douglas" and gave his date of birth and date of death, nothing more. Simple, clean, darkened by the drizzle of rain.

"Are you all right?" Chiswick asked.

We were two belated mourners in a spring churchyard cemetery beneath a slate gray sky. An English watercolor, I thought, and people might pass by our picture in a museum and murmur, "How lovely. How haunting." Then I looked down at my ridiculous black rubber boots, suddenly wishing I hadn't consented to wear them. They seemed disrespectful.

"Yes. I just, I . . . don't know what I should do."

"What do you feel like doing?"

I tried to smile. "Throwing up."

He slipped a steadying arm around me.

I reached out to touch the rose granite marker rising from the grass carpet. The mound seemed too small to contain Roger's height. "Goodbye, Roger," I said through my tears. "Goodbye, my love."

There was more that I wanted to say, but I didn't want Chiswick to hear it. I wanted to say thank you for so much and go to hell for so much and I hope it was good for you at least some of the time. And I'm lost without you, Roger. How could you have been so difficult to live with and so easy to love?

I bent over to kiss the cold stone, and then Chiswick gently pulled me away and guided me back to the car, holding me up and maneuvering me past obstacles I could no longer distinguish through the watery blur of tears.

If Roger's ghost watched me go, he didn't approve. Roger hated whining. He could have walked away from my grave dry-eyed, I told myself. Like Chiswick, Roger had control. He wouldn't have been sick with fear and sadness.

Chiswick must have seen my annoyance with myself. He reached into the back seat of the car and produced a box of tissues. "Cry," he said. "You're entitled."

I appreciated that. No long expressions of sympathy that would have intensified the tears, and no disapproval that would have intensified the guilt. He seemed to simply accept that in this situation for this person, tears were the proper reaction. That was rare, for a man, I decided.

We drove in comparative silence for a while. I sniffled and blew my nose and he watched the road, and then he said, "We'll be there soon."

"It's early. We'll be too early."

"We'll stop at a pub for a drink."

Any kind thoughts that I might have entertained toward him vanished. "That isn't funny."

He stared straight ahead. "It wasn't meant to be."

"Just a streak of sadism, I suppose."

"Just a matter of getting back on the horse that tossed you."

My cheeks flushed with anger. "Before the broken leg is set? Do the English have some arcane, cruel and revered tradition of riding about with casts on their legs?"

He sighed.

"Look at me. Look at me! Stop this goddamned car and look at me!"

He pulled over and looked at me, but there was nothing for me to see in his face, except steeled impasse.

"What's going on here? Why is it so important that I go in a pub today?"

"If you don't do it today, you may never do it again."

"And what difference will it make if I never do it again? It's beginning to seem highly unlikely that I will ever come back to England again and be presented with the opportunity."

"It's also highly unlikely," he said slowly, "that the fear will confine itself to pubs. You've already seen that open spaces frighten you. How will you feel at Mosby's, when all the other guests arrive and the rooms become crowded?"

I covered my face with my hands. Shit, I thought, and I said, "Shit."

81

"The pub is really just a trial run." He took something out of his pocket and offered it to me.

I opened the tiny manila envelope and found two small white pills inside. Tranquilizers. "This is too fast," I protested. "Everything is happening too fast. I don't need to be drugged. I need time to think, time to decide how I feel."

"We have about an hour," he said quietly. "But you should take the pills now."

"Shit," I said again.

"You want to watch that. People might start calling you Mrs. Shit."

I gave him a reluctant smile.

"That's better," he said. "Stiff upper lip, and all."

He had stopped before an old white stone building with a gaily painted sign that read The Swan. The side of the building bore the legend Young's. The bombed pub had been a Young's, too.

I opened my mouth to say something, but then closed it again. What was there to say? Chiswick produced a thermos and poured me a plastic cup of steaming tea, shrugging off my reproachful look. "Felicity insisted," he said.

I held the cup cradled in both hands, grateful for the warmth, if not the taste, and finally swallowed both of the pills he'd given me. But when he opened his door, I said, "I'm not going in there in these stupid boots."

Getting the boots off in the confines of the car proved to be too much for my injured shoulder. Chiswick watched my struggle for a few seconds and then got out and came around to my side of the car, opening the door and sitting on his heels on the roadway. He took the boots and socks off and accepted the evening sandal

I handed him.

"If this fits," he said, "you get to marry the prince."

"I just want to survive the ball," I answered. But the pills must have been working. I was starting to feel better.

The pub was dark and smoky inside, offering a choice of two rooms. Chiswick steered me away from one room, saying something about ladies and gentlemen that I didn't quite catch. Inside, conversation was even harder to understand, for the area was packed.

No one appeared to watch us, but I couldn't be sure. There were too many faces and too many hiding places. I inched closer to Chiswick.

"What'll ye have, guvner?" the bartender bellowed.

"Guinness," Chiswick shouted back. To me, he said, "What about you?"

"Guinness?"

"No, I don't think so. Want to try for a Coke?"

I looked around the room again and pulled him closer so I wouldn't have to yell my question. "What do women usually drink?"

The bartender evidently had fairly selective hearing. He smiled. "Oh, ye ne'er can tell!" he roared. "But, you, being an American lady, now . . ."

That effectively caught the attention of several patrons who turned to stare. My throat constricted, but I stood my ground.

"You might want to try some pale ale."

Chiswick shook his head. "Not with the pills."

I moved closer to his ear, and said quite distinctly, "To hell with the pills." To the bartender I said, "Pale ale!"

For a moment I thought the bartender might side

with Chiswick, but then he shrugged and drew a glass of golden liquid for me.

There was still a ray or two of afternoon sun peeking through the clouds, and when Chiswick said, "Out!" and gestured toward a side door, I needed no urging. I left him to pay for the drinks, not knowing whether that was the right thing to do in the circumstances, but unwilling to give it priority on my list of worries.

"Out" was lovely. The pub had a garden, not a flower garden, but a grassy lawn labeled Garden that looked out over a river. There were several tables with chairs, several sets of chairs without tables, a low stone wall and lots of grass to sit on during drier afternoons. It had stopped raining, and there were people here, too, shunning the noisy crowd inside for the quiet coolness of the river.

I took several deep breaths, willing my heart to stop its frantic pounding. I had lived. There hadn't been any bomb.

I walked to the edge of the garden, which ended at a sidewalk that ran alongside the river. Traffic was light this evening, consisting of a trio of swans and two rowboats. On the other bank, I could see backs of houses, complete with boat slips. The sound of vehicular traffic could hardly be heard here, despite its proximity. There was only the sound of the water and the muted conversations of the hardy souls enjoying the open air.

"Thames," Chiswick said behind me. I turned to accept a glass of golden beer.

"What?"

"Thames. The river."

"Oh. Thames." I followed him to a seat at a white-painted wrought-iron table. The chairs were still a bit damp, but Chiswick produced a handkerchief to dry them. I idly wondered if Scotland Yard issued hankies as well as guns. "What is that you're drinking?"

"Guinness. It's a kind of beer."

I stared at the dark brown liquid. It reminded me of the dirt-and-water drinks I had made to accompany mud pies as a child. "It looks gross."

"Try it."

I took a sip and made a face at the bitterness. "It *is* gross. I hope mine is better."

It was. Chiswick frowned at me, and I remembered the tranquilizers.

"Are they really tranquilizers?" I asked. "Or are they truth serum in pill form?"

"What makes you think I'd give you something like that?"

"I don't know, really. I just feel it. You're waiting to find out something from me. It started the second time you came to the hospital, and the feeling gets stronger every day. What do you want to know?"

Chiswick studied the murky depths of his drink. "If I knew, I'd ask you. You're . . . an incredible woman."

I snorted, buttoning the top button of my raincoat. "Nickie is an incredible woman. I am a sensible woman."

"Sensible?"

"Sensible. It must be true, because several men have told me. I'm also intelligent and sweet." I was beginning to feel considerably more cheerful. I drank more of my beer. "Sweet. Grandmothers are sweet."

He smiled. "And you always wanted to be a femme fatale."

It made me smile, too. "Only in high school. Must

have been all those spy movies of the sixties. Chasing cars through London on a rainy night . . ." I stopped for another swallow, and Chiswick waited patiently for me to continue. "What I always wanted to be was loved. The fairy princess. Major-league romance." I laughed at myself. "Now I prefer to just be liked. Maybe I am sweet, after all."

"But everyone wants to be loved."

"Even you?"

"Even me."

I thought for a moment, then asked, "By Nickie?"

"It's getting late," he said, rising. "We'd better be going."

It was dark before we reached Mosby's, but as we pulled into the drive leading to the huge house, the outside lights showed we were among the first to arrive. Getting out of the car, I looked at the building and wondered again why I was doing this.

I should have been back at Nickie's, sipping cocoa and listening to soothing music while Felicity pampered me. At the very least, I should have been trying to figure out how I felt about the random craziness that my life had become. Instead I was standing in the driveway of an elegant estate, about to go inside to greet a familiar face that belonged to a stranger. And I didn't know why.

Chiswick must have been having second thoughts of his own, for he eyed the house with what I thought was uncertainty, but then he said, "You could house a bloody army in there."

I looked at the house again. It was two stories, and looked well maintained from this angle, painted white, with dark, exposed beams framing the windows and crisscrossing on the second story above the door. The house made the same impression on me that Chiswick had made: solid, dramatic in appearance, and housing a wealth of mysteries. The stained-glass windows on either side of the entrance door were like Chiswick's eyes, too, revealing nothing about the interior. "Wealth and welfare," I said.

"What?"

"Wealth and welfare. Roger used to say that the government of developed nations was a continually negotiated compromise between those who wanted to maintain the status quo and those who wanted to eat."

Chiswick scowled at me to record his disapproval of this theory of economics and was about to ring the bell when the door was opened by a girl of no more than eight years. She had long, auburn hair and rosy cheeks, and she wore a blue wool jumper with a school badge on the right shoulder.

"Hello," she said. "Are you Valerie Douglas?"

"Yes."

She regarded Chiswick with distrust. "Who's he?"

"This is Mr. Chiswick. Who are you?"

"I'm Penelope Mosby," she announced. She moved out of the way, and Chiswick and I crossed the threshold.

"Did you really write *The Dandy Lion?*" she demanded. "Mummy said you did."

"I really did," I assured her, working myself out of the raincoat. I draped it over my arm and smiled at her. "Have you read it?"

"Oh, yes! Lots of times. Mummy bought it for my birthday. I think it's super."

"Thank you. It's nice to meet a fan. Would you like me to autograph it?"

"Oh, yes!" she cried, catching my hand and leading me up a large staircase. Chiswick followed at a respectful distance.

Penelope's room was richly furnished and impeccably neat. I felt like a long-expected guest; it was no accident that she had met me at the door. I was flattered.

"What shall I say?" I asked her, pen poised over the book's first page.

" 'To my super friend Penelope!' "

As I began to write, she added, "And please don't tell Daddy."

"I won't," I promised.

"Or Mr. Chiswick, either."

"Don't worry. He's very good at keeping secrets. Why don't you want Daddy to know?"

"Daddy says you're a dangerous woman."

I looked up, surprised. "Really? Dangerous?"

She nodded.

"Why?"

"He wouldn't tell me. He just made me promise to stay away from you. You're not dangerous, are you?"

"Of course not."

"Good. But don't tell him anything, anyway, okay?"

"I promise."

We followed her back down the stairs, went back outside, and after waiting patiently while I counted to fifty, Chiswick rang the bell.

"Am I dangerous?" I asked him.

"Not to me. I think you're sweet."

Chapter 6

A butler even more somber than Chiswick showed us into "the library." A library, with three walls of floor-to-ceiling bookcases and a fireplace, within which a cozy fire glowed. I stopped just inside the doorway, almost run over by Chiswick. I had forgotten how much I wanted a library of my own. The house in Houston had the space, but Roger had vetoed the idea, preferring to adorn the walls with "investment art." But Roger was gone, now, and the house was all mine. And if I wanted a library . . .

"Mrs. Douglas!" The boom of Mosby's voice preceded him across the room. "I'm delighted that you could come. I was afraid you might have been housebound after the bombing."

I frowned at him. "How did you know I was there?" I asked. "My name wasn't in the papers."

"Nicola's secretary told me when I called to inquire about your plans yesterday."

"Oh," I said, thinking Fierlan wouldn't have any trouble finding me. Chiswick's hand rested lightly on my back and I leaned back a little, remembering the gun he carried and the protection it represented.

"Of course," Mosby continued, "that's all behind you, now."

"It is?"

"You haven't heard? It was announced this afternoon. They've caught Fierlan."

Chiswick swore softly behind me. We'd been out of touch, visiting the cemetery and then the pub, traveling in an ordinary car without the usual communications link. I hadn't questioned the lack of equipment in the car. I hadn't thought about it, until now. But even so, Enders would have known, and Enders had been there. Or had he? I hadn't seen him.

"Mrs. Douglas?" Mosby was waiting for a response.

"You'd think," I muttered with unfeigned irritation, "they'd have told us before the news was released to the press."

Mosby's attention had shifted to Chiswick. "I'm certain they tried, Mrs. Douglas; the announcement was 'leaked' to the media. Not intentionally, you understand."

Mosby had either found the answer he was looking for in Chiswick's face or given up looking, for he steered us away from the door and toward the bar, where he left us to greet his other guests.

The bartender looked at Chiswick expectantly.

"Scotch and water," Chiswick said, "and the lady will have a Coke."

"The lady will have a Dubonnet on the rocks," I corrected him.

"No more alcohol," he said quietly.

The bartender hesitated, not willing to ignore a man of Chiswick's build. Other guests had gravitated toward the bar as well, and several were watching our little standoff with amused interest.

"Dubonnet isn't exactly hard liquor," I pointed out.

He had slipped an arm around my waist, and now he pulled me closer. His eyes, inches from mine, had gone steel gray. "No," he told me and to the bartender he repeated, "A Coke for the lady."

The bartender searched through his supply of bottles. "I'm sorry, sir," he stammered in embarrassment, "we don't have Coke. Will Pepsi do?"

The steadily growing audience tittered.

"Yes," I said, having abandoned the notion of fighting to get my way on a trivial matter. "Pepsi is fine."

When we finally had our drinks in hand, Chiswick took me by the arm and pulled me to an almost empty corner of the room.

"I need to talk to you," he began.

I glared at him. "I'm glad to see you're catching up with reality."

"You don't understand."

"Of course I don't understand! How can I understand what I haven't been told?" A young couple was strolling past us, arm in arm, and I waited until they were out of earshot to continue. My head was beginning to pound energetically.

He sighed with exaggerated patience. "Listen, Valerie . . ."

"This had better be good," I warned him. "If you made me go into that pub—"

"It isn't that simple!" he hissed. A woman standing in a group not far from us turned to look at him and he forced a smile.

"Then tell me in short sentences and don't use any hard words."

"Fierlan may be in custody, but that doesn't guarantee the threat is gone."

"I can understand that. See? It wasn't that difficult. Did you tell your boss that I was retarded or something?"

"We don't know for certain that the news report was even accurate."

I looked into my drink and my thoughts went off on another tangent. Why had I really been given the tranquilizers? What was the pub stop really meant to accomplish? I shook my head, trying to recapture control of my brain. Either I hadn't really been given tranquilizers, or they had stopped tranquilizing. "No, we don't know for certain. Why don't you call and find out?"

"No." He was looking off into the distance watching the door.

"It would *really* make me feel a lot better."

There was an eruption of laughter from a cluster in front of the fireplace. Chiswick waited until it had died down before he answered. "This isn't a good place. We'll call when we get back to Nickie's."

"This isn't a good place?" I had said it too loudly, and I caught myself and lowered my voice. "Are we in the lion's den here? Is Mosby Fierlan's cousin or something? What's going on?"

"Tonight," he promised, "when we're alone, I'll try to explain everything to you. Can you just trust me until then?"

"You are beginning to sound like a character in a television show. In fact, at the moment, the only things missing from my life are commercials for laundry soap. Who in the hell *are* you?"

His voice was low, and edged with huskiness. "Please, Valerie. Trust me."

I closed my eyes. "Trust you. Sure, why not? Since

I've met you I've been shot, bombed, drugged and life has ceased to make any sort of sense. One more bewildering evening won't make much difference."

He stood there for a moment longer without speaking, although he seemed to want to, and then he reached out to smooth a strand of my hair into place, turned, and drifted off toward a clump of gray-haired gentlemen. I frowned as I watched him go.

I would have enjoyed inspecting the books that lined the walls, but the room had rapidly filled with smoke and I wasn't willing to endure it just to find out what Mosby might have read. I drifted across the entryway hall to the parlor, dodging several well-intentioned but unwanted conversational offers along the way.

The parlor was smaller than the library and more densely furnished, but it was quieter and the air was relatively clear. My eyes settled on Mosby, huddled in a corner with a dark-haired man in a blue-and-gray striped tie.

It was a fairly ordinary tie, one that could pass in a crowd without notice, and yet it caught my notice. Had I seen that, too, somewhere before? Perhaps on Mosby?

"I say, aren't you Valerie Douglas?" said a deep voice beside me.

I turned just as he moved in front of me. I could still see Mr. Striped Tie over Mr. Deep Voice's shoulder. "Yes," I said, my interest still on the other side of the room.

"You're a writer, aren't you? A scholar of sorts, I believe."

"A writer yes," I said without looking at him. "But not a scholar."

"Ah, but Michael says you are quite well-read."

Quite well-read? How had Mosby come by that information? "I enjoy reading, especially well-written books. But I'm surprised to hear that Mr. Mosby thinks so highly of me."

Mr. Deep Voice ho-hoed in a way that would have made Santa Claus envious. "Michael's a clever one, he is. Have you any interest in history?"

I checked Mr. Striped Tie's position to make sure he was still with Mosby. "Not particularly," I admitted.

"I find it a fascinating subject myself. Particularly the Second World War." His silvered mustache quivered in anticipation of a rousing discussion. "It was very much a war of strategy, don't you think?"

Mosby and Striped Tie seemed to be disagreeing about something. "All wars involve strategy," I mumbled.

"Of course, of course. Quite right. But there are some particularly notable examples in the second great war. For instance, take your president."

I had no idea who had been president during the Second World War, and very little hope of successfully communicating this fact to Mr. Deep Voice.

He, however, was not dismayed by my silence. "He made several serious mistakes, you know."

I noted that Mosby and Striped Tie had moved a little closer to the door. "War is . . . always a serious mistake."

"True. Yes, yes . . ." His voice drifted away for a moment and then took up the cause with new vigor. "But these were particularly serious. They were mistakes of strategy. You do understand that, don't you?"

"I have to admit that military strategy isn't one of my

interests. I don't know very much about it."

"But you do realize that mistakes were made, don't you?" he pressed. "You Americans handled the situation poorly."

"I'm beginning to understand that," I growled, watching Striped Tie leave the room. "You must excuse me, Mr. Whoever, but the Second World War is ancient history as far as I'm concerned, and the study of wars in general isn't high on my list of leisure activities. I think you should discuss this with someone who actually lived through the war. Excuse me." I walked away, leaving him huffing and snorting in my wake.

In the hallway I stopped to look for Striped Tie, and thought I saw him disappear to the right from the end of the entryway. I followed, walking quickly but not running. Nevertheless, when I rounded the corner I bumped into him. "Oh!" I said in surprise. "I'm sorry. I—"

"Take this," he hissed, pressing something wrapped in a tissue into my hand.

"But I—"

"You're doing splendidly," he said. He had the same sort of accent Mosby had. The sort of accent I had first heard on the plane, from the man who had sat beside me.

I gently unwrapped the tissue and found a golden charm attached to a fine chain. I held it up to examine it in the dim light. "I'm glad you think so, but—" I began, looking up, but he was gone. Through the door at the end of the passage I could hear the clatter of dishes. I held up the necklace and looked at it again. It was a tiny gold skeleton key, pretty but a little young for me. It would have made a delightful gift for Penelope. But why me?

Behind me, I could hear the sound of running feet, and as I turned, Chiswick appeared, gun drawn. I closed my hand around the necklace. "What are you doing?" I snapped. "You scared the hell out of me!"

He darted past me, into what I assumed was the kitchen. I could hear some high-pitched squawks greeting his arrival. In a moment, he returned, holstering his gun.

"What's going on here?" demanded Mosby, who had appeared during the interim.

I looked at him and then at Chiswick, before shrugging. "Just a little policeman paranoia, I guess," I said

"What are you doing here?" Chiswick asked me, glaring.

The charm and its chain were suddenly heavy in my hand, but I kept them hidden, even while wondering why I was doing it. I trusted Chiswick, I told myself, and there wasn't any reason to keep secrets. But myself answered that I trusted Chiswick to take care of his business, and this wasn't his business.

Chiswick stared at me with an intensity that frightened me, as if he could read every thought in my face, and was angered by what appeared there. "Excuse me," I said, finally. "I admire chivalry, too, but an armed escort to the ladies' room seems a little extreme."

Mosby's face relaxed into a host's easy smile. "Don't be angry with him, Mrs. Douglas. The presence of a lady brings out the gentleman in all of us." He gestured to the passageway behind him. "You have taken a wrong turn. The toilet is this way."

I followed him without looking again at Chiswick, but the heat of his anger warmed my face, if not my icy hands. Safely inside the bathroom, I looked longingly at the tiny window. If I could escape, I could hide, and then I could think. I needed to think. I needed time to remember the things that were somewhere in my memory, to understand what fueled these strange impulses.

I didn't want to believe that I was falling apart, losing control, but that's the way it felt. When I had followed Striped Tie out of the library, I hadn't really known what I was doing, and now that it was done, I didn't know why. I didn't know what the necklace meant, or why I had kept the truth from Chiswick, or why I couldn't totally trust him. And the very worst feeling of all was that I didn't want to go back to Houston yet. Even given the chance of escape, I couldn't have taken it.

I closed the lid of the toilet and sat down on it, wondering what Roger would have told me to do. I'd had trouble placing names and faces before.

"You can't remember because you're not trying hard enough," Roger would say. "You've got to learn to concentrate. The fear of not knowing the person's name keeps you from remembering it."

I closed my eyes against the gay profusion of flowered wallpaper and tried to relax. Then I focused on Mosby: his face, his build, his voice. Where had I seen it before? New York? Houston? A company party?

The answer was almost there, but I couldn't quite take hold of the memory and bring it to the present. Outside, I could hear the sounds of a group of people being herded from one room to another, heralding either the serving of dinner or a group search for another bathroom. I sighed and got up to leave. I couldn't spend the rest of the evening hiding.

Chiswick was waiting for me outside the door. Without speaking or even particularly looking at me, he took my hand and tucked it into his arm, leading me to the dining room.

The mood of the party was lighthearted when we rejoined it. Whatever Mosby and Striped Tie had been arguing about hadn't spoiled Mosby's good humor, for he was recounting the history of the house and his family with gusto. Ordinarily I would have enjoyed this, but that night I heard very little. Roger was right. No concentration.

I looked around me, hunting for the reflection of the man in his possessions. It was a spacious room, flanked by two huge portraits, ancestors I presumed, on walls directly across from each other. There were also two massive china cabinets filled with china, even though there were at least twenty-five settings in use on the table. Even Mosby's wife, sat at the opposite end of the table, bore the evidence of his wealth in the emerald necklace she wore.

These were Roger's type of people, much more than I had ever been. They were wealthy and influential, the "movers and shakers," as Roger had dubbed others.

I remembered us returning from a banking affair in New York, arriving at the apartment in the early hours of the morning.

"Why did you spend all evening talking to —— [I had forgotten that name now, too]?" Roger had asked.

"Well, it wasn't for pleasure," I had assured him. "The man is a terrible bore. I did it for your career, out of love." I blew him a kiss.

"Save yourself the trouble next time."

"But he's a client," I protested. "I'm supposed to be

nice to clients."

Roger shrugged and shook his head. "He's nobody. We needed his agreement for one small transaction and the man expects to be courted for life. I don't know why Penning keeps him hanging on. It isn't as if he were important. He isn't a mover."

I must have looked surprised, for Roger laughed at my naïveté, and then, relenting, took me in his arms and vowed that was what he loved most about me. "But business," he'd added, "is business, and there's no place for innocent trust in business." I had kissed him and thought myself lucky to be loved by a mover of the movers.

"Mrs. Douglas?" Mosby was saying. He was seated at one end of the long table, and I was the first person to his right. Chiswick sat across from me. "Mrs. Douglas!" Mosby said again.

"Yes? I'm sorry. I was just . . . admiring the china."

Mosby smiled. "May I invite you to admire the wine, as well? As I'm fond of saying"—here he dipped his head to his wife—"the finest meal is no better than the wine that accompanies it."

He lifted his glass to propose a toast, but I didn't hear it. I was no longer in the room.

I was in New York, in a French restaurant, celebrating Roger's promotion with Roger and Nickie. We had eaten well, and drunk even better. Roger had called the waiter over and asked to see the wine steward for a third bottle of wine. The man appeared, and Roger asked him to recommend a wine that would go well with the meal we had eaten, saying, "The meal isn't over until the fat man pays the check." At the time, this struck me as extremely funny, and I had collapsed in laughter. When I finally got the better of my giggles, I looked up to see the steward had returned with a bottle of white wine.

"Vouvray," he said. "Because even a meal that's already been consumed is no better than the wine that accompanies it."

Mosby had been that steward.

"Mrs. Douglas?" Mosby said again. "Are you all right?"

"Oh . . . yes. Yes. I'm fine."

"I hadn't realized the china was so entrancing."

Several guests seated near us laughed quietly.

"Excuse me," I said testily. "This hasn't been the best vacation I've ever had. I'm a little the worse for wear."

Across the table, the corners of Chiswick's mouth twitched. Mosby was instantly apologetic; I wondered what he would say if I asked to see his résumé. I also wondered why Nickie had asked me if I remembered the waiter—Mosby—at the French restaurant. Nickie remembered him but she hadn't told me the truth about it. What else had she lied about?

I didn't know how Chiswick fitted into the scenario. It didn't seem likely to me that Nickie would try to have me killed. I could easily believe her capable of lying, cheating, and stealing. That was, by definition, high finance. Murder was another matter entirely. Maybe Chiswick was an almost-innocent, armed-to-the-teeth bystander. Maybe.

"Are you really a policeman?" I asked him, as soon as the door to Mosby's house had closed behind us.

"Yes, sort of."

"Sort of doesn't cut it. Are you a policeman or not?"

He was silent for the length of time it took us to

reach his car. Then he said, as he opened the door for me, "Are American treasury agents policemen?"

"Yes," I decided. "Treasury agents are policemen."

"So am I." He grinned, as if immensely pleased to be compared to that noble breed, and disappeared around the car.

"Can you prove it?" I asked, when he slid into the driver's seat.

"What kind of proof did you have in mind?"

What kind, indeed? I hadn't led a totally sheltered life, but this was definitely out of my experience. Roger played tennis with a man who once worked for the Drug Enforcement Administration, a man known to me as simply Stone. That wasn't his real name, of course, but it was an accurate description of his personality. Stone ran a security business, and Roger told me that he'd left the DEA voluntarily to go into business for himself. But after seeing a parade of bleached-blonde girlfriends with perpetually bloodshot eyes and cars that never seemed to remain undamaged for long, I decided Stone had probably been in business for himself long before he left the DEA. Even if I'd had Roger's address book with me, I wouldn't have wanted to consult Stone about Chiswick.

"Maybe you'd like to talk to Nickie about it," Chiswick said, starting up the car.

"No!" It was too loud and too quick and I instantly regretted it.

"Okay," he said easily. "Let's review the options. An audience with the Queen, perhaps?"

It took me a moment to realize that, for once, he wasn't serious. My anger followed quickly. "Forget it."

"Come on, Valerie. Relax a bit. Life isn't a spy

movie."

"No? Then why didn't the lady answer, 'Treasury Office,' or whatever the equivalent is, when I called you? What's all this about arranging meetings? And why didn't you tell me Fierlan had been caught?"

"Got a lot of questions, haven't you?"

"You can answer them one at a time. It's a long trip back to Nickie's."

"And if I answer them," he said, not looking at me, "will you answer mine?"

I looked at his profile. Why, I thought, was I so reluctant to trust him? If he was who he claimed to be I had nothing to hide from him. It wasn't an earthshaking thing, really, that Nickie hadn't told me about Mosby. And insisting that I call Ian after the bombing was probably due to the concussion she'd suffered, easily explainable. Roger's cuff link and the necklace, well . . .

"Well?"

I took a deep breath. "Okay."

Chapter 7

"What was your first question?" he asked. "Something about the way my phone is answered, wasn't it?"

"Yes."

"I do have an office, in an office building, with a uniformed guard at the door and a receptionist to answer phones. I even have a parking space, which in London is a sure sign of legitimacy. If we were to pull up to the next telephone we see and dial the number of that office, someone would answer — even in the middle of the night — 'Special Investigations.' If you were to ask that person my whereabouts, he or she wouldn't know. That person would never know my whereabouts when I am not in my office, and would never admit my identity over the phone."

"And if I called there, and really needed you?"

"The message would be routed through a series of relays that are changed daily. I would get it, but it would take time. You must realize, Valerie, that if you had called that office, and not said your message was urgent, you'd have been sitting in that café for hours, waiting for me."

I thought I *was* there for hours. And I wasn't waiting for you."

"Oh? What were you doing, then?"

"Recovering. Trying to think. It doesn't matter. Why did the woman who answered know who I was?"

He shrugged. "I didn't want Nickie to take you out yesterday. It was too soon. But she knew you'd insist, even though you were still weak. So I gave her the emergency number, in case you fainted somewhere." He smiled, and years slipped away from his face. "I may not wear a uniform, but I have a lot of influence with people who do. Of course," he added, "I wasn't expecting a bombing."

"No. Me neither." I looked out the window. It was late and there was little traffic. Then I realized we weren't in central London, although we'd been driving for what seemed like a very long time. I was tired, and ready for bed.

"You had another question, didn't you?" Chiswick asked. "Something about Fierlan?"

"Oh, yes. Why didn't you tell me about Fierlan?" I yawned. "And please, don't try to pretend you didn't know."

"Of course I knew. He's been in custody for over twelve hours."

"Twelve hours?" I was instantly wide awake. "Twelve hours?"

He checked his watch. "More like fourteen, actually."

All I could say was, "Why?" I would have demanded to be let out and walk, or take a cab, but it was late, cold, and we seemed to be driving through a residential area. There were no cabs in sight. "Why?" I said again.

He braked gently to a stop in front of an unassuming little two-story bungalow. "In order to explain that, I would have had to explain all of this, and we didn't have the time."

I leaned across him and looked at the house. "All of what?"

"This," he said, opening his door, "is my real office."

He opened the wooden gate set in a fragile-looking fence that seemed more or less held up by several large bushes behind it and let me lead the way to the front door. It was a nice little house, I supposed. Even in the dark, I could see well-kept flower beds and a tiny, neatly trimmed lawn. I wondered if Enders did the gardening. Although there was no porch light, a faint light glowed through the small stained-glass window beside the door. The noise we made walking up the winding stone path was quiet but apparently audible to those inside, for the door opened just as I reached it.

"Evening, Mrs. Douglas," said Enders when I walked through the door. "Evening, sir," he told Chiswick.

"Are the photos ready?" Chiswick asked.

Enders was helping me out of my coat. "Yes, sir." I followed them into the parlor, speechless, but processing information as fast as my brain could manage. From what I could see, the house seemed to be furnished modestly, but comfortably. There was an armchair on either side of the small fireplace, an occasional table bearing a chessboard in front of the bay window curtains, and a sofa, upholstered in fabric that might have dated from the late fifties, upon which Chiswick motioned me to sit.

He continued through a large, arched doorway to what must have been the dining room. At least there was a small dining table there, although half of the room was taken up by a large desk with a computer. There was another man there, younger even than Enders, punching keys and watching the monitor screen intently. Chiswick paused to look over the man's shoulder for a brief moment and then disappeared through another door.

"This is some office," I said to Enders when my voice returned.

"Office? Oh, yes, ma'am. Well, it has all the comforts of home." He smiled hopefully.

I thought about my home in Houston and looked around again. Not *all* the comforts of home, I was tempted to say. I wished that I were home, comfortable and safe, watching a late movie on the big-screen television and eating popcorn popped in the microwave.

"You wouldn't, by any chance"—I paused to listen to the tramp of feet on the floor above us—"happen to have a cold Coke handy, would you?" I looked around again. "And maybe another dose of Chiswick's tranquilizers. I think I'm going to need them."

"Tranquilizers?" Enders said.

"He *said* they were tranquilizers."

"I did not," Chiswick said from the doorway. "You assumed they were tranquilizers. The power of suggestion worked much better than chemicals could have done."

I sighed heavily and Enders excused himself and fled. "Have you told me the truth about anything?"

He took off his jacket and tossed it over the back of the couch before sitting down beside me, loosening his tie. "The out-and-out lies have been few," he said, plopping down a manila file folder on the low table before us. "I have elected not to tell you some things, though. Just as you have chosen not to tell me the whole truth." I held my peace and let him continue. He opened the file and took out a stack of pictures. "To get back to one of your earlier questions, Michael Mosby—"he paused to hand me Mosby's picture—"isn't exactly Fierlan's cousin, but they definitely aren't natural enemies. We have reason to believe Mosby has done a bit of work for Fierlan and his group."

I looked at the photo again. It had been taken at the party. "Work?" I said.

"Mosby is in the import business."

"Guns?"

"Weapons," he corrected me. "Of all types." He handed me a picture of Mr. Deep Voice, the war historian. "Mosby has powerful friends, as well."

Enders appeared with a cold can of Coke and an empty glass. I told them both about my conversation with Mr. Deep Voice, eliciting broad grins from the two of them.

"Isn't that just like his pompous . . . self," Enders said, substituting the last word in response to Chiswick's quick frown.

I looked from one to the other, charmed. "I'm pleased to see you're mending your ways," I said to Chiswick. Enders's eyebrows crept upward, which pleased me even more. Did Chiswick's staff also call him Bloody Hell behind his back?

Chiswick handed me another picture without comment. It was Striped Tie. "Who *is* this guy?" I asked.

"We were hoping you might know," Enders answered.

"Why did you go after him?" Chiswick demanded.

I shook my head. "You'll think I'm crazy. *I* think I'm crazy. It doesn't make sense."

Chiswick shook his head. "It may sound crazy, but it will make sense. Maybe not right away, but it will. Tell us about him."

"Well . . ." I was at a loss where to begin.

"Why did you follow him?" Chiswick asked again.

"His tie. I told you it didn't make sense. There was something about his tie. I just . . . *had* to go after him. I didn't even know what I wanted to ask him, or say, or anything. I just had to go."

Chiswick and Enders looked at each other, sharing a grave secret. "What is it?" I asked.

But Chiswick shook his head again. "Go on. What happened next?"

"I caught up with him just outside the kitchen. Before I could say anything, he gave me something wrapped in a tissue. Then he said something like, 'You're doing splendidly,' and just disappeared." I found the necklace in my purse and held it out to Chiswick. "This is what he gave me."

He examined it closely and passed it to Enders. "Does it mean anything to you?"

"No. It isn't mine. I mean, it isn't like Roger's cuff link, something that I once owned that had disappeared and then reappeared. I can't remember ever having seen it before."

"Does it remind you of anyone or anything?"

I looked from one to the other. They were literally sitting on the edge of their seats, waiting for some profound announcement. "No. What is it, what's wrong? Why is this so important?"

Chiswick's face relaxed into disciplined calm. "Anything that has to do with Mosby is important."

"Why was I invited to the party?"

He shrugged, and gave me back the necklace. "To get this."

I rubbed my temples. "I don't understand any of

this."

"Aspirin," Chiswick said to Enders, and then to me, "I'll check it out, see if I can identify Mr. X. There is one more question, I think, that you wanted me to answer."

I accepted the aspirin from Enders with suspicion. "What are these, really?"

"Aspirin. Really."

"Yes," I said to Chiswick, "there was one more question. Fierlan."

He leaned back against the sofa, resting his right ankle on his left knee, as if he were about to recount a long and complicated anecdote. "Fierlan," he began, "has to be viewed in perspective. He is, in some respects, a leader, but in the hierarchy of the organization, he is a lesser figure. He takes more orders than he gives. If we stop Fierlan—"

If?

"We stop his potential for harm. But if we stop those above him . . ."

"They're letting him go, aren't they?" Somehow the voice wasn't mine. The room had gotten so cold, so suddenly that I was shivering.

"Yes. He's . . . gone."

"No," I pleaded. "They can't."

"He won't be a danger to you anymore," Chiswick promised, putting an arm around me. "You can't hurt him anymore."

"They can't. All those people. Nickie. The people who died. They *can't* let him go."

"Think of the lives that might be saved, the bombings that might never happen," Enders said.

"Might. Might! He'll disappear. And nothing will be

accomplished. The people," I said again. "The sound of them, the sight of them, suffering . . . dying. How can the police let him go? Don't they understand? Don't they know?" I bent my head forward, hiding my face.

"They know," Chiswick whispered into my hair. "They know every victim by name. They know every next-of-kin. They know."

I felt the hardness of the gun between us and pulled away. Chiswick undid the harness with his right hand and slipped it off, reaching for me again.

I resisted. "What good is a gun, if it can't stop the killing? It's just more death, more killing, and innocent people are still dying."

He drew me closer, winning in a contest of many strengths. "I know, Valerie. Sometimes I feel the same way. But I have to keep trying. We can't give up."

He held me for what seemed like a very long time. Eventually my sobbing slowed, and the senses that it had blocked out returned. I could feel the warmth beneath Chiswick's shirt, the wetness that my tears left, and the even steadiness of a heart beating. And so I knew that he had a heart, although I had no other evidence to verify it.

When I had calmed down enough to breathe easily, Chiswick took my head in both hands and tilted it back, searching for something in my face, revealing nothing in his. Then, without warning, he pulled my head forward and kissed me on the forehead, his lips light on my skin, the way a father might kiss a child. But he held the pose longer than a father would, and when I drew back, the tenderness provoked an even greater confusion in me and I turned away, angry at that, too.

Enders eased me back into my coat and into the car with the gentlest of care, as though I might explode at any moment. After closing my door, he crept around the car to the driver's side. Or maybe he didn't. Maybe it was his normal mode of movement.

Probably, I thought, everyone who worked for and with Chiswick was accomplished in sneaking. Sneaking and lying. Maybe I wouldn't have been quite so angry if I'd had even one person in England that I could trust. But I didn't.

When we reached Nickie's door, I started to give Enders Nickie's key, and then pulled it back. "What's your name?" I asked him. "What's your first name?" I had never looked at him closely before, and now I was struck by his youth and the sweetness of his unlined face.

"Charles," he answered. "My friends call me Charlie."

"Do you have friends?" I wanted to ask, but I didn't. His role had been that of protector, and that, at least, I could appreciate. "Were you really there, at the cemetery?"

"I was there."

I opened the door myself. "Thanks for a swell evening," I said, going inside.

Lying in bed, with the opening chords of Mozart in my ears, I regretted that parting remark briefly, before surrendering to sleep.

I was walking down a long, dimly lit corridor, looking for something. The hallway was lined with doors, each of them named in large letters. I stopped in front of one and squinted to read it. "LON."

The doorknob was old and rusty, and I struggled to get the door open. Having finally gotten the knob twisted, I found I had to throw my entire weight against the door to budge it. My shoulder should have hurt, but didn't. I had to be dreaming. I looked back at the hallway, wanting to go back and wake up, but I couldn't wake up. I had to find something.

Behind the door, in a small, barren room, Nickie sat at a desk, punching out numbers on a calculator and humming to herself softly.

"Nickie?" I asked. "Where are we?"

She looked up. "You're dreaming. We're nowhere. We don't exist."

"But, Nickie, what am I supposed to find? I can't wake up until I find it and I don't know what I'm supposed to find. Help me." She wouldn't listen to me, and went back to humming and calculating.

I went out again and tried the next door down. CORP, it read. Behind this door, which opened easily, sat Dennis Penning, slumped in a straight backed chair.

"Dennis?" He wouldn't look at me. "What am I supposed to find? Can you help?" I touched him on the shoulder, and he sprang to his feet, shouting.

"Don't touch me! I don't know you! I can't help you!"

I backed out, shaken. Please, God, let me wake up, I prayed. I banged my head against the wall, but nothing happened. There was no pain and no reality. There was only the long, empty corridor.

The next door was marked CHIS. It opened by itself, to reveal a room full of people, all of whom immediately stopped talking and turned to stare at me. I found Chiswick in the crowd. "Please," I begged him.

"Please tell me what I'm supposed to find."

"I can't," he said "Keep going, Valerie. You have to keep going." He pushed me back out into the hall and closed the door.

I walked past miles of unmarked doors which opened to emptiness until at last I came to the end of the hallway. The door read NUMB. I tried to open it, but the knob wouldn't turn. No amount of banging or jerking made the slightest difference.

"You have to have the key," Roger said from behind me.

I whirled around. He was dressed for the theater: black suit, white shirt and a silk tie. I wanted to hug him and be held in his arms, but he backed away. "Roger, please," I said. "Help me. Help me find what I'm looking for. Tell me what I'm supposed to find."

Roger smiled, and I saw there was blood on his teeth. "You have to have the key, darling. That's the only way in." The blood dribbled down his chin and began dripping on his white shirt.

"I can't find the key!"

Roger's laugh was a high wail. "You don't have to find the key. The key finds you!"

Down the hallway, in the darkness, I could hear the sound of running and the growls of a nightmare beast.

"Roger, help me!" I screamed.

He laughed again, now drenched in blood. "It's coming, Valerie! It's coming!"

I felt it coming, the heavy tread of paws on a wooden floor and the heat of its panting. But the hall had dead-ended. My back was to the door and there was no way out.

I screamed into reality.

I couldn't seem to take a breath to replace the one I had expended in the scream, and that frightened me even more. I sat bolt upright, forgetting about the tape player and London guidebook that had been beside me on the bed. They fell to the floor with a double thump, leaving the cord of the earphones dangling. Still not fully awake, I was struggling for air in the dim lamp-light when the door flew open and Felicity burst inside.

She was gripping a gun in two hands. And it was pointed at me.

I didn't see my life pass in review, or regret the many mistakes I had made, or even offer a last-minute prayer. In the absolute stillness that the appearance of the gun produced, I remembered that Chiswick had used the word "we." "If *we* stop Fierlan," he'd said.

Felicity began to thoroughly search the room, and I noticed I was breathing again, probably in response to a massive jolt of adrenaline. She had satisfied herself and left the room to search the rest of the apartment before I gathered up the muscular control to retrieve my tape player.

The little stereo seemed intact, but it wouldn't play. "Damn," I said; as important as the music was to me, I hadn't brought another player. Then I noticed that the tape hadn't fully played out. The batteries had run down. I swung my feet to the floor and rummaged around in the drawer of the nightstand.

"What happened?" Felicity demanded from the doorway.

Her tone was imperious, as if I owed her an apology for dragging her out of bed. I knew I'd done that, because she was wearing a nightgown and her hair was tousled. And I supposed that I really ought to apologize, because I'd scared her enough to reveal her real profession. But she had frightened me, too, and lied to me at least by omission.

I gave her a cold glare. "I had a nightmare."

The tension eased out of her as she prepared to assume her former role. "It must have been a bad one. Want to talk about it?"

"Only to say that it pales in comparison to reality." I turned back to the drawer.

"I'm sorry, Mrs. Douglas. I can understand how you feel."

"That," I muttered, "implies a sensitivity that is unsupported by current evidence."

That silenced her, as it had silenced Roger so many times in the past. He was such a brilliant man with numbers and strategy, but where vocabulary and grammar were concerned, he was surprisingly unsophisticated. Pulling out the verbal stops could stop him shortly, boiling with rage but unwilling to damn himself further by speaking. Even in my memories, I tended to rewrite his dialogue. I just hadn't realized it, hadn't noticed myself doing that.

Felicity had said something else.

"What? I'm sorry . . . I was . . . just remembering something. What did you say?"

Felicity didn't seem at all surprised that my anger had dissipated. "I asked if you wanted something to help you sleep."

I'd found the batteries. "No. No thank you, I've got all I need to sleep. I always have nightmares when I don't listen to a tape. I'm a creature of habit. Very much a creature of habit." I exchanged the batteries in the little stereo with the deftness that accompanies frequent repetition, and then looked up. She was still standing there in the doorway, uncertain. "You really should go back to bed," I said.

I rewound the tape back to the beginning and settled down with the headphones again, this time turning off the lamp. Felicity hesitated, but finally surrendered and backed out, leaving the door open a few inches.

After she was gone I turned off the music and tried to figure out what the dream had meant, and what I could do about it. I had a key, strictly speaking, but I couldn't imagine what it could open, or why it had brought on such a frightening nightmare. I had nightmares when I didn't follow my bedtime routine, but they weren't like this. They weren't this real.

I thought about the cast of characters again. Nickie had performed up to my expectations, in a way. She had refused to say anything. Chiswick had been equally uncooperative. Again, no surprise. Roger's role was a shock, of course, but he was beyond my reach. That left Dennis Penning.

Chapter 8

Felicity was gone when I woke up. It was late, almost ten o'clock, when I walked into the tiny kitchen and found Enders frying eggs. He looked a little ridiculous, standing there in shirtsleeves with a spatula in one hand, the frying pan in another, and his gun holstered under his left arm.

He looked up and saw me. "You look cheerful this morning."

"I'm not cheerful. I'm amused. Do you have any idea how funny you look?"

He was confused, and then glanced down at his gun in realization. "I'll take it off."

"No. It's okay. I wouldn't want you to feel naked."

He suppressed a sigh, and I saw he'd been dreading this moment, my coming into the kitchen in a hostile mood. He'd been cooking breakfast as a peace offering, and it hadn't worked. He looked like I'd turned him down to attend the senior prom with someone else.

"I'm sorry," I said with true regret. In spite of everything, I really *liked* Enders. He reminded me of my brother in happier times. "I'll go back out into the hall, and we'll start over again."

"Good morning, Mrs. Douglas," he said when I reentered. He was smiling.

"Good morning, Mr. Enders." He slid the eggs onto two plates, and handing me one, beckoned towards the dining room. "Delighted as I am to see you here serving eggs instead of oatmeal, I hope nothing terrible has happened to Felicity."

He shrugged. "She overreacted. Aren't you mad at her, anyway?"

"Well, yes, a little, but not enough to warrant a crucifixion."

"Would you take her back, then?"

"Is it the only way I can save her life? I don't need a nurse anymore."

"The boss won't kill her," Enders said, fork in midair. "He'll just explain her mistake."

"Loudly."

He shrugged again. "Loudly."

"I'd like to do a little loud explaining myself. It's Chiswick's mistake as much as Felicity's."

Enders didn't look up from his plate. "You'll have to join the queue if you want to yell at him today."

"Cue?"

"Queue. Line."

I toyed with the last bite of bacon on my plate, thinking. "Mosby?"

"Among others. Guns and dinner parties don't mix in Mosby's social strata."

"Have you had any luck with Rumpelstiltskin?"

"Who?"

"The mysterious man who gives away gold."

"Aha. No, not yet. Have you remembered anything else that could help us?"

"No." That wasn't strictly untrue.

Enders traced his finger along the rim of his coffee

118

cup. "If you're going to give my boss the rough side of your tongue for not telling you everything, don't you think you should be a bit more truthful yourself?"

"I learn by example."

I could see the beginnings of Chiswick in him. He drew on an air of patient resignation that didn't quite hide his irritation; he was the father of a difficult child. Roger had done that, too, and I had never devised a successful strategy to defeat it. I always *felt* like a child when it happened.

"If it's any consolation to you, Mrs. Douglas, I'm not enjoying this, either."

I dropped my eyes.

"What do you want from us?" he pressed. "What could I do to prove we're not villains?"

"I don't know."

"Why don't you trust us?"

"I don't know." I looked up again, into those clear, calm eyes. What I wanted was to be held by strong arms, the way Roger had held me.

Roger traveled so much, I often felt he was gone more than he was home, and I hated it. But when he came back, he'd devote a whole evening to me. He'd bring home a bottle of champagne, and we'd light a candle and turn out the lights, and Roger would hold me. We'd talk for a while, and then after he'd filled my glass for the third time, I'd fall asleep in his arms. The next morning, all the loneliness and frustration I'd felt in his absence would be gone, as though by his holding me the poison had been leached away. I was in need of a leaching, now.

"It isn't that I don't believe you," I said softly. "It isn't that I don't want to trust you. I do. But something . . .

some part of me . . . doesn't want that to happen. And I don't know why."

"Intuition?" There was no mocking in his voice.

"No, I think even intuition would be supported by something, some fact or experience. But this, this . . ." I shook my head. "Nothing makes sense anymore. I do things — I *have* to do things — that I wouldn't ordinarily do, and I don't know why. It's like I've been possessed."

"Maybe you have been."

Startled, I looked for sarcasm, or disbelief, but his expression was deadpan. "Are you telling me I'm crazy?"

"No. I can promise you you're not crazy. People can be possessed and influenced in many different ways."

I gave him a dubious assessment.

"I've seen it happen," he assured me. "I'm a policeman, sort of, and I've had to deal with it before."

"Jesus!" I slapped a hand to my forehead. "What is it with you people? Everything is 'sort of.' Nickie is sort of involved with Chiswick, who is sort of a treasury agent, and I'm sort of being guarded by sort of a nurse and sort of a —" I squinted my eyes shut and shook my head, wanting to block it all out.

"Who signs your paycheck?" I finally demanded. It was what Roger would have asked.

He smiled, at ease with my frustration. "I've never studied it that closely. But I work for the Home Office."

"I know that you work in a home office. I've seen it. But who do you work *for*?"

"That's Home with a capital H and Office with a capital O. It's a division of the government. You know, James Bond."

"Ooooooh," I said. "You're James Bond?"

"Well, actually, I don't get paid that much, I don't have anyone devoting their life to making useful gadgets to get me out of tight situations, and there is no Miss Moneypenny. And I'm not a spy. I'm an investigator, junior grade."

"And what are you investigating, now?"

For a moment I thought he wasn't going to answer. He seemed to be weighing the pros and cons, watching me watching him, seeing more in my face than I could see in his. He must have seen frustration and anger walking side by side across my eyes.

"Terrorism," he said.

I took a breath without any idea of what I was going to say, and in the brief silence that ensued, I heard voices in the hallway.

Nickie's was the loudest. "She has a right to know," she said angrily as the door opened. "She has a right to choose!"

They couldn't see us from the doorway. Enders shifted in his chair, and I held up a hand to stop him.

"There is no choice for her. Do you think she'd be safe in America?" Chiswick demanded. "Do you think she'd be safe anywhere in the world? Or you, either?"

"I can take care of myself!"

"Oh, yes, you've done a wonderful job so far, taking care of yourself and Valerie."

Nickie didn't answer, but I could hear her stomping down the hallway to her room. I got up and walked far enough into the next room for Chiswick to see me.

"You were the one who decided to let Fierlan go, weren't you?" I asked.

He sighed heavily and closed the door behind him. "Nickie thinks you should be allowed to choose what you want to do, whether to stay and help us, or to change your identity and go into hiding."

"You said there is no choice for me."

"Yes. I believe that."

I looked hard at him, trying to find something I'd missed earlier, but he was the same man. With every conversation, my commitment to him grew, without my willing it. When he told me what he knew, would I, too, be driven by some dark force?

"You were the one who decided to let Fierlan go, weren't you?" I repeated.

He crossed the room to sink into the sofa, seeming to wish it would swallow him. At first, I thought he might refuse to answer my question, but then he said, "Fierlan is nobody. He's a henchman, a foot soldier. Even if we'd thrown him into prison and lost the key, you wouldn't be in any less danger. Someone else would take his place, and if we caught him there'd be another."

I sat down in an armchair, never taking my eyes off his face. "I didn't see just anyone after the explosion. I saw Fierlan. If he's a nobody, why am I still in danger?"

"It's a little more complicated than that." He paused to accept the cup of coffee that Enders had brought him. "I assume Enders has told you the nature of our investigations."

"Yes."

"It wasn't by accident that I took the car you'd been riding in on your way from the airport. Enders and I had been following you. He was the man who ran across the street, by the way."

"You kidnapped me?"

"In a way, I suppose. We had spotted trouble. Not

Fierlan, but someone just as dangerous. Someone who specialized in assassinations."

I shook my head. "Why would someone want to assassinate me? I'm not anybody."

"You're wrong about that. Very wrong. You hold the key to a great deal of money and a very important name, and someone is willing to sacrifice the money to ensure the name is kept secret."

"I don't understand. I don't know what you're talking about. What money? What name?"

"If I knew that, Valerie, I would confiscate the money and arrest the person."

I realized my jaw had dropped and closed my mouth, only to open it again in protest. "But I don't know anything. How could I?"

Chiswick studied the murky depths of his coffee. "In the beginning," he said, "there was a man named Roger Douglas. He came from a middle-class family, and although he was a good student in school, there wasn't enough money to send him to a good college. And Roger wanted to go to a good college."

"I know that. After graduating from high school he joined the military and was sent to Vietnam. And after that—"

"Not so fast. Have you ever seen his military records?"

Soon after Roger and I had moved into the house in Houston, I found him one afternoon, sitting on the edge of the bed, surrounded by packing boxes. In his hands he held a small box, the kind of hinged and padded box used to present jewelry, or a watch. He didn't see me when I first entered the room, but when he looked up, he snapped the box shut.

"Roger?" I asked uncertainly, unnerved by the lost expression on his face. "Is anything wrong?"

"Of course not," he answered, getting up suddenly and putting the box into a drawer. "I'm just unpacking. And you should be, too. I feel like I'm living in a warehouse, for Chrissake."

He resumed his normal manner easily, but that expression of distant sadness bothered me for days, until I finally had to find the box in the drawer and look inside. I found two medals bright with military shine, but I never asked about them, and he never told me.

"No, why should I? He didn't like to think about it. He never talked about it. I've always thought . . . he must have been good at it. He was such a methodical, efficient man."

"He was good," Chiswick said. "But he had friends who were better."

"Yes, I suppose he did," I said. I had caught the meaning of his tone. "But they were soldiers. They did what they were ordered to do. They were just good men in a bad war."

This pronouncement was met with a long silence. Chiswick's face was carefully composed. He took another sip of coffee from his cup before continuing. "I agree with you, of course; the majority of the men who fought the war were good men. But because the draft touched such a large cross section of American society, it found some dangerous men, too. Efficient men who were also greedy and ruthless. During the war they flourished, dealing on the black market and perfecting the art of killing, and after the war they found other markets for their talents."

I stared at him in disbelief. "Are you telling me that

Roger was a mercenary? When? He went to college immediately after the war, and began working for the bank straight out of college."

"I'm not telling you that he was a mercenary. I'm telling you that he had contacts. Some of the people he knew did become mercenaries, some of them gravitated toward terrorism because of the money involved, and some of them fell in with the Mafia."

"But Roger," I pointed out, "became an accountant."

"Yes, he did. A very good accountant, very successful very quickly. Doesn't that strike you as somewhat unusual, the speed with which he became successful?"

There was never a point at which Roger *became* anything, I thought. He was always becoming. One evening in the middle of the week, soon after our marriage, he came home and told me he'd been promoted, with an appropriate raise in salary. I was ecstatic, ready for a night on the town to celebrate.

"Tomorrow is a working day," Roger reminded me. "And I have a lot more work to do, now. We can go out Saturday night."

We did go out, but we didn't stay late. Roger went to the office Sunday morning.

"No. He worked very hard for it. He worked *all the time*. He stayed late at the office, brought work home — he even took his work with him when we traveled for pleasure." I stopped for a moment. "Not that we traveled very often."

"Even so, the companies he invested in paid exceptionally well. It should come as no surprise that he was eventually approached by some of his army friends to manage their investments."

"No," I admitted, "it's no surprise. And it wouldn't

surprise me to learn that some of the investments were quasilegal at best. But terrorists?"

Enders had produced a large manila envelope, and at Chiswick's nod, gave it to me. I opened it slowly, knowing I wouldn't want to believe whatever evidence was inside. I was surprised, but I wasn't shocked. I wanted to be shocked, but I couldn't be. The knowledge had been there all along, but I hadn't wanted to see it, so I had been blind. Now, in hindsight, I was confronted by the truth.

I took out the pictures. Roger had been photographed with a variety of men, walking on a city street, eating in a restaurant, entering offices and bars. One photo had even been taken inside his racket club, as he walked past a court with someone, deep in conversation. I didn't know the other faces, with the exception of Mosby's, but I could guess at their identity. "Bad guys," I said.

"Bad guys," Chiswick confirmed.

How big of a leap is it, I wondered, from shady to definitely illegal? Maybe Roger hadn't known what he was doing.

Roger's ghost appeared behind the sofa, laughing. "Didn't know what I was doing? Did I ever not know what I was doing?"

I looked past Chiswick. Maybe you knew where the money was going, but didn't break any laws to get it there.

"Sure, and I donated my time," Roger sneered. "Terrorism is one of my favorite charities. It was just money, Valerie. It was just people who had some money and wanted to make more."

"Maybe . . ." I started, but let my voice trail away.

Maybe he just hadn't cared.

Chiswick and Enders waited in quiet patience, not staring at me but not ignoring me, either. I put the pictures back into the envelope. "Did he lose their money?"

"No. He made excellent choices that paid well. There was a death among the investors, which left a position of some power vacant. The organization was split between the 'old guard' and the 'new radicals,' and there was a struggle for power. Roger sided with the losers, and diverted the assets."

"Meaning the money disappeared."

"Completely. The investors hadn't counted on loyalty. They saw Roger as a tool, a means to an end. They didn't realize he had fought beside some of those he supported, he had saved lives and his life had been saved. He moved the money and erased the trail, and then flew to London to be present at a negotiation meeting between the factions." He stopped talking, but the connection was too obvious to miss.

"So they killed him," I said.

The car that I drove in Houston was an aging but beloved Volvo. It was equipped with overdrive, and there was a switch on the gearshift to turn it off during stop-and-go city driving. When it was off, a small red square appeared on the instrument panel, reading "OD off." "OD off" saved the engine, but it slowed the acceleration. I enjoyed getting on the freeway, clicking off that red light, and flooring the gas pedal, even though I would always ease off at about 60 miles per hour. For me, the satisfaction was knowing the power was there when I needed it.

What I felt in that room, sitting across from

Chiswick and with Enders hovering nearby, was that red light inside me going out, and my mind shifting into overdrive. "That wasn't very smart."

Chiswick was visibly startled. "Eh?"

"I said, that wasn't very smart. They should have gotten the money before they killed Roger."

"Well," Chiswick said, regrouping, "it's possible that Roger was killed not by the faction he was opposing, but by those he intended to support."

"Why?"

"Probably to protect someone's identity. Someone who doesn't want his involvement known. Coups of this sort are rarely bloodless."

"And this is the person who tried to have me killed?"

"It's a possibility."

I thought, It would be hard to pin Chiswick down on the color of the sky. "Well, *sometimes* it's blue," he would say. "Except, of course, when it's gray or black. And then there is always the slight possibility it might turn up green. . . ." Would he know the truth when he heard it?

"Who wants the money back?" I asked.

"Pretty much everyone, I should expect. Except Mr. X."

"Yes. He just wants me dead. How much money are we talking about? More than a million dollars?"

"Considerably."

I raked my hair back with both hands. "Shit. I don't know anything about this. Can you understand that? I don't know *anything*."

"You knew it was important to go to Mosby's dinner."

"I *felt* it was important to go. I *felt* it was important to follow Rumpelstiltskin. But I'm not any closer to the money. Has it occurred to you that I might be cracking up?"

"No. You survived five years of marriage to Roger Douglas." His gaze was steady. "You can do this, too."

"You knew Roger pretty well, didn't you?"

"During the last three years of your marriage to him, yes. We couldn't prove anything, but we kept a close watch on him during his trips to Britain."

"But you never felt it was necessary to tell me about any of this."

Chiswick spread his hands. "You were never here to tell."

"No?" My voice was rising. "Is it just my imagination, or is this *not* my first day in London? When were you planning to fill me in on this? Were you just going to wait until a third attempt was made on my life, when I said, 'Gee, it sure does seem like someone wants me dead,' and then you were going to say, 'Oh, yes, sorry, I forgot to tell you that your husband was a criminal and your life is in danger, would you like to see Stonehenge?'? Can you give me a reason, one good reason, why I shouldn't pack my bags and get out of here?"

"I can give you two," Chiswick said quietly. "First, the countdown sequence has been started by your arrival in London, and it can't be stopped. Mr. X knows you may know something, and you can't erase the problem by leaving the country. The world is just too small to hide in. And second, you can t leave the country without your passport, and you no longer have one in your possession."

"My God," said Nickie, from behind me.

"Can he do that, Nickie?" I asked, turning in my

chair.

She shook her head, not in answer to my question, but in amazement. "You fucking bastard. She's an American citizen."

Chiswick met her eyes without flinching. "Mrs. Douglas is merely being detained for questioning."

"You can't hold her forever on that pretense."

"I don't intend to. I'm just giving her twenty-four hours to exercise her right to choose."

I could see the fire banking in Nickie's eyes. "Her right to choose? She doesn't have any goddamn rights with you. I'm calling the American Embassy."

"I could arrest her, if that would make you happier." He waited for a response, but there was none. "Go to bed, Nickie. There's nothing you can do for her now."

I had no choice, he'd said, and I realized he'd been right. Nickie would have seen that if she had been told the whole story, or if she'd been told the true story. If *I* had been told the truth. If Chiswick knew what the truth really was.

I stood up. "I'm going to my room," I announced to Chiswick and Enders. "Get Felicity back here, and lay in a supply of chocolate bars and Cokes." I turned and put my arms around Nickie. "Don't fight him," I whispered into her ear. "Give me some time to think about this."

I stepped back and put my hands on her shoulders. There was a bandage above her right eye, and her face was heavily bruised. Despite her seething anger, I saw that she was as much in need of protection at that moment as I was. Had her plans gone awry? "Get some rest, Nickie. We'll talk later."

Then I turned her around and led her out of the

room and down the hall. When I left her to go into my room, she opened her mouth to say something, but then changed her mind. I closed the door of my room behind me, and then sat down on the chaise by the window.

Who was Roger? Who was Chiswick? Who was I? It was midafternoon on a spring day in London, but I couldn't decide whether the sky was gray-blue or blue-gray.

Chapter 9

I remembered that Roger always carried a loaded gun. He had two: one for traveling and one that he kept underneath the bed, within his reach. It had shocked me at first.

"Surely we're safe inside the apartment, I said "Is the crime in Houston really that bad?"

"It isn't crime," Roger answered.

"Well, what, then?"

He was reluctant to answer but I pressed him. "In Vietnam, my life depended on a gun," he finally said, "and on my ability to use it. It got to be instinct."

"But the war is over."

"No, it isn't, Vallie. It'll never be over for me."

"I don't understand."

"No," he said softly, "how could you understand? You weren't there. How could anyone who wasn't there understand?"

The look on his face had frightened me, and I hadn't asked any more questions that night, or for many nights after. What I learned about the war, I learned gradually, on my own initiative.

The war was always in the news when I was in college, but I never heard it. Had I subscribed to a newspaper, I might have realized at least in part the enormity of it. But I was a student, removed from everything except the rumbling of fear among my male classmates and the strident lectures of social injustice by the politically active minority. I saw them as a minority, anyway. They were always marching somewhere, carrying signs and generally carrying on. I spent most of my time studying.

If I had understood then what I knew later, I would have been at the airport on a regular basis, bestowing flowers and kisses, throwing confetti and serving champagne to every returning soldier. I would have attended funerals; I would have sat with the bereaved. For while I studied my children's literature, my fairy tales, and dreamed of faraway lands and handsome princes, the knights were buried all around me, unknown and unmourned by the subjects for whom they had died.

Alone in my room, I cried awhile, for the loss of innocence, and the loss of life the terrorists continued to cause, but mostly I cried for the loss of even my memories of happiness. The man I loved had never really existed. I had wreathed myself in foolish illusion once again to escape a harsh reality. I should have known. I should have done something.

Eventually, the tears dried up and I dozed, to wake up uncomfortable and unrested when Felicity knocked on my door.

"Come in," I said half expecting Nickie's face to appear.

Felicity stood uncertainly in the doorway, not sure of her welcome.

"Come in," I said again, wincing as I readjusted my position on the chaise.

Felicity took the neatly folded blanket from the foot

of the bed and covered me with it before sitting down on the bed herself. "Are you all right?" she asked.

"I'll be okay. How about you?"

She shrugged. "I *did* overreact."

"Which, to Chiswick, is roughly akin to treason. And unjustified, considering his performance at Mosby's."

Her lips threatened to smile.

"Anyway," I continued, "I want you to know I wasn't really angry with you, and I apologize for being rude."

"You weren't unjustified. I shouldn't have burst in. You looked petrified."

"That was the nightmare, mostly."

She tried not to look too interested. "Nightmare?"

"We'll get to that in a minute. Are you a doctor?" She shook her head. "A nurse?"

"A psychiatric nurse, with some training in therapy," she said with deadpan professionalism. Then she dropped her eyes and added, "Among other things."

"Among other things. Yes, I should have realized that sooner." I waved it away, not wanting a side issue to cloud the air just then. "I want your opinion, as someone who has worked with, well, mental illness. Am I losing my mind? Cracking under pressure? Can I still trust my perception?"

"To the limit of my experience, you aren't disintegrating. On the contrary, you are handling stress rather well. Better than most."

"Better than Chiswick?"

She grinned. "I couldn't say."

"Aha. There are no private conversations in this apartment, are there? Take it easy, Felicity. Elementary logic got me that far. Here's my psychological problem:

when Chiswick told me about Roger, he was surprised that I didn't go into hysterics. Now, maybe Chiswick is just a rabid chauvinist, but if he *isn't*, if he's convinced of my mental prowess and he was just plain *surprised* . . . perhaps I shouldn't trust his judgment that somewhere in my collection of strange urges and nightmares and premonitions there's an answer to the riddle."

She thought for a moment. "You describe Roger as a practical efficient man, but you don't seem to realize that you, too, are practical. You have your own, unique perspective, and your sense of humor does incline toward the whimsical, but that's largely an extension of your creativity. Think of your marriage as the impartial observer would see it. You married a man who was financially secure and who traveled frequently, leaving you plenty of time to continue writing. On a basic level, you have managed very well. What you're experiencing now may seem at variance with that basic, pragmatic self, but it isn't without its own pattern." She stopped to draw a breath and shrugged. "An impulse shouldn't be considered crazy just because its foundation in experience isn't immediately apparent."

I had misjudged Felicity the night before. She knew some impressively long words. "Is that a vote of confidence?"

"Yes."

I smoothed the blanket across my legs. "Ah, but can I trust *you?*"

Her face had relaxed into the same warm welcome that I had felt when I first met her. "You don't have to trust me on this. Elementary logic can get you that far."

"Yes, I suppose it can. One more thing. How is

Nickie?"

"She'll be fine. She's had a mild concussion, and the doctor wants her to take it easy for a few days, so I've given her a sedative, hoping things might calm down a bit by tomorrow."

I threw back the blanket and stood up. "Meaning, I should get a grip on myself." I shook my head to forestall her protest. "I can handle myself, but the thing between Nickie and Chiswick . . . They'll have to hammer that out for themselves. Come on. It's almost dark outside, and I'm hungry. Fix me a sandwich and I'll tell you a story." She followed me out of the room. "I don't know if this will help, but . . . Once upon a time, there was a lady who dreamed she was in a long corridor lined with doors . . ."

Felicity heard me out and responded, "Hmmm . . ."

I was sitting at the dining room table, a sandwich before me and Felicity across from me. "I recognize the 'medical hmmm,'" I said, "but I don't know what it means."

"It means I'm thinking."

"About what?"

"Give me a moment. Eat your sandwich."

"Mmph." I was coming to like Felicity's sandwiches. They were made with butter instead of mayonnaise, one slice of ham, a piece of very limp lettuce and several slices of small, tasteless tomato. Felicity called it a "ham sandwich with salad." I observed that limp lettuce and artificial-tasting tomato slices could hardly be called salad, and tried to explain about iceberg lettuce and American tomatoes. Felicity, however, remained unimpressed by brags of Yank vegetables. I quickly learned to concentrate on the luxurious taste of real butter spread on generous slabs of hand-sliced bread.

"The key finds you," Felicity said at last. "That sounds suspiciously like hypnotism. Have you ever been hypnotized?"

"I don't think so. But Roger's been dead for two years now. If what Chiswick needs to know is something Roger hypnotized me to remember—would it last that long?"

"It could if you had a daily reinforcement. And you do."

"I do?"

"The tapes. What happens when you don't listen to the tapes?"

"I have nightmares. I see what you mean. I don't suppose it's possible to just hypnotize me again to find out what you want to know."

"I'm afraid not. Temporal precedence."

"Which is?"

"Roger would have instructed you not to tell unless the proper command were given, and that overrides any commands I might give. He got to you first. He got the golden ring. Anyone else has to have the key."

" 'The key,' " I mused. "Someone gave me a key recently."

"I know." She was stirring sugar into her cup of steaming tea, around and around, and watching the liquid swirl. "But that key wasn't *the* key."

"Maybe you could give me drugs and ask me what the key is, or where to find it."

"I won't do that," she said firmly. "And Chiswick wouldn't agree to it. It's too dangerous."

I wasn't ready to share her faith in Chiswick's concern for my welfare, but I held my peace.

"And besides," she continued, "you may—Have you ever been sick, very ill, before?"

"Yes."

"While Roger was alive?"

"Well, yeah . . ."

"About two years after you married?"

"Uh-huh."

She leaned back in her chair. "Tell me about it."

"One winter I had pneumonia. It started out as just a cold, but then I developed asthma. My doctor couldn't figure out what was going on, and I kept getting worse and worse until it became pneumonia." I shook my head, remembering. "It was scary. I don't know what I'd have done without Roger. My doctor wanted me to go into the hospital and I didn't want to. It was Christmas, and I wanted to be home with Roger. Roger found a doctor who'd make house calls every other day to give me penicillin shots." I began to listen to myself. "He was a friend of Roger's from the war. . . ." The sound of my words died away to a silence so complete that I could almost hear Chiswick's hidden tape recorders rolling.

"Drug-reinforced hypnotism could last indefinitely." Felicity's voice was softened almost to a whisper.

"I think I'm going to be sick," I said, but I wasn't sick. My face turned white enough to get Felicity out of her seat, and I began to shiver, but I wasn't sick.

"Put your head between your knees," she said, pulling my chair away from the table and forcing my head downward. She was about to add more instructions when the phone rang in the next room. She hesitated a moment, torn between her dual identity as a nurse and Chiswick's minion.

"Go!" I said, and she left. I got up slowly, testing every movement, and went through the kitchen so I wouldn't be seen on my way to Nickie's room.

It was almost dark outside, and her form was indistinguishable from the bunched comforter of her bed. I pulled a chair to the side of the bed and turned on the small lamp that stood on her nightstand. Her eyelids fluttered slightly, but the deep, even breathing wasn't disturbed.

"Everything is suspect now," I said softly. "Every kindness and every kiss. They've taken seven years of my life, Nickie, and Roger and maybe you, too. Why did you help them?"

I waited for a moment, as if I expected her to answer, but of course I didn't. At that moment I didn't expect to ever have any acceptable answers. A tear spilled onto my cheek.

"There's no difference now between nightmare and reality," I whispered, leaning closer. "Chiswick says that someone wants to kill me, and I'm not sure I really care."

She moaned quietly, and I reached out to touch her face. Her eyes opened and tried to focus "Val?"

"I remember, Nickie."

"Remember?"

"I remember the waiter from the restaurant."

"Val. I wanted—to tell you—" She fought the grogginess.

"Was it Roger? Did you do it for Roger?"

"She did it for me," Chiswick said from the doorway, "and for you."

"For you," I said, without looking up. Nickie's eyes had closed again. "You control Nickie, too."

I thought I heard him sigh, but I wasn't sure.

"Control? No. The best I've gotten is reluctant cooperation."

I looked up at him then, a dark silhouette beyond the circle of lamplight. "Why now?" I asked. "Why did you wait so long?"

"We're following Roger's schedule, not mine."

"Roger's schedule?"

He reached inside his jacket and pulled out a business-sized envelope, dangling it like a reward I would have to earn. "Nickie got a letter from Roger. Recently."

I let him lead me back into my own room and then took the envelope. It was one of the bank's imprinted envelopes, from the London office, but I couldn't quite make out the date on the postmark.

"February tenth," Chiswick supplied.

I took out the letter inside. It was typewritten on the bank's expensive letterhead, and the date was February tenth, the year of Roger's death. The inside address, as well as the address on the envelope, was Nickie's.

"My dearest Nickie," it began, "I shall have been dead two years by the time you receive this letter. I'm sorry to have to shock you, writing from the grave, but I have one last favor to ask of you.

"Knowing Valerie as I do, I can predict with certainty that she won't have come to my burial. She won't have visited my grave and she won't have said that final goodbye. Without your help she'll never manage it, and she'll never remarry and find the happiness she deserves.

"I want you to ask her to visit you here in London. No, more than that, I want you to *insist* she come, and force her, if you have to, to look at my grave. Valerie will know what she has to do next.

"Nickie, darling, you know what you mean to me, and how I have always felt about you. I hope that by helping Valerie, you'll be helped, too.

"All my love," it concluded, "Roger." There was no signature; his name had been typed.

I refolded the letter, but continued to stare down at it, hoping to prolong the silence. I wasn't sure what Nickie had meant to Roger. But when I thought about the unraveling lies with which he had cloaked himself, I found it more and more difficult to care. Was that what he had intended? Wasn't a tangled web of lies the spider's best work?

Chiswick shifted his weight from one foot to the other, having chosen not to sit.

"Now I understand why it was so important to Nickie that I visit Roger's grave?" I said. "But I didn't have any revelations there. I don't know what to do next."

He had moved to look out of the window, pulling back the curtains with one hand, a spy looking for a signal from the street below. "Things got a bit out of order. Roger wasn't expecting you to be injured."

"That was woefully shortsighted of him. But no worse, I guess, than thinking he could negotiate with terrorists." My voice was flat, and Chiswick seemed disturbed by it. Or perhaps his quick, appraising glance was meant to assess how far he could push me in the next few minutes. I hadn't made up my mind about that, myself. "So what do we do next?" I asked.

"You said you *felt* you should go to Mosby's. What do you feel now?"

"Shock and revulsion, mainly."

"Understandable, but not very helpful. Lie down and relax. Close your eyes," he said without turning around.

How could he not understand, I wondered, that I could not turn off the chaos in my mind? I wanted an argument, a real screamer. Of course, it was Roger I wanted to yell at, or at the very least, Nickie, and I knew Chiswick wouldn't let me do that. I thought about telling him I felt I should go back to Houston, where he had no jurisdiction, but I wasn't at all sure that would stop him from coming.

"Lie down," he said again. "And relax."

"I can't relax!" I snapped. "I hate to be a disappointment to you, but this has been, without a doubt, the worst day in my life, and I can't relax!" I waited for a reply, but I didn't get one. He was restless, but that wouldn't interfere with his patience, if patience were the best course. Evidently that was the course he had chosen. "If I choose not to—" I searched for a word. "If I choose not to cooperate with you, will you drug me the way Roger did?"

"No."

I wished I could see his face. "Will you let me go?"

Silence.

"What's the difference between you and Roger? What's the difference to me?" I couldn't keep the cry out of my voice.

He turned, but his face was still half-hidden by shadow. "I care what happens to you."

Roger and I had been to a concert of chamber music the night he proposed. We left the concert hall contented and silent, and when we got into his car, instead of starting the motor, he turned to me and said,

"Marry me."

I was startled, not yet used to Roger's habit of issuing commands rather than asking questions. "Darling, I—I—" I realized I was stuttering and stopped to regain control. "You know I love you, but isn't this a little sudden? Shouldn't we give ourselves a little more time?"

"We have time," he answered. "We'll have the rest of our lives together. I want to spend mine making sure that nothing bad ever happens to the woman I love."

I looked at Chiswick and thought, perhaps Roger had been telling the truth, after all. Perhaps he had spent his life making sure nothing bad happened to Nickie.

"I've danced to that song before," I said softly.

Chiswick stepped forward and, lifting me to my feet, put his arms around me and drew me close to his chest. "I can't protect you from the past, Valerie." His voice was low and husky, and it didn't sound calculated. "But I swear to you I'll do my best to protect you in the here and now."

I didn't try to pull away. He had tried, as far as I knew, to protect me. He had surrounded me with sort-of-policemen, encircling and isolating me like Rapunzel in her tower. But if I let down my hair, who would climb the braids?

"What do you remember about Mosby?" he asked quietly.

"He was there, at the restaurant in New York, at Roger's birthday party," I answered, not wanting to, slurring the words a little. "He was . . . pretending to be a waiter." It still sounded strange to me.

"That was the birthday you gave Roger the cuff

links."

"Yes."

There was a moment of silence, and then he asked, "What should we do now, Valerie?"

Run. My heart was pounding out a message. Don't talk. Don't tell him. Run. I thought about the dream, remembering the sound of the nameless horror running toward me in the black corridor. "I think we should talk to Dennis Penning."

I could hear the smile of approval in his voice. "I'll be back for you in the morning." He released me and I pulled back a step, fighting my own reluctance to do so. "Try to get some sleep."

"Sleep?" I never wanted to sleep again. Sleep was no longer my friend.

"I can have Felicity give you something."

"No!"

"You'll have to listen to the tape."

Roger had even ruined Mozart, I thought.

"There will be nightmares if you don't," Chiswick cautioned.

"I know. I'll listen to the damn thing. Now please, go."

After he left, I undressed in slow motion, dreading the moment I would have to turn out the light and press the "play" button. But when the first chords filled my head, the tension and terror slipped away, and I drifted into sleep remembering the beauty of spring azaleas.

Chapter 10

I didn't want to leave my room the next morning. I was completely dressed, teeth brushed, hair combed and ready to take on the world, except . . . When I left the room I *would* be taking on the world, or at least a sizable portion of it. I sat down on the bed.

At first the knock on the door was tentative, easily ignored. Then it became stronger, and finally Felicity came in without invitation.

"There's no need to hide from breakfast," she said. "The boss got you some Frosted Flakes."

I sighed. "It'll take more than Tony the Tiger to get me through today."

"You've got more than Tony."

"Yeah. I think that's part of my problem."

"Well," she said, sitting down beside me, "you can't stay in here forever. Your troubles will find you here as easily as anywhere else."

"I know," I said, but I didn't get up.

She pretended to study the carpet. "What do you really want to do?"

"I think, before I decide to do anything, I want to talk to Nickie."

It was Felicity's turn to sigh. "Leave it for a few more hours. You can talk to her this afternoon."

"You're sedating her," I accused. "You're drugging her to keep us apart."

"We talked about this yesterday. She needs peace and quiet. Time to recover."

"Yes." I looked down at my feet. "Okay. I want to wake up in my own bed and find out this was just a nightmare."

She thought for a moment. "If you had the choice, then, would you want to go back to America today?"

I shook my head. "Well, no. I guess not. I mean, I wish the problem would disappear, but since it won't . . . I can't just run away."

"No, you're going to hide, instead."

"Any second now, I'm going to stand up and go."

"Any second."

Yes, I thought to myself, any second. A crystal-clear image will appear in my mind and I'll know what to do. An ever-helpful impulse will force me into motion. The machinations of a man dead for two years will churn out the proper response.

"But I don't know what to do," I said. "I don't know what to ask Dennis, or what to tell him. Maybe I'll just wander around London indefinitely, until I'm killed, not knowing what to do next. It's been two years. Things might have changed. Someone might have died unexpectedly, or . . ." I stopped because I'd looked up and seen Chiswick leaning against the doorframe, arms crossed across his chest.

"You'll tell Dennis you want some investment advice," he said. "That will get you into his office."

I snorted. "Investment advice? I'd have better luck making a random selection. Everybody knows that. Even Dennis."

"That does seem to be the general consensus." He crossed the room and, taking me by both hands, pulled me to my feet and led me to the dining room, still talking. "Nickie's judgment was even harsher. How did he get this far?"

I recognized it as a rhetorical question, but I couldn't help remembering that Roger had spent a great deal of energy trying to find the answer, to undo what he considered to be a great deal of damage to the company.

"Somebody screwed up." I was pouring milk on the Frosted Flakes and thinking that I had managed to acquire at least one of the comforts of home.

"Nickie said that, too."

I looked up sharply. "You've talked to Nickie?"

"Frequently over the last few years."

Glaring at him would have been useless. I stirred my cereal, watching the sugary flakes swim round and round, slowly drowning. "Okay, I can get into Dennis's office. He might not believe my excuse, but he'll see me. How am I supposed to explain your presence?"

"Somebody has to look out for you. You're an innocent tourist who's been injured and frightened."

"But not too scared to ask an imbecile for investment advice."

"People under stress do strange things."

I saw Felicity bow her head in reluctant agreement. "But there's no apparent reason for a police escort. Fierlan won't be prosecuted. As a policeman, you should have no further interest in me."

"As a policeman, no. But as a close friend of Nickie's, I am naturally concerned about you. So I have hired a private bodyguard for you."

"A private bodyguard?"

He smiled without humor. "I'm a busy man, Valerie. I can't neglect my work to chauffeur you around London."

"I wish. Who is my private bodyguard going to be, then? I don't suppose you could spare Enders?"

"It's already been arranged. He's waiting for you downstairs." He got up to leave, but I reached out to touch his arm, and he turned.

"I need my passport," I said. "I want to buy some things, and I can't cash my traveler's checks without it. Can Charlie be trusted with it, or are you afraid I might make a mad dash for the airport and leave the country?"

He reached into the inside pocket of his worn leather jacket and tossed my passport onto the table in front of me. "I trust you," he said, and when I didn't answer, he left.

I could feel Felicity watching me, trying to will me to stop him, and after the door had closed behind him, she got up and turned toward the kitchen.

"I want to trust him," I said to her back, "but I can't."

She stopped but she didn't turn around. "You could do it if you let yourself."

"No. I trusted Roger—"

She swung around then, her face dark with disapproval. "Are you going to hide behind that excuse for the rest of your life? Don't you realize what's at risk here, not just for the boss and the terrorists, but for you?" She raised her hands in frustration, but then let them fall again. "You can't *not* trust him."

I lowered my head in surrender, but we both knew it was a surrender to logic and not to Chiswick. She made a soft, despairing sigh and disappeared into the kitchen to vent her irritation on the dishes. I stirred my now soggy cereal and admitted to myself that it was true, I had become a coward. Felicity obviously thought that being a coward and trusting no one was worse than being idiotically brave and screwing up, but I couldn't be so sure. If I had never trusted Roger, terrorists might not, at this moment, be making up a shopping list for weapons. Oh, well, of course they would, I told myself, but at least I wouldn't be an accomplice.

I gave up trying to get food down a constricted throat and, stuffing my passport, traveler's checks and guidebook into my purse, let myself out of the apartment. I felt less vulnerable than I, the coward, had expected, and then wondered if Chiswick also considered the danger to be less, or if he had supreme faith in the unseen men he had assigned to protect the apartment. Were they watching me on the elevator, and in the lobby? Was I only in danger among crowds? Enders was waiting directly in front of the door to the building, so that I only had a few feet of open space to cover between the building's door and the car door.

I got inside the car, closed my door, and buckled the seat belt. Enders closed the book he had been reading and waited, as a cab driver awaiting the passenger's instructions. "To the bank, Jeeves," I said.

He put the book he had been reading down between the front bucket seats and started the engine. It was a slim book, and the color of the cover looked familiar, but I was surprised when I opened it.

"This is my book," I said. *"The Dandy Lion.* You bought a copy of my last book." I riffled through some of the pages, just to make sure. "I'm flattered," I said, looking up. "Would you like me to autograph it?"

He was smiling. "Actually," he said, "I borrowed it from a friend."

"You have friends who are beginning readers?" It didn't occur to me that this could be considered an insult until after I'd said it. "I mean—" I began.

He laughed, shrugging off my apology. "You can't guess who lent it to me?"

"Nickie? No," I answered, myself, "it can't be Nickie. Nickie wouldn't waste time reading a child's book." I closed my eyes and clapped a hand over my mouth, prompting another chuckle from Charlie.

"I'm not that thin-skinned. I think it's a nice little story, anyway. Better than cheap romance novels."

My mouth dropped open. "You're kidding," I said. "Romance novels? Nickie reads romance novels?"

"Only at night. She reads the financial news in the morning. But you still haven't guessed who lent me the book."

"That only leaves Felicity and Chiswick, and I just can't believe Chiswick would buy one of my books."

"Not one. All."

"All?"

Charlie nodded. "Every single one. He had to get a mate of his to send several from America."

"He asked an adult man to buy children's books for him?"

"Well, he is an uncle, as far as that goes. But he kept them all. I've seen them."

I shook my head, stunned. "That's incredible. Roger never read my books."

"Roger was a twit," he said cheerfully. "The Cap'n

likes a thorough job. He never discounts anything."

"Yes, I can see that. I just . . . Why do you call him the Captain?"

"He's like that, don't you think? The captain of his ship."

"Yes, I guess so. But buying my books and reading and keeping them." I stared through the window at the passing buildings and heavy traffic. "That's — well — I'm . . ."

"You're what?"

"I . . . don't know." I watched the buildings outside slip past us, and thought how easily time and opportunity escape, and how permanently regret scars a heart. "I don't know what I feel anymore. This is all happening too fast. It's like running through a strange room in the dark and not knowing if the next step will be on solid ground or into the bottomless pit." I closed my eyes and laid my face against the coolness of the window.

Charlie rested his hand lightly on my shoulder. "I know it's hard," he said, and something in his voice made me look across at him. He was older than I had thought; he had probably never been as young as I felt at that moment. "You're not running through this, Valerie. You're not even walking. You're being dragged. And honestly, about the only thing I can personally guarantee is to try to keep your face out of the mud so that you can catch a breath once in a while. Okay?"

I nodded. It seemed to be all anyone could promise.

"Right. Let's see what this Penning chap has to say for himself, then."

I realized that the car had stopped, and that we were

in a parking lot with numbered spaces. Charlie opened my door, and I looked around a little uncertainly before getting out. "Are you sure we can park here? This looks like a private lot."

He laughed and patted the car's roof. "This car could park in the lot at Parliament at a moment's notice."

"But won't the—the bad guys know that?"

"I certainly hope so."

"But—"

He shushed me and straighted my coat on my shoulders. "We want 'the bad guys' to know there's no point in trying anything, don't we? Right." He tucked my hand under his arm. "Tell me why we're going to see this fellow."

He was steering me around the puddles on the pavement. "Well," I said. "You know about the dream, don't you?" It was a silly question, really. Everyone had known about the dream minutes after I had told Felicity. But Charlie wasn't bothered.

"I know. But in the dream he said he couldn't help you."

"But he said it as though he really could, but was just afraid to. And he worked with Roger. He was Roger's boss when Roger died."

"Did they get along?"

"No. Roger hated him." I told him what Roger had said about Penning being worth killing.

We had come out of the parking lot onto a busy sidewalk. Charlie stopped, causing a minor traffic jam of human bodies around us. "That sounds like a threat."

"It was just temper. If Roger had decided to get rid of Penning, he wouldn't have killed him. He would have

152

ruined him financially and professionally, but he wouldn't have murdered him."

Charlie started walking again. "Maybe he did. Penning's career hasn't been doing too well, lately. Hey, where are you going?" He pulled me back and pointed across the street. "There's the bank."

I looked at it, a big, modern dinosaur. "Oh." There was disappointment in my voice. "I didn't think it would be so ugly."

"You've never seen the bank?"

"I've never been here before. How could I have seen the bank?"

"But—you've never even seen a picture of it?"

I frowned at him. "Of course I've never seen a picture of it. What did you think, that Roger brought back snapshots? 'And this is Dennis and me in front of the bank.' Sure."

"Right," he said to himself, and then to me, "You will let me know if something jogs a memory, won't you?"

I had time to say, "Oh," before Charlie pulled me into the street after him. He was a fearless pedestrian, and I could see how he had managed to get across the roadway alive on that first day. It was a game of chicken, the challenge of a human life (or in this case, two human lives) against the cab driver's God-given right to drive like a maniac. He walked in front of them with a confidence that they would stop, reminding me somewhat of the biblical story of Christ walking on water. By the time we got to the other side, my heart was pounding and I was gasping for breath.

"Are you all right?" he asked in surprise.

"I think so. Maybe. But I'll never be the same again."

He shrugged at the street. "Cab drivers. Never let on

that you value your own life. Are you ready to go in? Do you know what you're going to say? I can't be in charge in there, you know. I'll just be your bodyguard, silent and respectful."

I had to smile at that. We went through the glass doors and sought out the information desk in the bank's lobby, proceeding by instruction to the elevators and the third floor. The elevator doors opened to maroon carpeting and chrome, guarded by a middle-aged woman with steel gray hair and an iron will.

I made a pretense of needing something in my purse.

"What's the matter?" Charlie whispered.

"I think we should have made an appointment."

"Best to keep the opposition off guard. Stare her down and walk right past. You can do it." He gave my arm a squeeze. I wondered if he coached Little League teams on the weekends. No, of course not. Maybe Little Rugby.

"You'll have to have an appointment to see Mr. Penning," the woman informed me smugly.

"That's fine," I said, recalling Roger's water-freezing tone, "as long as it's within the next five minutes."

She scowled. "I'm afraid that won't be possible."

I tried next to imitate the fearless disdain Charlie had used in the street. "I am not afraid," I said. "If you wish to call Dennis's secretary and announce our arrival, you may. However, I am going to see him. Now." I walked past her, with Charlie a respectful but amused two paces behind.

"Now just a moment!" Her voice had risen a notch. "You can't do that."

"Of course I can do it." I looked at her as though she

had lost her mind. "Are you going to personally assault me, fling yourself between me and the door? Pull out a gun, perhaps? I should warn you that this gentleman is my bodyguard, and would feel obligated to respond in kind." Charlie was maintaining his solemn expression with difficulty.

"I'll call security!" she threatened.

"You do that, Miss . . ." I read her name. "Miss Martin. Call them and tell them that Mrs. Roger Douglas is here and you want her arrested."

She reached for the phone, and I was disappointed that she hadn't recognized Roger's name, but I walked on. Security wouldn't be so forgetful.

"I'm impressed," Charlie said, when we had gained the comparative privacy of the hallway.

I leaned against the coolness of vinyl-papered wall. "So am I. But I don't know how much more of this my heart can take."

Charlie pulled me away from the wall and pushed me along in front of him. "Nonsense. You're doing splendidly."

I started to remind him that Rumpelstiltskin had said the same thing, but we had come upon a large glass door leading to a plush waiting area, and I thought perhaps I'd better take a moment to think about exactly what I would say to Penning. Charlie had other ideas. He opened the door and pushed me through.

When I turned to glare at him, he winked and said, "You hate Penning."

I hadn't given it much thought until then. I'd pretty much assumed that I felt the same way about Penning that Roger did. Roger had always assumed that I felt

155

the same way about Penning that Roger did, anyway. Roger always assumed I was feeling exactly the way I'd been instructed to feel. Maybe Charlie was making that assumption, too, and maybe I didn't want to play along this time.

"Mrs. Douglas?" a voice asked. This woman was younger, efficient in manner, but more polite. She was pretty, smiling at me in a welcoming way.

"Yes. I'd like to see Mr. Penning," I said quietly, willing to rely on Roger's name more than my ability to bluff.

"Go right in, he's expecting you." She gestured toward a large wooden door behind her. "Can I get you a cup of coffee?"

"Uh . . . no, thank you." I frowned at the door. What was I doing here?

Charlie's hand was instantly under my arm. "Are you all right?" he asked, his face asking much more.

"Yes, I'm fine," I said, with more confidence, moving toward the door. I didn't give him an opportunity to open the door for me, but grasped the cold knob myself. I wouldn't know how I felt about Dennis Penning until I looked him in the eye, and if Roger had left instructions not to trust him, they would have to be evaluated against that look.

Chapter 11

I had seen Dennis Penning at Nickie's party, but I hadn't really paid that much attention to his physical appearance. I had been thinking of him in the past, in relationship to Roger, and so my mental image of Dennis was at least two years old.

The man that looked up from a pile of papers as I entered his office had aged in the last several years. He had lost his country-club tan and tennis-playing physique, growing grayer and heavier, and as he rose to shake my hand, I noticed that he no longer moved with his old quickness. But his handshake was firmer and his smile warmer than I remembered, and when he spoke to me, his voice was quiet and without the cockiness of superiority that had once annoyed me so.

"Valerie, how nice to see you," he said. "Please sit down."

He didn't seem at all surprised or unnerved by Charlie's presence, but I thought introductions were in order in any case. "This is Charles Enders." I realized too late that I hadn't asked Charlie if I should use his real name. Assuming that I *knew* his real name. It was possible that Dennis knew his real name even though I didn't. "He's my, uh . . ."

"Minder," Dennis supplied. He offered his hand to

Charlie. "Dennis Penning."

Rather than retreating behind the oversized desk, Dennis had pulled up another chair, so that we were seated in a semicircle off to one side. "I heard about the bombing," he said to me. "I hope you're not expecting any more trouble from that."

I shook my head. "No. I think that's over and done. But I did come to see London, and I'm still pretty wobbly, and now Nickie . . ."

"Yes, Nicola. There's no need to explain that."

We all observed a brief moment of silence for Nickie, and then I cleared my throat. "I'm afraid, Dennis, that I was a little rough with the receptionist by the elevators—"

His laughter cut me off. "So I heard. Good for you. I would have loved to see the old dragon's face."

He had lost some of his confidence, I saw. The old Dennis wouldn't have been bothered by Satan as a receptionist. And even if he had, he would simply have walked into his office one morning, picked up the phone, and told personnel, "Get rid of Brunhilda."

"Anyway," I continued, "I'm sorry for barging in like this."

"You're welcome any time. I'm glad to see that you're, well, getting on with your life." His gaze shifted to the window behind the desk. "Roger's death was a shock to all of us. The company hasn't seemed the same since."

"No, I expect it hasn't." He was first puzzled, then pleased by the smile I couldn't suppress. Dennis must have had his own memories of Roger, I thought.

"I came to ask a favor," I said. It wasn't what I had planned to say, but Chiswick had wanted me to act on

158

impulse. "I wonder if I could see the office Roger was using when he died."

Dennis didn't seem at all flustered, although Charlie may have been surprised. "Of course. It's just down the hall. I'll take you myself."

His secretary's face, as we passed her desk, reminded me that not everybody got this much personal attention from Dennis. Had I not been Roger's widow, I might not have been so well received. It was probably still true that single, beautiful women were treated with elaborate chivalry, but now I had at least some reason to believe that colleagues and employees received their share of respect. Their widows did.

Roger's office was a short stroll down the hallway. It wasn't quite as large as Dennis's, but it was appropriately furnished in the same formal, impersonal style. There was no secretary at the outside desk, and the office door was open. Dennis led the way and entered without bothering to announce us. The man behind the desk was about my age or a little younger, perhaps in his late twenties. He was attractive, and when he looked up and saw Dennis, his face took on a cheerful smile. I couldn't imagine Roger doing that.

"Will you excuse us for a moment, please?" Dennis's voice didn't rise at the end of the question, so it came out as a quiet command. The man was startled, but he wasted no time in fleeing. Some things never change, I told myself.

I didn't know what I was looking for in that room, other than a clue to lead me to the next clue, but there wasn't anything of Roger left there. I decided, after turning slowly in a circle, that there probably had never been very much of Roger in that office. Roger had the ability to pass through interior space without leaving anything of himself behind except demands and instructions. And though they may have remained even in the bank, they weren't visible.

It was just an executive's office, with a standard-sized desk much messier now than Roger would have tolerated, a few side chairs upholstered in rust velvet, and three oak file cabinets. And no matter how long I stared at it, it wouldn't become anything else.

I turned back to Dennis. "Thank you," I said.

"Is there anything else?" he asked, becoming a little curious. "If I can help . . ." His voice trailed off suggestively.

"Maybe what I need is a priest experienced in exorcism."

Dennis managed a weak smile. "There is something you could do for me, if you wouldn't mind."

"Of course. If I can."

We were back out to the hallway by this time, and Dennis leaned against the wall, choosing his words carefully. "It's about young Bromley." He hesitated.

"Yes, I remember him. We talked at Nickie's party."

"He feels, you know, that since he arranged for the plane that Roger . . . well, you know what I mean. Several times he's seemed almost ready to leave the company. He's a good man, and I'd hate to lose him."

"I can understand that." It was nonsense, I knew. I understood very little, if anything, about what was going on. I did understand, however, that if I didn't urge him along, Dennis might decide that the favor wasn't worth the embarrassment of asking it.

Dennis cleared his throat. "Yes, well. After the party, after you talked to him, he looked so much better that I thought, well, we're finally exorcising the company ghost. But then the bombing . . ." He shrugged.

I hadn't thought about how the pub incident would affect Bromley and the bank. I hadn't thought, in fact, about how it would have affected anyone else except Nickie and me. Other people had been hurt. Perhaps some of them had died.

I said, "Just point me toward his office."

"Down this hall, second door to the left." He gave me a quick, not quite impersonal hug. "Thank you, Valerie. I know I wasn't one of Roger's favorite people, but . . . if there's anything at all I can do . . . well, call me."

His sincerity surprised me, and I stepped back to look at him closely once again. He was a nice man. How could I have been so wrong about him? How could he have changed so much? I said, "I will. And next time I'll use my own name, instead of Roger's."

Dennis smiled, reached out one last time to squeeze my hand, and turned back to his office.

"I don't hate that man," I told Charlie, accusingly.

"So it would seem."

I hesitated. "But he isn't the same."

"How so?"

Charlie had started toward Bromley's office and I fell into step beside him. "He's quieter . . . kinder."

"Older. Wiser," Charlie added.

"Yes, I guess so. But when did it happen, and why? Was it Roger's death that caused it?"

He shook his head, looking old and wise himself. "It's difficult to guess. His wife left him about the time Roger died, and then the bank had some difficult years and he had some personal financial setbacks."

"Dennis has lost a lot, too."

"Some of it he just threw away," he said flatly.

Typical, I thought, stealing a glance at his deadpan face. You would have calculated it better, I suppose.

Bromley, when we found him, was hard at work, his head bent industriously low over a computer printout.

"Hello," I said from his open doorway.

"Mrs. Douglas!" I doubted that he would have received the Queen with more enthusiasm. "Let me get you a chair. Would you like some coffee?"

Charlie and I sat down in the chairs he dragged from the small waiting area outside. The three of us had to sit in close quarters; there wasn't room for a fourth.

"Please, sit down," I said, pointing back to his desk. "There isn't room in here for dancing." He seemed about to accept the guilt for that, too, so I distracted him. "This is Charles Enders."

Bromley shook hands with Charlie and arched his eyebrows at me, confused but too polite to ask questions.

"Charlie is my minder." I saw that he wasn't going to venture anything by way of conversation on this point, so I went on. "I suppose you heard about the bombing. I thought you might like to know I survived it intact." I thought again about the others who didn't and had even more sympathy for Bromley's feelings of guilt.

He ducked his head. So much for the direct approach.

"I came to see Dennis Penning, and while I was in the neighborhood I thought I'd drop in and say hi." I was beginning to understand Chiswick's frustration at his early attempts to talk to me. "I wanted to change some traveler's checks and I thought perhaps you could spare me the waiting in line in the lobby."

Bromley looked up at last, delighted to have a concrete problem that he could work on, and he picked up his phone to make the arrangements. Charlie shot me a you-are-blowing-this look.

"What am I supposed to say?" I hissed at him.

"Tell him you're having a nice time," he whispered back.

"I am not having a nice time!"

"Lie!"

"I beg your pardon?" Bromley asked.

"I said, 'I'm having a nice time in London,'" I lied.

He looked at me as if I were crazy, and then at Charlie, who shrugged and smiled. "Women," Charlie's shrug seemed to say. "We'll never understand them."

But having made the statement, I felt obligated to defend it. "The bombing was a shock, of course, but I wasn't injured. And Nickie will be all right. And, well, I couldn't just sit around the apartment and mope, and so . . . I'm trying very hard to have a nice time," I finished lamely.

"I, uh, certainly hope things will go well for you," Bromley fumbled.

"Listen," I blurted in desperation, "the truth is, I was worried about you. You looked so miserable at the party, and I feel responsible for that, and I just wanted to see how you were doing and if there was anything I could do to help." I stopped for breath, half expecting Bromley to bolt for the door, but he didn't. His consternation resolved into an expression of pleased surprise. Out of the corner of my eye I saw Charlie nod in approval. I thought that might be nothing more than an indication of the prevailing wind's direction; I had discovered that Charlie was changeable.

"Thank you, Mrs. Douglas, that's very kind." Bromley allowed himself a small smile, relaxing just a little. "I hope I didn't embarrass you at the party. You seemed . . . a little upset when I left you."

I thought back. The cuff links. Roger hadn't come back to his hotel room the night before his death. "That wasn't your doing," I reassured him. "In light of recent events, it isn't even important anymore."

"You might ask Catherine Woolsey about them."

My ears pricked up and were frustrated by the arrival of an older woman with a cash drawer and the forms required for exchanging my traveler's checks. I signed the checks, then filled out the papers, produced a passport and watched her count out the money.

I smiled as I singled out a five-pound note. "It's so small," I said. "This couldn't hold plenty of money. Unless they wrapped it around a hundred-pound bill."

Charlie frowned, and Bromley told him, "'The Owl and the Pusssy-Cat,' don't you remember? 'They took some honey, and plenty of money, Wrapped up in a five-pound note.' The notes used to be bigger, Mrs. Douglas. Excuse me for a moment."

He stepped outside for a final word with the cashier, and I took the opportunity to glare at Charlie. "Who is Catherine Woolsey?"

"Roger's secretary. Didn't he mention her?"

It didn't sound quite right. Charlie's face was open and friendly and the tone of his voice was pleasant, but something kept me from answering. I shivered a little, even though I wasn't cold.

"What's wrong?" Charlie asked.

"It's . . ." I couldn't get my throat to say the words. Charlie had caught the scent of prey. "It's what? Try,

Valerie! What is it?"

"You . . ." Inside, my voice was hammering away at a repulsive truth. You knew. Chiswick knew. Chiswick knew the night of Nickie's party. He knew where Roger had been the night before he was killed, and he'd known for two years. He lied to me.

"I what? Tell me!" He was crouching in front of my chair, his face inches from mine.

"Mrs. Douglas?" Bromley said from behind us. "Is everything all right?"

I looked at Charlie and let my face relax so that he could see it, and then turned in my chair. "I'm fine. Just a little weak, still. It's nothing, really. I'm *okay*," I added for Charlie, who reluctantly returned to his seat. Heat from his displeasure raised the room temperature several degrees.

Bromley, too, was hesitant about sitting down again. "What were you going to say about Miss Woolsey?" I prompted him.

"Oh, Catherine. Yes. She might know if Roger had any appointments after the concert was over. He did that, sometimes. Saw people late in the evening, I mean. He may have left the cuff links somewhere along the way." He was fidgeting, and so was Charlie.

"Thank you," I said, letting Charlie help me stand up. "I don't seem to be able to hold up in your company, I know, but I want you to understand that it has nothing to do with you."

"He knows," Charlie grumbled, pulling me toward the door.

"But—"

"I understand, Mrs. Douglas. Really I do." He looked as though he really did. I hoped it would be enough for him.

Charlie didn't turn on me until we were in the elevator. "Talk!" he demanded.

Roger got angry, too, but it was hard to see if you didn't know him. It was self-contained fury, held in by the tightness of his lips and controlled, deliberate breathing. He had ways, of course, of letting people know when they had displeased him, but they rarely saw it coming, like a flash of lightning out of a clear sky. His quiet anger scared me more than yelling and threats could have done, and I was always watching for it.

"I will talk, count on it," I told Charlie. "But not here. And not to just you. I want everybody there. Felicity, Nickie, you, and most of all, Chiswick."

He left me waiting in a chair in the lobby within his line of vision while he made the phone call that would assemble the combatants and Felicity, the referee. Charlie was in constant movement as he dialed the call, pacing and shifting. But as he talked he calmed, standing still again, losing the tension in his posture.

He was talking to Chiswick, I thought. Even Felicity wouldn't have been able to siphon away that anger. But I couldn't decide whether Chiswick was simply calming an employee or whether Chiswick wasn't worried about the fact that I knew he had lied to me and might not trust him again, and was communicating his confidence to Charlie.

"What did he say?" I asked when he returned.

A small smile played around the corners of his mouth. "He said to cool you down first."

I leaned back in the chair, trying to appear nonchalant. "I'm cool."

He walked behind the chair and tested the muscles along my right shoulder. "The hell you are. You could bounce bullets off here."

"It didn't work the last time. What else did he say?" Charlie had begun to rub my shoulder with the sort of skill that had probably been gained by years of experience loosening up tense informants.

"He didn't have anything else to say to *you*. We've got about an hour. What would you like to see?"

"See?"

"You're a tourist, aren't you? Trying to have a good time?"

"Only when it suits your purpose, apparently."

"Well, it suits my purpose now. What do you want to see?"

He had moved on to my injured shoulder, rubbing more lightly now. I would have been content to sit there indefinitely, anger notwithstanding.

"How about Saint Paul's Cathedral?" he asked, mostly to himself.

"Wherever."

"It looks like a cupcake," I told Charlie.

He frowned at me and then looked again at the cathedral's dome as we approached it. "I'm not sure I want to hear this," he muttered, "but tell me why, anyway."

"Well, back home—"

"In Texas."

"Yes, in Texas, but probably in other states, too, although I've never investigated it . . . Anyway, the grocery stores have bakeries in them, and one of the things that they bake are cupcakes. For kids, you know.

They frost them with colored icing and then stick a little plastic ornament on top."

"A plastic ornament." It wasn't a question.

"Sure, like a turkey for Thanksgiving, a Santa for Christmas, that sort of thing."

"What holiday would get a gold cross?"

"I just said it *reminded* me of a cupcake with a plastic ornament."

He was maneuvering into a parking space. "Right. A cupcake. Do me a favor, Valerie. Don't talk to the other tourists. Particularly the British ones. People will be queuing up to throttle you."

My first sight of the entire church was jarred by the modern building standing next to it, but Charlie explained that many structures had been destroyed by the bombing in the last war. Then, after I had given the white stone building a cursory glance, the garden in front caught my eye. It was the first time I had been so close to English grass in the daylight, and I couldn't resist kneeling down to touch it.

"It's beautiful! As soft as velvet."

"It's grass," Charlie answered. "You don't have grass in Texas?"

"Not like this. And flowers!"

Charlie shook his head. "The dome looks like a cupcake to you, but you rave over the flowers."

"Beauty is in the eye of the beholder."

"Evidently."

Once inside the building, however, I forgot about the flowers, and Charlie's pride was appeased by the permanent "oh!" of my lips. I looked up.

The ceiling consisted of arches and saucer domes framed by exquisite carvings, and then, past the cupcake dome, the ceiling turned to gold. It was a bright day outside, and the sun came in through the high, arched windows and the lower, stained-glass windows, reflected off that golden ceiling, and bathed the interior of the church in a red-golden glow. I wouldn't have been surprised to see Christ himself standing at the high altar, instead of sculpted in gold, triumphant on the top of a small domed roof constructed over the altar.

"Charlie."

He had circled me with a supporting arm to keep me from falling backward. "What."

"We have nothing — absolutely *nothing*—like this in Texas."

"It's better than cupcakes?"

"This is better than sex!" I caught myself too late to stop, and promptly blushed.

Charlie laughed, and led me to one of the chairs set up for worshipers under the great dome. "I don't know whether that's high praise from a Texan, or a proposition."

I tried ducking my head, but the floor was only done in black and white tile, so I slouched down in my chair and tilted my head back far enough to try to memorize the glory above me. " 'I will lift up mine eyes,' " I said softly to myself. "They knew what they were doing.

"I've embarrassed you. I'm sorry."

"Yes, you have and no, you're not."

"Okay, I'm not. You're still carrying the torch for Roger."

"No."

He smiled knowingly. "The Captain, then."

"No!" It was too quick, and too loud, but I had been

startled by the way my pulse quickened at the suggestion.

"Aha! So it is the Captain. Why don't you let him know?"

"Why don't you mind your own business."

"It is my business, close enough. Why don't you tell him?"

"Tell him what?"

"Tell him how you feel."

"I haven't admitted to feeling anything."

"You haven't made a convincing denial, either."

I finally sat up and glared at him. "What is it that you really want from me?"

"I want to know why you haven't told Chiswick how you feel. But I would settle for knowing how to get the truth out of you."

"That's it, isn't it? That's what this is all about. Manipulation. The faces change but the game doesn't."

He blew out a noisy sigh. "God, you are infuriating! Let me introduce you to a radical new technique. It's called cooperation. Everybody works together on the problem instead of on each other."

But it wouldn't be that way, I thought, if I admitted to Chiswick that he attracted me. It would be one more way for him to control me.

I was composing a stinging reply when something behind him caught my attention. "Stone!"

"What?"

"Stone," I repeated, already on my feet and moving. "It's Stone."

He jogged easily beside me as we dodged tourists down the hallway. There were cubbyholes all down the side of the building, chapels and memorials I supposed. The people stopping to admire them obscured my vision just enough to lose Stone. I finally had to stop, out of breath and uncertain which way the figure had gone.

"What's going on?" Charlie demanded.

"Stone," I panted.

"You keep *saying* that. What does it mean?"

"Stone is a person. A man. Roger's friend."

"Are you sure it was him?"

I leaned against somebody's honorary plaque on the wall, getting my wind back. "No, I'm not sure. It looked like him, but . . ."

"Is he part of the plan? Do you need to talk to him? I could put out a description."

I shook my head.

"Come on, Valerie!"

"No. It isn't that. I just don't think I need to see him. There's something, but . . ." I pushed my hair back. "Can we pick up some lunch on the way to the office? I need some time to think about this."

We walked out of the church slowly. I looked around, not expecting to see Stone lurking in the vicinity and not finding him.

Of all Roger's friends, Stone seemed the least likely to be met by chance in London. Why would he have come? To enjoy the culture? Stone's idea of a good time was to get stoned and go drinking in sleazy bars.

But the idea that Roger might have included him in the plan seemed even more farfetched. Stone and drugs, yes. But Stone and terrorists?

Chapter 12

The lunch was ominously quiet. The tension flowed around us like static electricity, making even a casual touch dangerous, building inside me until I thought my hair must be streaming out behind me on invisible currents. Charlie and I ate, Nickie stared at her plate, unable to even pick up a fork, and Chiswick refused everything except a cup of coffee that Felicity brought from the tiny kitchen.

They were all waiting for me to talk. I had rehearsed what I wanted to say and what I wanted to yell, but when I finished eating and pushed the plate away, I edited the speech severely. "You lied to me," I accused Chiswick.

He sighed, a quiet but weary sound. "I see I haven't exactly impressed you with my talent for investigation."

"What?"

"Investigation. You haven't credited me with much intelligence, have you?"

The rest of my tirade evaporated. I had gone from injured victim to wrongful aggressor in the space of one sentence.

"It hasn't occurred to you, has it," Chiswick went on, "that in the course of my normal duty I kept track of Roger's movements, and after his death I reconstructed his last days as closely as possible?"

I shook my head. It hadn't.

"No. And I don't suppose you remember sitting on your bed the night of Nickie's party and telling me that you didn't want to know where Roger was the night before he was killed."

I did remember that, but I couldn't say it.

"And you've never realized that I've held back as much as possible in order to spare you as much as possible." He waited for an answer, and then continued, his irritation mounting but his voice level. "You said, in the hospital, that you could produce proof that you were intelligent. I think I'd like to see that proof, Valerie, because I just can't believe that any intelligent person would think that she could run this investigation on her own. I just can't believe that an intelligent person would talk to strangers on airplanes about Roger, but not to the people who could help her."

"Strangers?" I squeaked. What had I said to the man sitting next to me on the airplane? I could barely remember speaking to him.

"He was insurance." His voice was perfectly even. "So tell me, Valerie, because I'm *really* interested in hearing this. Tell me one intelligent thing you've done since you've been here. One smart move that you haven't been pushed into making."

I had been sitting still, but I couldn't stop panting long enough to speak, and the sound of my heart pounding in my ears almost drowned out his last words. They seemed to echo faintly across the immense distance between us, fading as rapidly as the focus of his face. Then someone pulled my chair back and forced my head between my knees.

"Just relax and breathe," Felicity said into my ear. "Calm down and relax." She drew back and said, "I hope you're satisfied."

"Bloody hell!" Chiswick said, but it was faint. Perhaps he said it over his shoulder as he left the room.

"Sarcasm won't do any good," Charlie said.

"Neither will yelling at her!" Felicity snapped. Their voices were becoming closer, less distant, and I was beginning to breathe easier.

"It's just frustration."

"I know that."

"An interesting little contest, don't you think?" He sounded as though he were discussing the weather. "Two people with a lot to say to each other and both of them too stubborn to be the first one to speak. I should take bets." He leaned closer to me, so close that I could feel his breath on the back of my neck. "What about it, love? Should I bet on you to hold out the longest? You're the one who hasn't yet realized the importance of what we're playing for here. How many people will this affect, I wonder. Hundreds? Thousands? How many lives will be lost because you don't have the courage to go up those stairs—"

"Stop it!" Felicity cried.

"Shut up," Charlie answered her.

"You can't—"

His head snapped up. "Shut up or I'll have you thrown out!"

I raised my head, too, and looked at him, chilled by the smile on his face.

"Whatever is in that head of yours that doesn't want to trust him," he said softly, "has an enemy, now. And the enemy's name is hunger. How long can you carry on with a war in your head? That would make an interesting bet, too. Maybe I'll bet on Chiswick, after all." He got up and walked out of the room, slowly.

I watched him go and then got up unsteadily, shrugging off Felicity's offer of help, and went out the other door, the one that led to the kitchen and the bathroom beyond it. It was hardly more than a cubbyhole, and unheated, but it was private and the cold kept my nausea at bay. I splashed some icy water on my face and then sat down on the toilet lid, staring down at the cracked linoleum.

Felicity had thought that I was devasted by the double blow of Chiswick's and Charlie's anger. But neither one of them, I decided, had really been angry. Chiswick had been irritated in the way that Roger had been when people acted independently of his will, and Charlie, well, I had to admit that Charlie was a species unto himself.

But I had almost fainted. Chiswick hadn't done wonders for my self-esteem, but feeling like an idiot had never made me faint before. Looking stupid had never produced an anxiety attack.

I sat there in the refrigerated confines of the tiny toilet until my hands were as cold as the lifeless porcelain without coming up with a reasonable answer. But there were just a few things I wanted to say to Chiswick, so I mustered my courage and emerged to climb the stairs to his office.

As I climbed, I tried not to think about what Charlie had said. I tried not to wonder if there was even the slightest possibility that he was right, that I was something more to Chiswick than a case he was investigating. And most of all, I tried not to care.

Chiswick's office was the right-hand door at the top of the stairs. I knew it was his because I could hear him yelling behind the closed door. He wasn't yelling loudly. The decibel level was somewhere in the middle range, not loud enough to threaten imminent death, but about right for a boss ready to fire an employee. I knocked on the door.

I could hear muttered curses, and then Chiswick yanked the door open with unnecessary force. Yes, I thought, now he *is* angry. But so am I.

I marched past him into the room, an office only slightly larger than Bromley's, but furnished in a more personal style. Chiswick's hand was everywhere in the room: a cluttered desk; an overstuffed armchair that had seen better days, but looked comfortable; and a file cabinet that bore fist-sized indentations on one side.

I was about to turn on my heel to face Chiswick and Charlie, who was leaning against the opposite wall, when I noticed the pictures. They were pinned to a large corkboard that almost covered one wall, and they were all of me. Roger and I were together in some of them; I judged the oldest to be about five years old. Nickie was there, too, but the one that caught my eye and held it was Mr. Striped Tie, Rumpelstiltskin. We were standing outside a store that I frequented in Houston, a small boutique in a shopping mall, and I was talking to him. It looked like a casual conversation, pleasantries passing between two friends. But he wasn't my friend. I didn't know him and I couldn't remember talking to him before Mosby's party.

I could feel the floor almost shift underneath my feet. Maybe, I thought, I should go back to the bathroom. No.

"Yes?" Chiswick asked sharply. I could tell he was still angry. It seemed to be his day for it. That, and lying.

"You wanted proof of my mental acuity," I reminded them, building up steam again.

"I remember," Chiswick answered.

"I'm afraid that, being so far from home, the evidence I have available at short notice is somewhat circumstantial. And I find myself hard pressed to defend one smart move I have made since arriving in London." I forced myself to wait for a comment, and then continued, letting the anger carry me along. "So I may be, as you say, a fool, but even I am smart enough to know that no matter how hard you pound the buttons on a video game, you're not going to get any points until you put in your quarter."

"What the hell does that mean?" Chiswick demanded, glaring.

I glared back. "Why don't you ask Charlie? He knows a lot about playing games. Don't you, Charlie?" Chiswick had returned to the chair behind the desk, leaving me a clear avenue to my target. I walked over slowly, imitating the casual stroll he had used to leave me. "You know, Roger used to gamble, too. But he stayed away from games he could lose. He never bet heavily on a fair competition. I guess that makes you two kindred spirits, doesn't it?" I looked into eyes that were cold and deep without flinching.

We stayed like that for a moment, and then Chiswick cleared his throat. "I think you've been dismissed, Enders," he said.

After Charlie had closed the door after himself, Chiswick leaned back in his chair, and said, too casually, "Now I can't ask him to explain about the video game."

His fury had dissipated, but mine held on for a parting shot. "Well, I guess you'll just have to use some of your investigational expertise, then."

He swiveled in the chair to look out of the window behind him, onto a pleasant little back garden. Over his shoulder I could see tulips and daffodils edging a small square of green grass. There was a small terrace with a pair of heavy metal lawn chairs just off the kitchen, and I could imagine him there, in quieter times, sipping a dark, frothy Guinness and thinking. I didn't solicit the image, and when it came to me it was unwelcome, but it made me see that I wasn't really angry with him. I was fighting something else.

When he finally spoke again, his voice registered a defeat. "Do you kick all the dogs you meet, or is it just me?"

"No. I kick all of the ones who bite me and most of the ones who growl."

"You didn't kick Roger."

I turned my back to the window and sat on the corner of the desk, too tired, suddenly, to stand up anymore. "No," I answered heavily, "but I should have. Only with Roger I was the dog, and he led me around on a leash and told me who to bite and who to growl at."

"Roger's gone."

"Do you really believe that? I can still hear my master's voice."

I could hear him getting up behind me. "So what are you going to do, Valerie? Just continue being Roger's helpless victim?"

"But that's what you want, isn't it? I'm supposed to just say the lines I've been taught, and make the right moves, and then when the man and the money show up, you'll take them both and hand them over to your master and get your pat on the head."

"I don't want to use you."

"Yes you do! Yes you are!" My voice was stretched to the point of breaking, and I struggled to keep it under control long enough to say what I had to say. "You want to know every secret, every private, painful thing. You want to drag it out and examine it and hold it up to the light. You're the judge and the jury and I'm the one being stripped naked in the courtroom. And for what? What's my crime? I loved someone. I trusted a man who was powerful. Just like you." I had to stop then, unable to talk and cry at the same time.

He gathered me up in his arms and held me tightly, pressing my head against his shoulder. "And I don't want to be spared anything, anymore," I managed to gasp out between sobs, "because I don't ever want to go through this again."

When I had calmed enough to breathe fairly easily, he said, without releasing me, "Do you really want to know about Catherine Woolsey?"

"Yes."

"She's young, pretty. Roger saw a lot of her, on the job and off, but I don't think there was anything between them. He was using her."

I buried my face against his neck.

"Do you want me to stop?" he asked.

"No."

"She was the last person we know to have seen Roger alive. He went to the concert with Nickie, but after he took her home, he went to Catherine's instead of back to the hotel."

He stopped. "And then?" I whispered.

"And then, early in the morning, a man left the flat wearing Roger's clothes, with a scarf around his face and a hat pulled low. Not an unusual practice, considering the time of year. He went back to the hotel, asked for the key, and went up in the elevator. And disappeared."

"Because he wasn't Roger."

"No. Roger was at Heathrow, boarding a company plane."

I relaxed a little, being supported by his arms. "And what did Miss Woolsey have to say?"

"Roger had told her that competitors would do anything to stop him from completing his business in Scotland, and she believed him."

"And she believed him," I echoed. "And she sent the cuff link."

He hesitated. "She had the cuff link. Roger had told her that when he called, she should send it to you at Nickie's, with a note explaining that she'd found it at the office."

"But he never called. And there was no note." I pulled back enough to see his face, but he turned it to one side.

"No." His voice was very quiet. "If there had been a note, you would have wanted to see her, and I couldn't let that happen. She had insisted on that as part of the deal for helping us." There was a long pause, and then he said, barely above a whisper, "I sent the cuff link."

Without planning it, I drew back my fist and punched him in the ribs as hard as I could. I felt the bones flex inward as his breath expelled in a "hunh!" and he bent forward a little from the blow. But he didn't fall and he didn't let go.

I was unprepared for my own violence, and I shrank from it, stuffing my fist into my mouth to stop a new wave of sobs.

"It's all right, I'm okay," he said, gingerly feeling the spot where the blow had landed. "Lucky for me you were standing so close. A few more inches and you might have broken something." He pulled me closer. "Just take a few deep breaths. It's all right."

"I'm sorry. I've never hit anyone before."

"No? I think you've got a natural talent there. We might give you a bit of training and put you up against Charlie."

"No, thanks. He'd probably wear brass knuckles." I wiped the tears away and blew my nose with the tissue he had produced from somewhere. "Do you have an endless supply of handkerchiefs and Kleenex?"

"I have a supply." He was looking off toward the garden again, but not really seeing anything, and I stole a quick glance at his face. His expression was sweet, almost tender. "It's something I can do to make things easier. A little thing, but something."

I didn't want to lose the moment, but I had to ask the question, and it felt like the right time to do it. "Who is the man in the striped tie?"

He looked at the pictures. "You mean Rumpelstiltskin? He's a courier. He delivers messages, mainly. Sometimes money."

"I don't remember meeting him in Houston. I don't remember meeting him at all before Mosby's party."

"I know." His voice had grown quiet again, and

soothing. "You never really knew him. If you took the time to study those pictures, you'd find that you don't remember most of the other people in them." He paused a moment to let it sink in. "Roger used you to pass and receive messages and instructions, and sometimes even money. It was worked into your routine. He would ask you to go to the grocery store, or the liquor store, or pick up dry cleaning, and somewhere along the way, you'd meet someone. Just a chance meeting, in passing, except that the person would say a code word, and the information would be passed. You don't remember it because you were programmed not to remember."

I closed my eyes. "How long?"

"I came onto the case about five years ago, briefly. Of course, the messages stopped after Roger's death . . ." He hesitated, not wanting to continue.

"But the surveillance didn't," I finished for him. "Did you bug the house and the phone lines, too?"

"The Americans wouldn't go for that. Anyway, I don't think we could have kept the taps going while Roger was alive. He checked too often and too thoroughly; he would have found them."

"So you just followed me. And you listened when you could."

"Yes."

I knew that he was expecting me to blow up again, but I felt very calm. A fog was lifting inside of me, and I could see a patch of clear blue beyond it. "You've known me for a long time," I said.

"Yes. I wasn't actively working on the case for the whole time, but I kept up with it." He let his voice die away, and then added, "With you."

The phone rang then, and he reached behind with one hand and picked it up, still holding me with his left arm. He needn't have bothered. I wouldn't have moved away.

Charlie had told me the truth in his own inimitable, brutal way. Chiswick had things he wanted to say to me, things that weren't harsh and painful, but he was holding back. And he wasn't holding back because it would interfere with the investigation, either. I could see it now, so clearly that it seemed foolish that I hadn't realized it earlier. He was afraid he would be rejected.

I laid my head back on his shoulder and breathed in the light fragrance of soap. He had seemed to me to be always in control, the unassailable fortress who knew everything and controlled everything. Just like Roger. But he wasn't just like Roger. Chiswick knew and controlled, but he wasn't a cold, unassailable fortress. He was a man capable of loving, and that made him vulnerable.

I looked up at his hair and saw for the first time that it was streaked with gray, and that his close-cropped haircut made it curl gently around his face and neck. I smoothed my hand gently across his stomach and the ribs I had punched and found that his leanness was lightly veneered with the beginnings of the fleshiness of a man who ate too much fast food and had too little time for exercise.

He wasn't perfect. But when I wrapped my arms around his middle and pressed my ear to his chest, I could hear his voice rumbling up from his chest as he talked on the phone, and I could hear his breathing and his heartbeat as he listened, and I could almost feel the blood pulsing in his veins and arteries. And I was pleased by the look and the feel of this man who loved me.

He put the telephone receiver back on its resting place, thought for a moment, and then took a breath. "Have I . . . missed something here?"

"No," I answered from my contentment. "Actually, *I* had been missing something. But I've figured it out now." I brushed his neck above the shirt collar lightly with my lips, making a wonderful, slow journey along his chin.

"If this keeps up," he said, before I reached his lips, "it's going to get very warm in here."

"Good. I haven't been warm since I got off the plane."

He kissed me fiercely, and if I had had any second thoughts, they would have melted away. Roger had been a cool, delicious lover, but Chiswick was going to be all fire.

"Now?"

"Now," he said.

I looked around. "Here?"

"I know a place, close by." He pulled me into the hallway, poking his head into the adjacent room. "The Bull."

"Oooooh!" a woman's voice replied, knowingly.

"None of that," Chiswick replied, but he was smiling.

"Nice," I said on the way down the stairs. "Are you sure you wouldn't like to take out an ad in the newspaper, too?"

He pulled me close for another kiss. "Does it bother you?"

"I don't know. Has she ever been to 'the Bull'?"

"Not with me."

It was only a few blocks away, a red brick building with a sign reading The White Bull hanging from a timber. Beneath the words was a picture of a white bull gazing placidly off into the distance. Chiswick parked beside a sign that warned, "Absolutely no parking anytime."

"Has this car ever been towed?" I asked

He laughed. "Once. But it'll never be towed again."

The barman recognized Chiswick as an old friend. "Captain!" He came out from behind the bar and extended his hand to Chiswick. "And who's this, then? A special lady?"

"A special lady. Valerie Douglas, may I present Duncan Lowerden."

Duncan favored me with a bear hug. "Delighted! What can I get you? A Guinness, as usual? And what for Miss Douglas?"

"Actually," Chiswick stopped him, "we were on our way upstairs."

Duncan stopped and looked at me with new interest. "Upstairs. It's been a while, hasn't it? You're the American lady, then."

"Yes," I answered, surprised.

He gave me another hug, this time accompanied by a kiss on the cheek. "My house is your house," he said. "Anything, anytime."

I would have liked to stop and question that, but Chiswick pulled me away. "He's an old friend. You can trust him."

The room was small, but comfortably furnished in a homey sort of way. There was a bureau, a straight-backed chair and a double bed covered with a worn floral spread. Chiswick drew the curtains while I tested the bed.

"Second thoughts?" he asked, sitting down beside me. He slipped off his jacket, took off his shoulder holster, and looped it over a bedpost before turning back to me.

I began unbuttoning his shirt. "Lewd, lascivious thoughts."

When his shirt was completely unbuttoned, he dropped his arms to his sides and let me slide it off his shoulders. I slid my hands back up his chest and then across his shoulders again, feeling the ripple of muscles as he raised his arms to remove my blouse.

There were scars on his chest: a long row of stitches just above his right nipple and a shorter one along his left collarbone. I remembered that he'd told me in the hospital that he knew what it felt like to be shot. He knew more than I; his stitching was longer.

He pulled me closer to undo my bra. "I didn't know women still wore these things," he muttered into my neck.

I stroked his back with my fingertips, smiling. "You were supposed to be excited by the satin and lace."

"I'm more excited," he said, finally getting it unhooked, "by what's inside the lace. Ah." He gently caressed a breast with one hand. "You're brown everywhere. And beautiful."

He insisted on removing the rest of my clothes himself, even my shoes and socks, smoothing away the clothing with strokes that left tremors in their wake. "Beautiful," he said again, when I stood fully naked before him. Then he stepped back to shed the remainder of his clothing while I sat on the bed and watched.

The fat that I had felt in his office disappeared with

his clothes; he was lean and slim-hipped. The sunlight peeked through a gap in the curtains and streaked across his milky shoulders as he lay down beside me, light and shadow.

He kissed my lips and then, tilting my head back, continued over my chin and neck, working his way downward. When he had reached the point on my chest where cleavage would begin, he paused long enough to ask, "Has there been anyone since Roger?"

"No," I said, my voice deep, throaty.

He kissed a wide circle around my left breast and spiraled inward. "Was he good in bed?"

"He was enough. At the time."

He moved back up to my face, kissing my forehead, my closed eyes, and then my lips. "I won't betray you, Valerie," he whispered. The touch of his hand along the inside of my thigh made my body arc in desire. Simple, raw hunger. "I will use you, if I have to, but I won't betray you. Will you trust me?"

I reached for him without answering. What could I entrust to him, that I hadn't already?

Spent and content, I watched him trace a gentle circle around the stitches of my shoulder. "What Roger did to you shouldn't have happened," he said, mostly to himself.

I caught his hand and kissed the fingers. "Let's pretend it didn't. Let's stay here forever, just like this."

"Can you do that?" he asked.

"No."

"Neither of us can. The only way we can get out of this is to go all the way through. And we will go all the way through, because I want more than just a day with you." He leaned down to kiss me, and then sat up.

"Don't go," I pleaded.

"We have to go, Valerie."

"No, we don't. Stay here and interrogate me some more."

He turned back, grinning. "About what?"

"About Stone."

"Who's Stone?" He rolled back onto his side.

I let my hand slide over his hip, snuggling closer so that I could reach down to his buttocks.

He caught my hand and brought it back between us. "No points until you put in your quarter. Who's Stone?"

"Stone is a friend of Roger's. It's a very *big* quarter."

"Then you'll get a lot of points."

"He used to work for the DEA . . ."

Chapter 13

"Do you think Stone is here?"

"I don't know," Chiswick said, "but I can find out." He was lying on his back, staring at the ceiling. "What worries me is why he's here. Could he be part of the plan?"

"No, I don't think so. Stone was never included in parties or dinners or that sort of thing. Roger invested money in Stone's business, but . . ."

"But that was probably part of a laundering operation for drug money," he finished for me. "Yes, I think you're right about that. Still, Stone must have owed Roger. He might be here to fill a last request."

"Stone as an honorable man?" I sat up and looked down at him. "He's more of an anything-for-money type. I think the DEA threw him out, and it wasn't because they didn't like his looks. No. If Stone is here, there has to be a payoff waiting."

"We'll see. Now, get out of bed, you insatiable wench, and go downstairs. I'll never live this down as it is."

"You're not coming?"

"I have to make some phone calls first. Anyway, Duncan will have tea waiting for you. And questions."

"Questions?"

"You can trust him. Tell him as much or as little as you like."

Duncan was waiting, at the foot of the stairs.

"Ah!" he exclaimed. "Thought I heard footsteps. Well, come in, sit down." He beckoned me to a table in the now-empty pub. "You must be exhausted; you've been up there for two hours. The randy old goat."

I grinned at the image, as Duncan retrieved a plate of pastries from the bar counter.

"Eh, so that's the way of it," he said, shaking his sandy brown curls. "Pity. You being such a sweet young thing."

"I'm not young, and he isn't old."

"Well, that's as may be, but you're well and truly caught now, my girl. He won't let you go."

"I wouldn't go."

He stopped and, teasing aside, smiled, looking as lovable as a giant teddy bear. "I'm happy for you. And happy for him. Shall we celebrate with champagne?"

"I'd like to do that, sometime soon. But not today. How about something nonalcoholic?"

"Tea?" He saw my expression. "No, of course not. You're American, aren't you? I know. Just the thing. Orange squash."

"Squash?" I shook my head. "I don't mind a little tomato juice occasionally, but squash juice?"

"Squash juice?"

Now we were both confused, staring at each other. "You said it first," I reminded him.

"I said orange squash, not squash juice."

"Orange squash, yellow squash. Squash is squash."

A light began to dawn across his ruddy features. "No, I don't think so. When you say squash, you're

190

thinking of a vegetable, aren't you?" I nodded. "Well, here," he went on, "those are called marrows. Orange squash is a orange-flavored drink — like lemonade, only it isn't fizzy."

"Lemonade is fizzy?"

He laughed. "Please! Let's get orange squash sorted out first."

"I like it," I said, when I tasted the drink he brought.

He had drawn himself a beer and settled into the chair opposite me. "I'm glad. I wouldn't want to have the Captain's lady leave thirsty."

"Why do you call him the Captain?"

"Because that's who he is." He looked puzzled, as if I'd asked for information that was already obvious.

I remembered Charlie's explanation. "But you don't work for him."

"No, not now. But I did my time in the military. We were mates together, until he promoted past me. I owe him my life several times over, as he owes me his." His expression darkened momentarily, remembering. "I left for this," he indicated the building around us, "and he stayed."

Chiswick, the English equivalent of G.I. Joe. "Why did he stay?"

Duncan smiled in gentle reproof. "There are things that want doing. And the Captain, he's a great one for doing what needs doing. And it's *my* turn to ask questions."

I selected a pastry. "Okay."

"Is it bad, the trouble you're in?"

"I'm not an intentional criminal. But yes, it's bad trouble. It's dangerous. There's a lot of money involved."

He folded his arms on the table in front of him and stared into his beer. "It's the old game, isn't it? Innocent people and guilty money. And he's in it again."

"Well, it is his job."

"Yes, but it's his life, too."

"I don't understand. What do you mean?"

He shook his head slowly. "I think that's a tale that has to come from him."

"But there's so little *time*. There's so much I want to say and ask, but . . ." I raised my hand and let it fall again in frustration.

Duncan sighed. "That's true." Then his grin returned. "Loving the body can be done in an afternoon, but love in the heart takes a bit longer."

This was such an unexpected statement that my eyes must have widened.

"Oho!" he laughed. "You're surprised to find a simple publican talking about love."

I blushed for answer.

"Here, now," he said gently. "I didn't mean to embarrass you. But I . . . I just wanted . . ." He tried to make an apology, and then abandoned the effort. "Do you love him?"

"I, well . . ." I stammered, caught completely unawares. "As much as it's possible in the space of an afternoon, yes."

He smiled to himself, and wanting to avenge my embarrassment, I asked, "Does he love me?"

I expected Duncan to laugh at the question and reprimand me again, but he said, quite seriously, "You could be the one. It's been a couple of years, now, since he's brought a lady here."

I shrugged. "Maybe he's been taking them somewhere else."

"Maybe," he said, but he didn't sound convinced.

I started to suggest another alternative, slightly more risqué, when Duncan held up his hand for silence. I listened, but could hear nothing. Chiswick's men were out there somewhere, I knew. And perhaps Duncan did, too, but he had heard something I had not. Soundlessly, he rose from the table and started for the bar. We heard the click behind us at the same moment, but Duncan turned faster. By the time I had turned to see him, Stone had raised the gun and pointed it at me.

He made no attempt to say anything, and I saw no hatred in his face. At that moment the name "Stone" seemed to fit his chiseled indifference very well. He had come to kill me, and he would. Time seemed to freeze for a brief but endless second, but before the cry in my mind formed on my lips, he pitched forward, crumpling at the foot of the stairs.

Duncan was almost to the bar, but a new voice stopped him, a voice I'd heard before.

"Sit down, Mr. Lowerden," Fierlan said. His gun was aimed at a point midway between Duncan and me. "You can't serve drinks in the middle of the afternoon. And we don't have time to stay." He stepped carefully over Stone's body. Another man appeared behind him, watching the stairs.

"You've been invited to tea, Mrs. Douglas," Fierlan told me. "And we've come to fetch you."

I looked to the stairs in desperate hope.

Fierlan shook his head and then nodded back toward the stairs. "If he comes down, I'll have to kill him." He took my hand and helped me to my feet. "There's no need to be frightened. You'll come to no harm with me."

We walked around Stone and the blood that had puddled beneath his head, and through the kitchen, where Fierlan handed me a pair of workmen's coveralls and a cap. My hands were shaking enough to make the task of putting them on difficult.

"Really, Mrs. Douglas," Fierlan said, helping me with the buttons, "Chiswick has exaggerated my ferocity. Put your hair under the cap. That's it. And keep your head down. Excellent."

He picked up his gun and a clipboard that had been resting on a stack of boxes. "Now you and I are going out the back door, where we will get into a delivery van. You will get in on the left-hand side. Don't forget that. I will get in on the right-hand side. If you try anything foolish, my friend will kill Mr. Lowerden, and if possible, Captain Chiswick as well."

"And if I don't — will they be all right?" My voice was little more than a croak.

He smiled in icy benevolence. "Then we'll *all* be all right."

I kept expecting my legs to fold underneath me, to have Duncan, Chiswick and myself all killed because of my inability to function in an emergency. But I walked the short distance from the back door of the pub to the door of the delivery truck without incident. I closed the truck's door and sat rigidly still on the seat beside Fierlan.

"Very good," he said, starting the motor. He maneuvered the truck carefully yet easily out of the alley, one arm resting nonchalantly on the door, elbow through the open window as he watched the traffic for a suitable opening. "Keep your head down," he reminded me.

I looked down at my trembling hands. "Are you going to kill me?"

He pulled out onto the street. "That's a fine thank-you for a man who's just saved your life for the third time. Though I'm sure that you've been told I was the one wanting to kill you. And that's a blow to my pride, all right. If I wanted you dead, I could have killed you many times over."

"For the third time?" Surprise had momentarily overcome my fear.

"Indeed. The first time was the day of your arrival in London."

"But you tried to kill me that day."

"Did I? Stone tried to kill you. Chiswick pretended to be chasing another car, but he wasn't. Didn't it seem strange to you that he made you get out of the car and hide? Under normal conditions, surely, you would have been safer with him. Yet he left you alone while he turned on your attacker. Have you never wondered why?"

"No, I've never thought about it that way. But it does . . . seem a little unusual."

"He knew I was there, and that I would look after you. And I did, although I must apologize for my ignorance of your wound. I saw you fall, but I thought you had simply stumbled, out of fear." He stole a sidelong glance. "You are more than Roger described."

I had to ignore that. "And the second time?"

"Come now, surely you can figure that out for yourself. I didn't set the bomb in the pub. I merely wanted to see you out of the way when Stone moved in for the kill. Chiswick's men should have been there. It worried me to see you wandering alone. Almost alone." He smiled to himself, enjoying the joke. "I've done their work for them twice, but you won't find them admitting it. One side's white and the other one's black, that's the way they've always seen it."

"But . . . then . . . if you're on the side that isn't trying to kill me—" I stopped, uncertain of what I wanted to ask.

"You can raise your head now. And get out of those coveralls."

I had calmed a bit without noticing it, and was able to wriggle out of the disguise on my own. "But I don't understand—" I began again.

"In due time, Mrs. Douglas." He pulled the truck off into a side street and after shedding his coveralls herded me into the back seat of a waiting car. There were questions I wanted to ask, but I lacked the courage. I waited for "due time."

I thought mostly about Chiswick, and the possibilities that would never be realized. I hoped that Duncan had been wrong, and that Chiswick didn't love me. I hoped that I had just been part of his job, a minor battle lost in a war that would ultimately be won. But I didn't believe it.

Nor did I believe Fierlan's assurance that no harm would come to me. He was a terrorist, and the death of another innocent wouldn't weigh on his conscience. In his eyes, I wasn't even innocent.

Presently the car slowed to a stop in front of a small house half hidden behind trees and bushes and a sturdy-looking stone fence. As we walked through the gate, I saw someone watching us from an upper-story window. Fierlan opened the door himself and motioned me through an entryway papered in atrocious pink-

and-gray wallpaper, to a sitting room somewhat more conservatively decorated. I sat on the edge of a small sofa, ready to run at a moment's notice although there was nowhere to go.

"Mrs. Douglas! How delightful to meet you at last," said a voice from the doorway. The effusive greeting reminded me of Mosby, and I looked up quickly.

But it wasn't Mosby. I could tell that, even though the man's face was hidden beneath a black hood that covered his head. Nothing showed except brief flashes of his eyes through the holes that had been cut for that purpose. He was taller than Mosby, and slimmer, although his voice held the same modulated gentility.

"Bring the tea," he said to someone behind him, and then sat in an armchair at an angle to the sofa. He hiked his trouser leg and crossed his legs with deliberate slowness. If this was an act to convince me he was a cold-blooded and casual killer, he was a poor judge of people. I was long past that.

"Please. Sit back and relax," he said, waving a vague arm.

I wondered what he would do if I didn't, but I didn't want to find out. Not in the conventional way, anyway. I eased deeper into the cushions of the sofa and tried to look comfortable.

We sat silently until Fierlan brought in a tray with a chipped teapot, mismatched mugs, cookies, and a glass of Coke for me. I accepted the drink gratefully, a familiar prop in a demented play.

The hooded man cleared his throat. "I wish I could introduce myself, but I'm afraid that would be unwise, as well as inconvenient for you. Chiswick will give you no rest until he's gotten every detail of your trip here as it is." He caught my expression and turned to Fierlan with a silent question.

"I told her," Fierlan said, shrugging. "But we're the blood-drinking enemy." He raised his cup of tea in a mock toast.

"An attitude which is disappointing, but understandable. You may call me the Black Knight, then, Mrs. Douglas, since you think of us in terms of absolute evil."

I wondered if an apology for my unacceptable attitude would improve my chances for a long life.

"We shall return you to Captain Chiswick's care at the conclusion of your visit, alive and unharmed." He paused, obviously waiting for some acknowledgment from me.

"I'd appreciate that," I said.

He affected an amused chuckle. "Humor in the face of danger! I'm impressed."

I hadn't intended the remark to be humorous, but I tried to smile anyway.

"Brendan told you the truth when he said that we haven't tried to kill you," Mr. Black Knight went on. "Mr. Stone has been waiting for you to arrive in London for several weeks."

"Mr. Stone should be referred to in the past tense," Fierlan interjected from the position he had taken behind the Black Knight's chair.

"Indeed. Hardly regrettable, though I expect Captain Chiswick will be disappointed." He turned to look at me again. "And that surprises you, too, doesn't it? But of course, you weren't told that the identity of your attacker has been common knowledge for some time now. Oh, yes, Chiswick knew. He had Stone followed, hoping he would somehow reveal his employer, but Stone slipped away from his surveillance."

"But not from you."

"No, not from us." There was pride in his voice. "Or, I should say, not from Brendan. Though you caused a stir, heading off for The White Bull like that."

I remembered that Fierlan had known Chiswick was upstairs, and the color rose in my face.

The Knight chuckled again. "I quite understand, my dear. It's in our best interest to keep you as comfortable as possible."

"Except for the group that wants me dead," I reminded him.

Fierlan and the Knight shared a look in which inaudible information was passed. "I wonder if you were really meant to die," the hooded man mused.

I turned my glass around and around in my hand before taking another drink, trying to make something of this statement. "I don't understand."

"Stone seemed quite deadly to you," Fierlan explained, "but he was a rank amateur. Even you could go into the streets of London and find someone more capable."

I doubted that, but I had remembered an earlier question. "If you don't want to kill me — and I am beginning to actually believe that — why am I here? If you knew Roger, then surely you must know that I have no control over the outcome of his little production. I can't tell you what you need to know until the drama is played out to the end."

"We're quite aware of that," the Knight assured me. "We aren't planning to torture you for information we know isn't accessible to you. We aren't monsters."

"It wouldn't work, anyway," Fierlan added. "Roger would have provided a failsafe procedure. I should think that would tip you over the border into madness. Or at least instability."

I shuddered. "You're so urbane. Just a couple of businessmen."

The Knight shrugged. "But we *are* businessmen. We had a contract with Roger and he failed to uphold his end of the bargain."

"Then . . . you aren't the ones for whom the money is intended."

"But we are the ones to whom the money is *owed*." The Knight smoothed the material of his slacks over his knee with long, elegant fingers. "We didn't ask you here, however, to solve our problem. We want to help you solve yours."

"Mine?"

"Stone."

"Stone is dead," I reminded him.

"But his employer is not, my dear. Why didn't Chiswick tell you about Stone?"

"I don't know."

"*Think,* Mrs. Douglas!" Too agitated to sit now, he rose and began pacing, reminding me of Charlie, two hunters stalking an elusive prey. "There must be a reason why Chiswick didn't tell you about Stone. You must know something. Something that, added to Stone's appearance, would lead you to a conclusion Chiswick doesn't want you to reach."

"But I really don't know. Stone was a tennis partner, someone Roger could beat without too much effort. And a drug dealer, I suppose, in a minor sort of way. But I'm not involved with that. Although . . . it's getting harder and harder to say for certain exactly what I'm involved with. . . ." I let my voice trail away for a moment. "Nothing makes sense anymore, and I'm tired. I'm so tired of all of this."

Fierlan sat down beside me. "Of course you are. Just relax and take your time. There's no need to be frightened of us. We want the same thing you want, to see this thing finished."

I was beginning to feel a little drowsy, so I took another drink of Cola to clear my head. A voice inside me warned that this was the enemy, no matter how civil they appeared. The use they would make of the money separated our interests severely.

And yet, they obviously had information that I didn't, information that Chiswick knew, but had kept from me. I wasn't confident of my ability to play perfectly the part that had been written in my subconscious. I wanted all the help I could get.

I felt my head nodding forward and brought it up with a jerk.

"Are you all right?" Fierlan asked gently.

I wanted to tell him that I was, but I couldn't get my mouth to move. Then I began to fall.

Chapter 14

I was cold and my legs and back hurt. I felt for the blanket that I knew I must have kicked off, but it wasn't there, and the movement almost caused me to topple forward. I needed to wake up, I told myself, and get another blanket for the bed. Roger must have left early, and tossed the blanket back at the foot of the bed. Or maybe it had slipped to the floor. In any case, I wasn't going to sleep comfortably until I found it.

I tried to make my eyes open, but they kept closing again, wanting to drown the physical sensation of pain in sleep. I fought for wakefulness, for the control of movement that would start the blood moving.

What finally brought me to awareness was the trickle of cold water down a part of my neck that had heretofore remained inexplicably dry. My eyes focussed slowly in a darkness that was unfamiliar, and I found that my bed was no more than a stone step in a doorway that hadn't managed to keep me dry in the drizzling rain.

I sat there, leaning against the doorframe, for several minutes, trying to make sense of the situation and to remember how I'd gotten there. I was surprised to discover that I still had my watch and that it was almost two o'clock in the morning. I knew I hadn't just fallen asleep for a little nap, of course. Fierlan had drugged me. But I was surprised that it had taken so long; the Knight had only asked for one piece of information. Did the lateness of the hour mean that he had miscalculated the dosage of the drug, or that I had been an uncooperative subject?

I made the slow and painful journey of getting to my feet, cursing Fierlan every inch of the way. Perhaps he didn't count waking up in that condition and situation as coming to harm, but I certainly did. I pushed my dripping hair back from my eyes and thought, looking around, that being left in a strange place in the middle of the night wasn't even close to my definition of being returned to Chiswick's care.

But it was better than being dead.

The thought made me draw back into the doorway. Stone was dead, but his employer wasn't, and as far as I knew, I had no protection. There was no one visible on the dark, rain-washed street or in the parked cars that lined it, and the windows of the stores opposite me were black, but I couldn't fool myself into thinking that that meant there was no one there. But I couldn't stay where I was for the rest of the night, either. That raised the inevitable question of where to go.

I was in the suburbs, I decided. I could pick out the shops that I had come to realize were essential to small neighborhood shopping areas: a tobacconist, a newsagent, a betting shop, a small grocery store, a bakery, a butcher shop and a greengrocer. And yet, as I looked around, I could see that there was one thing missing. There was no pub. And I knew there should have been at least one pub.

I was standing in the doorway of a small bank.

There was a bakery to my right, and after that, a corner. Praying that Fierlan had at least left me within walking distance of the place he had picked me up, I started off unsteadily toward the corner. Cars passed from time to time, which frightened me at first, but after the first few whizzed by without paying me any notice, I began to pay more notice to my surroundings than to the likelihood of being suddenly separated from them.

There was a pub around the corner, but it wasn't the one I was hoping to see. There was also an "Estate Agent" office, with shadowy pictures of expensive properties half obscuring the dark window, and a dry cleaner's. I stopped and stared again at both sides of the street before me. It looked vaguely familiar.

Fierlan had insisted that I ride with my head down leaving the pub, and that was why I couldn't be sure about the street upon which I now stood. Beyond the few businesses were a row of ancient dingy townhouses on one side of the street and a tiny church on the other.

As I crossed the street, I realized that I remembered the church. It wasn't the building so much as the large hydrangea bushes. They were dark and dripping tears now, but they had been ablaze, in the afternoon, with pink flowers on either side of the gravel drive. I had seen that splash of color as we drove by and turned my head slightly for a better look. That meant that The White Bull should be on a side street a little further down and to the left.

The side street was a little bit farther than I had expected and the pub was a little farther down it, but I was pleased with myself for finding it at all under the circumstances. We had, after all, come out of an alley, necessitating extra turns, and I had been terrified. I forced my frozen, cramping legs to hurry the last half-block.

Duncan's answer to my knock was relatively swift, although when he opened the door and pulled me inside, I saw that he was wearing a bathrobe and his hair was disheveled as though he had been in bed. He immediately enveloped me in a hug that was warm in more than one sense of the word.

"Thank God!" he sighed. "I thought you were done for!"

"Me too." My voice was no more than a whispering croak.

He closed and locked the heavy door behind me and then bellowed over his shoulder, "DORIS!," which produced the sound of hurrying footsteps on the stairs. "Are you all right?" he asked, turning back to me.

"Yes," I said. "I think so. I guess so."

"What happened?"

I shook my head slowly, not wanting to provoke the steady ache that was pounding there any more than necessary. "I don't know much. The last thing I remember before waking up on the street was falling off a sofa with a glass of—something—in my hand. Up until that point, things were pretty sane. Or maybe not. Maybe I just thought they were." I leaned against him, seeming to have used up most of my remaining strength and concentration just to get there.

He had been guiding me toward the stairs, and it was there that we met Doris. The lighting was bad and I was in generally poor condition to be meeting people: I wanted to be warm in my bed, drinking hot

205

chocolate and secure in the knowledge that this experience was truly and definitely over instead of a constant threat. I didn't want Doris. I wasn't even sure that I wanted Chiswick anymore. I wanted warmth and solitude.

None of this would have mattered to Doris even if I had taken the trouble and effort to articulate it. She gathered me up in her sturdy arms and half carried me up the stairs. "You poor thing! You're half drowned."

I wanted to tell her that drowning had been among the least of my worries.

"Get a doctor!" she called back to Duncan.

"No!" I managed to gasp.

"Don't get a doctor," she amended herself. "But get the heat on, she'll need a hot bath to thaw. And if you're calling your mate the storm trooper, tell him she won't answer questions for at least a half-hour."

The bed had been remade in the room that Chiswick and I had shared, and Doris threw back the bedspread and pulled off the top blanket with one practiced hand. Even relatively unheated, the room was warmer than the street outside, and the difference made my numbed hands even stiffer. When Doris settled me on the bed, I found I had difficulty even undoing the large buttons of my sweater.

"Here," she said. "Let me do that. The sooner you get out of those wet clothes, the better."

I thought she seemed particularly good at the task, and, as if to answer an unspoken question, she said, "I nursed me mum for six months before she died. Just relax and leave everything to me."

As she bent over me, her loosely curled blond hair

spilled forward, smelling of hair spray and cigarette smoke. Her breasts made prominent bulges under the robe. Called upon to describe her under Chiswick's interrogation, I would have said she was buxom. Comfortably padded, but shapely. Her fingernails were painted with a bright red polish. Roger hated red nail polish. I liked Doris.

"You gave them a bit of a fright, all right," she said to me, peeling the clothes away from my shivering body. "We had the place crawling with coppers for the longest. Missed our evening opening hours."

I mumbled something about being sorry.

"Not your fault, was it? Can't blame the dart for a bad throw. I came in for work at five, and Lord! what a mess. And Duncan and his pal as sorry a sight as you'd ever want to see. Stand up. We'll have these pants off and then give you a good, hot soak in the tub."

"Is Stone—is the man who was shot dead?"

"Too right. Dead as a doornail, and justice done, I say. But what about you?" She wrapped the blanket around me and walked me out of the room to the bathroom across the hall. I could hear the pipes clanking as steam filled them.

"They were civil to me," I said, still surprised by the fact. "It started off pretty well, I guess. Fierlan took me to a house not far from here—it didn't seem far— and there was a man wearing a hood and he wanted to know about Stone but I didn't know anything . . ." I stopped, suddenly aware that the trail of sense was being drowned in the flood of words. But Doris seemed not to notice, giving indication that for her, at least, this wasn't an interrogation. "And then I lost consciousness. I guess they'd put something in my drink." I watched the water fill the large, detached tub.

Doris unwrapped the blanket and helped me into the hot water. "And something into your arm, too," she said, pointing to a bruise on the inside of my left elbow. "But you'll be none the worse for it over the long run."

I took this to mean she expected me to recover. "Yes. Physically, anyway. But I'd appreciate some aspirin."

She found the aspirin in a bottle in the medicine chest and rinsed out a glass for me that had formerly held two toothbrushes. I wondered if one of them was hers.

"How did you find us again?" she asked, taking back the glass when I was finished. She had settled herself on the fuzzy rug, hugging her knees against her chest, so that her face was just about level with mine.

"They didn't leave me too far away. And I remembered a church. Mostly just luck, I guess."

There was a knock on the door. "Sod off!" Doris growled.

"Tea, Dorrie," said Duncan's voice.

"Thanks, love." Doris's voice had softened with affection. "Leave it outside the door before you sod off. The lady needs her privacy."

"They're coming," Duncan added, and then we heard his retreating footsteps.

"They're coming," Doris snorted. She crawled over to the door, opened it, pulled the tray inside and closed the door again. "Too right, they're coming. Won't give you a moment's rest and you'll be sick tomorrow for certain." She poured me a cup of tea, dosed it liberally with milk and sugar, and handed it to me. "Better drink it, love. You want warming up inside and out."

I fought down a sip that my queasy stomach didn't want and thought of Chiswick, and how easy it had been to get warm yesterday afternoon. Had I made a mistake? "I won't betray you," he had said. He hadn't, really. Yet.

"How did he take it?" I asked.

"D'ya mean Chiswick?"

I slid down further into the tub, until my head was resting on the back rim. The steamy water was relaxing.

"He fancies you, you know," Doris said.

"Yes, I know, but . . ."

She sighed. " 'Tisn't in my nature to trust a copper, either. But you're in a right mess, love, and you've got to trust somebody. Ian's a cheeky devil, but he's been a good friend to Duncan. And to me. You could do a lot worse."

"I did a lot worse, once."

"Haven't we all."

"Why did you call him a storm trooper?"

She shrugged. "That's what he is, close enough. Didn't you know?"

"No." My fingers felt again for the bruise inside my elbow.

Doris pulled my hand away, but as soon as she released it, it returned to the bruise, rubbing as if to wash it away.

"It's the SAS," she said quietly. "No ordinary copper could get away with this." She took my hand again.

"The SAS," I repeated. "The Special Air Service? The people that dangle out of helicopters and storm embassies?"

She nodded. "You must have seen that on television, the report of the Iranian Embassy seizure."

A faint noise at the door caused us both to turn. Chiswick was standing in the open door, listening. Before either of us could respond, he stepped over Doris and, grabbing me under my arms, pulled me up and wrapped his arms around me. He held me tightly, as if, even now, he expected someone to come in and attempt to prise me away from him again.

Doris left, closing the door softly.

I let him hold me for a long time, surprised that the position felt no less safe now than it had before the kidnapping. At last his grip loosened. "I missed you, too," I said.

He let me slide back into the warm water and took off his jacket and the shirt which I had gotten fairly wet, draping them over the warm radiator next to the towel Doris had gotten for me. His scars looked almost blue under the single hanging bulb above him.

I splashed my hand in the water. "There's room in here for two very friendly people."

He smiled, and I saw a weight of weariness lift from his face. I wondered if he had burst in without invitation because he was afraid he might not get one, and grabbed me up because he was afraid I might not come willingly. He kneeled where Doris had sat, and leaned forward for a kiss. "You taste like tea."

"She made me drink it. And anyway, I'm thinking of giving up Cokes. Fierlan drugged the last one I drank."

He found the needle mark on my arm. "You should be checked by a doctor."

I covered the bruise with my hand, drawing the arm close to my chest.

"I have been, already, I'm sure. That's the way this game is played, isn't it? Every team is issued an arsenal and a doctor, complete with medical kit and an unlimited supply of drugs. Fierlan and his boss want me alive; I'm sure they took precautions. They were even concerned about my comfort, can you believe that? Of course, they could have lied about that. Considering the condition I woke up in, they probably did."

"They brought you back. But they didn't want to get you any closer for fear of catching surveillance."

"What surveillance? I should think they could figure that out after Stone walked in waving a gun. *I* did. And surveillance wasn't there tonight, either."

His face was perfectly expressionless. "They were there."

"Damn!" I got up and wrapped the towel around myself. I didn't want to be naked before him anymore; I needed a disguise for the impotence of my anger. "I wonder if they enjoyed that, watching me stumble past them in the dark and the rain. Did they go along with Fierlan and me, too?"

"No."

"Too bad. They would *really* have enjoyed that, watching the needle go in and me reduced to a babbling idiot. You could have all gone down to the pub and had a good laugh over that one."

"Valerie."

"Shut up!" I yelled. "Just shut up." I slipped a little

in the tub, and he rose and instinctively caught me by the shoulders, but after regaining my balance, I turned away. The silence after my shout was heavy in the rising steam.

It might have been better, I knew, to cower, to emphasize my helplessness and fear, to cry. That would have worked better on Roger, and it would have done its damage on Chiswick, too, although for a different reason. But what I might have gotten from that were more assurances that were simply lies, or at best halftruths. And it occurred to me that what was becoming hardest wasn't the shock of the harsh truth, but the acceptance of the devious lies used to disguise it.

With my shaking fingers, I brushed my hair, still damp from the rain, sleekly back from my face. I wouldn't show him any softness that I could conceal. That, I thought, would be a response Chiswick could well understand.

"Is Stone dead?" I asked.

"Yes."

"Did he say anything before he died?"

He thought for a moment, and I saw the weariness return to his features. I wanted that, and yet it hurt me. I shook my head, causing echoing throbs of pain that reminded me why I was there.

"No," he said.

"Would you have let Stone kill me?"

"No."

"How would you have prevented it?"

"I was standing at the top of the stairs, just out of your sight. I would have killed him." He spoke with the quiet surrender of a doomed prisoner under interrogation.

"How did you know he was coming?"

"I had a beeper, in my jacket pocket. It went off, just after you went downstairs."

"Did Duncan know?"

"No."

"You're not above using your friends, either, are you?"

For the first time, I saw a little of the fire return. "That's between Duncan and me."

"I guess it is. Why did you lie to me about Stone?"

"I didn't want . . ." He dropped his gaze.

"To worry me? Cut the crap. Why did you lie to me about Stone?"

He remained stubbornly mute, not looking up. The power was being held in check, and I thought I knew why. And yet it puzzled me, because I could see no reason to withhold the truth any longer. "What were you expecting me to say when I saw him?" I asked.

He looked at me again, with the steady strength of the unshakeable convert. "I didn't expect you to say anything. I expected him to say something. I hoped he would say something."

"He didn't," I added unnecessarily, swallowing against the nausea.

"He didn't have time."

For one wild moment I thought about hitting him again. "Christ! How fucking long were you going to wait, asshole? He'd already cocked the trigger! Were you expecting him to take a *practice* shot?"

"There was a slight safety margin," he said tonelessly. "By the time he entered the room, Duncan was far enough away from you to make killing you both difficult. Stone wasn't an experienced assassin. He would have had to think, to realize that it would be wiser to kill Duncan first, and then you."

My throat had constricted, making my words difficult. "That assumes he cared about his survival."

"Yes."

The words that he hadn't said rose up in my throat, and I convulsed in a dry heave. He caught me easily, lifting me out of the tub, and then lowered us both to the floor, cradling me on his lap. "You're all right," he assured me gently. "There's nothing in your stomach. Just breathe deep and relax." He pressed my head into his shoulder and stroked my hair, and I wanted to hide forever in the curve of his neck and strangle him at the same time.

"Why didn't you just drug Stone?" I choked out the words as the retching quieted. "The way you did me the night of Mosby's party?" I'd known, I suppose, in the back of my mind, that something strange had happened that night of the nightmare, something more than I could explain, but I hadn't admitted it to myself before.

"Because, as you have discovered, that takes time. His absence would have been noticed. And he wouldn't have known anything. He wouldn't have known who he was working for; Stone owed a lot of favors to a lot of people. He and Roger had more than one mutual associate."

I struggled violently to get free, but he seemed to have been expecting it, holding me tighter, closer.

"It's a game to you!" I cried. "I'm a chess piece, a pawn, and if I die, what difference does it make to you?"

He pulled my head back and kissed me hard. When

he finally released my lips, he cradled my face in his hands and asked, softly, "Do you really believe that?"

"Please let me go," I pleaded. "Let me go."

He stood up and picked me up, carrying me out of the room. In the hallway, Dorrie stood before the bedroom door like a guard.

"No," she said.

Chiswick turned his head slightly, toward the darkness of the hall. "Duncan," he called quietly.

"Come away, Dorrie," Duncan said in answer. He stepped out of the shadows and took her gently by the arm.

She resisted enough to look at Chiswick one last time. "You bastard!" she hissed.

He carried me on into the bedroom, kicking the door closed after him. "Don't let her go like that," I was surprised that it came out so clearly. "She thinks—"

"It's an old hurt," he said, sitting down on the bed beside me to take off his shoes, "and it can't be talked away in a night."

I watched him take off the rest of his clothes, a lithe ghost in the darkness of the room. "You are a bastard," I accused him. "And this is your needle."

His breath was warm on my cheek. "One strong emotion replaces another. And you don't want to hit me again, do you? Let me work it out of you, and then we'll talk. Don't you want me, still?"

"I wanted Roger . . . once."

He drew back enough for me to see his face in the dim glow from the streetlamp outside. For one brief moment, I saw a flash of pain in his features. It washed over me like a burst of sunlight through a break in the clouds of a stormy day, and as any green and growing thing will, I reached out for it.

Chapter 15

"You're right, I do feel better," I said. I was lying with my head on his chest, with his arm across my shoulders, as if even now he feared I might still try to run away. "But I'm still angry."

"Of course you are," he answered mildly.

I turned and raised my head, so that I could see his face. "What happened when Fierlan came in?"

There was no change of expression. He'd been expecting this. "I dropped the gun. Fierlan is well versed in these sort of things. I wouldn't press our luck that far. So you left, and after about five minutes, Fierlan's friend left, too. And, yes, I let him go without stopping him, because I wanted you back." He stroked my hair almost absentmindedly. "Fierlan and his mates are dangerous men, but they can be depended upon to act in their own best interests, and giving you back was to their advantage."

"Yet, when you grabbed me up out of the bath, I would have sworn that you thought you'd never see me again."

He smiled like an indulgent parent. "You aren't the only one in this mess who has to live with fear."

I closed my eyes. "God, why don't I hate you for what you're doing to both of us?"

He pressed my head to his chest once again. "You're special."

"Uh-huh."

"You are. You've got gut instinct. Intuition, if you like. Maybe it's because you pay such close attention to people. When we first met, I was on pins and needles all the time with you, because you watched everything I did and listened to everything I said as intently as if your life depended on it. Which it did, of course, but you couldn't have known it then. I had to be so careful about controlling every expression and every movement that sometimes I'd come back to your room after you'd gone to sleep, just so I could look at you without having to worry about your noticing." He laughed, remembering. "You're such a *tourist*, Val, and yet I think I could have walked you through Buckingham Palace sometimes and you wouldn't have noticed it for watching me." His arm tightened around me. "Roger underestimated you, and that's why we'll beat him."

"Did he really?" I asked bitterly.

He squeezed me. "Yes, he did. You're getting stronger every day. Can't you feel it? Roger controlled you when he was alive, because you trusted him, I admit that. A little trust and a lot of brainwashing can go a long way, love. I've seen it happen to older and wiser than you. But he's gone now and you're finding your own way, one step at a time. You walked out of the pub bombing on your own, almost, and you did finally make the call. You didn't collapse when Fierlan marched you out of this pub, and you found your own way back. Bloody hell, you even stood up to Charlie! Roger never knew you."

"Fierlan said that, too. He said I was more than Roger described."

"What else did he say?"

I told him as much as I could remember, from the point at which we left the pub until I lost consciousness on the Knight's sofa. The story came out calmly, each detail as precise as I could make it in retrospect, and much more clearly than I would have expected. Chiswick had known it would, had known how to bring about that peace in the eye of the storm that would make the telling possible.

When I had finished, I looked up and saw that he had produced a microcassette recorder from somewhere, probably under his pillow. Even that had been finessed for me.

"Could you find the house again?" he asked.

"I don't know. Maybe. I'd know that pink-and-gray wallpaper in a minute."

"The local police won't like that, having to make a house-to-house search for wallpaper," he teased.

"They won't have to," I retorted. "All they have to do is just call the local real-estate agents and ask them. Any agent worth his salt is going to know in a flash if he has that house listed. There can't be that many furnished, vacant houses with horrible wallpaper in this part of London.

"Very good," he said, snapping the recorder off. "You see, you're even becoming a fair detective. Now all we have to do is find the general neighborhood. The house will be easy enough to find to have made it worth Fierlan's time to leave it very, very clean, so we needn't bother to go looking for it until after sunrise. I reckon we've got about an hour and a half. Do you fancy a nap?"

I shifted in the bed so that I could put my head on the other pillow, snuggled warm against him.

"Me, too," he said, reaching for the bedside lamp.

I was surprised at the amount of cars on the streets at six A.M. As I explained to Chiswick, I'd always pictured the typical Englishman riding to work on a train, carrying an umbrella and wearing a three-piece suit.

"The brolly brigade still exists," he said. "But it doesn't help my job to have large numbers of people concentrated in a small area, so you'll pardon me if I don't wax nostalgic."

I wondered if we should have stopped for more breakfast than the coffee and roll he'd eaten at the Bull before we started out. I wouldn't be hungry until after we'd done what we could to find the house, but I hadn't thought about Chiswick's hunger. When had he last eaten?

"Watch the *scenery*, Val," he reminded me "Should I turn here?"

I studied the surroundings. Ahead of us lay a traffic circle filled with the sort of traffic that would have intimidated even a New York cabbie. Had Fierlan and I gone through that, at a more leisurely time? Chiswick pulled over to the side of the road and braked behind a tiny electric milk cart, incongruously making its slow, clanking progress up the side of an otherwise very busy street. I was amused to see that even the shops took one or two of the pint bottles.

"For tea," Chiswick answered my unspoken question. "Do we turn here?"

220

I looked around once more. "No, but soon we'll turn left. Just a few blocks more."

He merged into the stream of cars again without comment, but I knew what he was thinking. In England, a few blocks might mean a hundred yards or a couple of miles. I watched the trees and bushes roll by until I found the house I was looking for, and laid a hand on his arm. "There."

It was a winding street, deeply shaded from the first rays of an indecisive sun by the tall trees that lined it. "Left again there."

And there was the house again, a narrow two story with black-and-white trim, rising behind a small overgrown garden. I was suddenly as frightened to see it as I had been the first time, and for a moment I saw again the man's face, watching from an upper-story window. I shivered. "That's it," I said. "My God, I found it."

"Of course you found it," he said, reaching for the car telephone. "Fear is a trance, too, isn't it? And you're used to learning things in a trance." After a short exchange, presumably with Charlie, he started the car again. "Right," he said to me. "It's time for a proper English breakfast."

"Aren't we going to . . ."

"Get in the technical team's way? No. We have more important things to do than to make a nuisance of ourselves here."

"What kind of things?"

"Eating breakfast, for one."

"Please don't patronize me."

He sighed and smiled at me, but it was a weary smile. "I'm not patronizing you. It's a simple case of logistics: you need to eat in order to carry on, and therefore *I* need for you to eat. And besides, I'm hungry."

As concerned as I had previously been about his hunger, I said, "And if you told me what's waiting for me today, I wouldn't eat, would I?"

He shifted the car into gear and pulled away from the curb, pretending not to hear. I looked out of the window and remembered another spring day.

"Why do you have to go on such short notice?" I asked, sitting on the bed beside his suitcase, tempted to take out the shirts he had just packed.

"Because I'm the only one available," Roger answered.

"But you're *not* available," I insisted. "The award dinner is tomorrow night. And you promised. You *promised* that this time . . ." I took a tissue from the table beside the bed and wiped away the tears as they welled in my eyes, and then wadded it savagely into a ball in my clenched fist, angry at myself for the demeaning weakness. Roger was standing in front of his closet, and when he turned, I stood up and walked to the other side of the room, to stare out of the window. The brief south Texas winter was almost over, and the sunlight through the sliding glass doors was warm, but not hot enough to thaw the chill that had overtaken me.

"It's just another award dinner," Roger said quietly behind me. "You don't need another piece of paper to know you're good."

"It isn't just another award. It's important to me."

He joined me at the window and slipped his arms around me. "Vallie, I'm sorry. But it's my job. I have to go. It's that simple."

I stood rigid, not yet yielding to him, thinking, "That's what I hate the most about it. That it's so simple."

The houses and gardens rolled past the window of Chiswick's car, and I pretended to look at them, but I couldn't see them. I was searching out the less visible lies in an old landscape and thinking that ignorance was an uncertain and treacherous bliss.

I used to believe the old cliché about your life passing before your eyes in the moment before death. But, thinking about it, I realized it wasn't true. When Roger died, I regretted not so much the ending of the life that we had shared as the loss of a life we might have had. Sitting beside Fierlan and thinking I would never see Chiswick again, I was keenly aware of the possibilities that would never be explored. So it seemed to me, that in the last living breath, I wouldn't regret the life that I had lived nearly so much as the life I *hadn't* lived. That's what I was thinking about when Chiswick finally told me his news.

He'd waited until I had finished the greater part of the eggs and bacon that Doris served me in the tiny dining room of Duncan's apartment above the pub. When I put my fork down for the last time and pushed my plate away, Chiswick looked at me steadily over the rim of his coffee cup and said quietly, "Dennis Penning was murdered last night."

Dennis and I might have become good friends. We might have spent a few evenings together exploring who Roger had really been and how he had manipulated and changed our lives, and we might both have gained from that. Now it would never happen. Now his children would lose completely the man who had been their father. Their lives would be forever saddened and changed.

My mind began whirling. If I hadn't come to London, if I hadn't let Roger control and use me, if I hadn't trusted him so completely, if I hadn't married him, if I hadn't gone to a music store at a particular time on a particular day and met him there . . .

"Valerie?" Dorrie's voice was soft and a little hoarse. I didn't answer her, because I knew she was talking to the body of a woman sitting beside her, and not to me. Across the table Chiswick was watching with careful clinical interest, waiting for a signal, a sudden stranger.

My body got up and began to pace around the outer perimeter of the room, walking as close to the walls as was possible without bumping into furniture. I wasn't controlling my movements. I was watching myself much as Chiswick was, caught in a waking nightmare, unable to scream myself awake.

"Where are you going?" He was walking beside me.

"Looking," my lifeless voice answered.

"What are you looking for?"

"Looking."

He stepped in front of me, and when I moved to walk around him, took me by the shoulders and held me gently but firmly. "What are you looking for, Valerie?" he asked again.

I found myself looking around the room, unable to focus on what was there, looking for something that wasn't. But I didn't know what it was. I turned and tugged myself from Chiswick's grasp without too much effort and went into the rest of the rooms of the upper floor, one at a time, making a single journey around each, with Chiswick close behind me. I wasn't moving quickly, but my breath came faster and faster, and the heat of my flushed face provoked a sheen of perspiration.

By the time I had finished searching the upper story and headed for the stairs, I was panting in ragged gasps, my fear producing a pounding heartbeat to match. I tried to calm myself with the assurance that soon my legs would collapse beneath me and the madness would have to stop, at least for a while. I descended the stairs slowly, but with the physical effort of running, so that by the time I reached the ground floor I was dragging myself forward.

At the bottom of the stairs, just off to the right, was the chalk outline of Stone's body, and when I reached it, I stopped, refusing to go further, biting my lower lip to halt the scream rising in me. The pain was stronger than the urge that had propelled me, and I groped for the banister post and sank down on the bottom step.

"Not this time, Roger," I said.

Chiswick reached out for the doorknob of Dennis Penning's apartment, and then, seeing my face, drew back and hugged me tightly. The uniformed policeman guarding the door looked tactfully away.

Chiswick had already assured me that the body had been taken away, and that the single shot between Penning's eyes had left only a very small bloodstain inside the outline taped on the carpet. "Will there be anyone else there?" I asked.

"Enders, and a woman who cleaned the place once a week."

At least, I thought, if I do start acting crazy I won't have a large audience. "Okay," I sighed. "I'm ready."

Dennis had been shot as he opened the door, staggering backward a few steps before falling, thudding quietly in the thick carpeting. To his neighbors below, it would have sounded fairly innocuous. Someone moving furniture, I thought, or dropping a heavy book.

"As near as we can figure, it happened around midnight," Chiswick said gently, guiding me around the spot. "No one saw anything, of course. The killer used a silencer, and no one heard any loud noises."

"Who found him?"

Chiswick looked surprised, but Charlie, behind him, nodded as if that were a natural question for me to ask.

"A security guard. Penning was supposed to take a transatlantic phone call at around twelve-thirty, and when he didn't answer, the caller rang the security desk downstairs."

I looked around the room. It looked like a bachelor's place, comfortable enough but furnished in a random style that encompassed everything from Danish modern to French provincial. The sofa was tastefully upholstered in a subdued blue-and-white floral print, but the drapes behind it were patterned with large pink roses splashed on a pale green field. I remembered Penning's house as well-appointed, but that had been in the days before his wife left.

I couldn't remember any specific piece of furniture from a previous time, but I made a swift circuit of the entire apartment, hoping to find what I was looking for quickly, then ending up where I'd begun, knowing I'd have to begin again.

"I caused this," I told Chiswick. "I told Fierlan . . . something."

"We don't know that."

I opened a side drawer of Penning's desk, flipping through the bills and personal letters, feeling like a voyeur. I knew I wouldn't find any surprises, following behind Chiswick and Charlie, but I didn't know what else to do.

"If Fierlan didn't kill him, then who did?"

"There is no if," he insisted. "You can't claim the guilt for this. Dennis was the next link in a chain that Fierlan wants completed."

I closed the drawer and decided against opening the others. The desk was set in a corner of the living room, between two long windows, facing a blank wall. "But the other side, Forbin's group, I guess, couldn't want him dead, either."

"I know." His look was reproving.

"Sorry." I gave up on the desk and moved on to the bedroom. Penning had lain down before he was killed. He'd thrown his suit jacket over the back of a chair, sat down on the edge of the bed and taken off his shoes and then stretched out for an unknown period of time, rumpling the bedspread. I could almost see him there, fingers laced behind his head and eyes closed, letting the weariness of the day slip away. On the small bedside table was a glass half full of clear liquid, probably the remains of a drink. I reached out to touch the bedspread gently and then straightened up and forced myself to look around me. But nothing caught my eye.

"Should I search his closet?" I asked.

"Do you want to?"

"Christ. No."

He laid a hand on my shoulder, lightly. "Then don't."

"Who killed him?"

"I don't know."

"Do you know why he was killed?"

"The why is obvious. To obscure the next clue." His eyes were gentle, but there was no leniency in the voice.

I looked around the room once more and shrugged. "There isn't anything here. I just can't . . . I can't believe that the man I spoke to yesterday would willingly have helped Roger."

"Not willingly." Chiswick waited for me to turn back to him before continuing. "Whatever you were meant to find here, you were supposed to find without any collusion on Penning's part. When I told you he was dead, you got up from Duncan's table and began searching for something, something that you expected to find in open sight. Whatever you need to see here should be in open sight."

"Maybe it was in open sight two years ago," I said softly, "but it isn't now."

"Maybe." He led me out of the bedroom and into the guest room next to it. "Maybe the killer knew exactly what to take. Maybe it's gone. But you have to try, Val."

I nodded mutely, perilously close to tears. I wanted control, to be able to do this as quickly as possible.

Closer examination of Penning's guest room yielded

proof that he was a family man. The walls were almost completely covered with pictures, from pencil and charcoal sketches to crude and more refined oil paintings. I remembered that Penning's daughter, now in her late teens I supposed, was an artist. Several of the paintings on display, presumably the most recent, were quite good. So many paintings . . . Without speaking, I backed out of the door and went back to Dennis's desk in the sitting room.

"What is it?" Chiswick asked, his voice sounding distant.

"It's not *here*," I heard myself mumble. "It should be here, but it isn't." I shifted from one foot to the other, unable to keep still, ready to go but without a destination.

"Enders!" Chiswick barked.

"Sir?"

"Where's the woman?"

"In the kitchen."

"Fetch her."

I heard the footsteps behind me, but I didn't turn. I couldn't turn.

"What's missing from this part of the room?" Chiswick asked her.

"Well, like I told the constables, there wasn't nothing of value taken. And Mr. Dennis had some nice things, he did."

"It needn't be anything valuable," Chiswick explained patiently. "But it's probably something that would have been easily seen, even by a casual visitor."

"Well . . ." She glanced around herself, frowning. "Oh, yes. There was the picture. It was hanging over the desk." She laughed a little self-consciously. "Fancy me forgetting that! As many times as I dusted it!"

"What kind of picture was it?"

"It was a painting. Mr. Penning's daughter done it for him. Mind you, it wasn't a very *good* one. There's better in the bedroom. 'The gallery,' he used to call it . . ."

"What did the painting look like?" Chiswick interrupted her.

"It was a picture of Stonehenge," she answered. "From high up, like, in the early morning . . ."

Her voice droned on, but I had stopped listening. I didn't need the rest of her description, for as I stared at the wall, I could see it as clearly as if it hung before me. A double ring of huge, vertical slab-shaped stones, some with lintels, on a barren hill, with the winter sun just peeking over the horizon, tentative yellow light defining the darker stones. Snow covered the ground in hues of black and gray and slate blue, turning to white where the sun streaked across it.

I felt the urge to go, the same need for action that had sent me after Stone in St. Paul's. Stone and Stonehenge. Had it only been the likeness of his name that had drawn me that day? I remembered the coldness of the stone walls beneath my touch.

Chiswick was still talking to the woman, and Charlie appeared not to notice me. I moved a step closer to the door, and then another.

"I take it this means you've found what you were looking for," Chiswick said in my ear.

I stiffened and then relaxed, taking a deep breath, glad to be spared another robotic episode.

"Where were you going?" he asked.

"I don't know." I turned to look at him, needing to

see the quiet confidence in his dark eyes. "But I think this is the last step, the finale of the dance."

I looked back at the wall above the desk, able now to see the darker space where the picture had hung. Dennis had been killed for an amateur rendering of a tourist postcard. I wondered if the killer knew how futile the effort had been, how easily I had found the clue I was looking for. I wondered if he knew but didn't care, and then I wondered if my successful delivery of the money would stop him.

Chapter 16

"Where are we going?" I asked Chiswick. We had driven from Penning's apartment to a part of London that grew less and less scenic as we progressed.

"To lunch."

I looked doubtfully at the warehouses and the run-down buildings. "I hope you brought your gun."

"There won't be any trouble," he grinned. "They know me around here."

He parked legally and, instructing me to stay in the car, vanished inside a door beneath a sign that proclaimed, "Fish & Chips." I locked the car doors and waited.

After a few minutes he emerged, both hands full, and signaled me with a jerk of his head to get out of the car.

"Are you sure this is a good idea?" I asked as I closed the car door behind me.

He shook his head, smiling at my wariness. "Houston must have a terrible crime rate."

"There are places there that I wouldn't visit alone."

"Well, you're not alone, are you?"

I thought about Fierlan. "No, I'm not."

He caught the meaning of my reply and shrugged. "The more, the merrier. Here."

I looked at what he handed me, an aroma of fried fish rising from a cone of newspaper. "What is this?"

"Fish and chips. Very British."

"I know that. I mean *this*." I tugged on a corner of the newspaper. "This is *newspaper*."

He leaned over to inspect the corner. "One of the evening rags, I think."

I looked closer into the cone, pushing the fried potatoes to one side. "There's a picture of a naked woman on this page!"

"So there is. Want to trade? I got the sports section." He chewed a piece of fish with elaborate casualness, but I could see the laughter dancing in his eyes.

"Civilized people do not eat out of newspaper. We wrap *garbage* in newspaper." A passing couple turned to stare at us.

"Eat your lunch, Yankee snob," he said.

So we ate, leaning against the car, while I tried not to think about the calories I was consuming. If he had asked me, I would have had to admit that the food tasted better than many fast-food burgers I had eaten in Houston, but he didn't. After we'd finished and wiped our greasy fingers, he produced two cans of soda from his pockets and said, "Let's walk."

I hesitated.

"There isn't much traffic on this street," he pointed out. "And strangers are noticed."

We were being eyed with a good deal of suspicion by those whom we passed on our leisurely stroll. He took me by the hand, capable, strong fingers curling protectively around mine. "Okay," I said "A short walk."

We turned left at the corner and then left again, and I heard the sound of lapping water and the cry of scavenger birds overhead. I hadn't realized how close we were to the river.

Chiswick stopped and pointed to a warehouse across the street, weathered and aging. "Does that one look familiar?" he asked.

I frowned first at the building and then at him. "No. Why—?" I caught myself, understanding. "This isn't where I was going, if that's what you're asking."

"I'm just asking if it looks familiar."

"Well it doesn't."

He led me across the quiet street. I breathed the smell of ancient damp through the open door, and then stepped back as a body suddenly appeared out of the darkness beyond.

"Afternoon, Constable," Chiswick greeted him, nodding.

The young policeman's face was carefully respectful as he stepped aside to let us pass. "Afternoon, sir," he said.

I had noticed the bulge under his uniform. "Friend of Charlie's?" I whispered.

Chiswick ignored me. "Look around."

I moved closer to him, uneasy in this artificial night and still restless to reach another destination. "All I can see is dark."

"Lights!" he called over his shoulder, and I was momentarily blinded by the immediate brilliance.

But it was only a warehouse, mostly empty, with various pieces of large, unidentifiable equipment and a scattering of ropes, curled like sleeping snakes in the musty corners "What am I supposed to see?"

He sighed. "Nothing, it seems. Thank you, Constable, you can kill the lights."

I blinked again in the enveloping darkness. "This belongs to Mosby, doesn't it?" I asked quietly.

"Yes."

I tried to conjure up the picture of Mosby in the restaurant, to add to it in some way, but I couldn't. "What did I tell you, when you drugged me after Mosby's party?"

He pulled me closer. "You said it wasn't time."

This raised a barrage of questions I didn't want to think about. "Well, it's time now, but this isn't the place."

"I know."

"Can I go, then?"

"No, not yet. I'll take you back to the house in Surrey, where you'll be safe. I have to see my boss."

I tried to pull away from him. "I have to go, can't you see that? It's time, and for me there isn't time to talk anymore. Put a map in my hand and let me go. You can follow me, you and Fierlan and—"

"The killer," he interrupted softly.

"Damn it!" I swore out of frustration "I don't have a *choice*. If I hadn't been so spooked by this part of town, I'd have left when you went inside the fish shop. I have to go!"

His grip on me tightened. "If you go now, you'll have very little chance of actually getting there."

"It stopped me this time, but it won't work again. I *know* the killer is out there. But Roger doesn't seem to have planned for that; it doesn't matter. The robot inside me knows that it's time to go, and it can't recognize anything else."

235

He let go of my hand only to take me by the shoulders and shake me roughly. "Listen to me! I know that it's hard, that it's going to get harder. But the killer knows where you're going, Valerie. You'd be walking into a trap. I won't let you do that."

"There are things worse than death," I said softly, remembering what Fierlan had said about a possible failsafe procedure that could send me into the dark regions of insanity. In the silence that followed, I wished desperately that I could see his face. Only the vague outline of his head was distinguishable in the darkness. Maybe, I thought, that was why we were there: to speak the words that had to be said, but hide the truth.

"I can't play this game any longer!" My words were muffled against his chest.

"You can do it," he said. "We can beat him." I drew back my fist, but even in the darkness, he caught it easily. "Use your left this time. Old bones are brittle."

I let out a long breath of surrender. "At least let me tell you where I'd go."

"No. The doctor says that would be worse than not letting you go at all."

He waited for a response from me, a sign of acquiescence, but the silence stretched between us. I had lived my life for Roger, even after his death, and I had given him everything I had to give and had not won his love. I didn't even believe he had ever really liked me, although he'd assured me daily that he loved me.

Chiswick's words said that I was a tool to him and that his concern for me, though genuine, was strictly impersonal, but when he touched me, when he held me and laid his cheek on the top of my head, as he did at that moment, the tenderness was overwhelming. I knew that he loved me. I knew that if he lost me he would be devastated, but I didn't understand why he couldn't say it.

My voice was barely a whisper. "Okay."

Outside, I looked at his face and saw nothing but the carefully composed, professional control. We walked back to the car without speaking.

I paced the house in Surrey all afternoon, setting everyone in the office on edge, until a discreet telephone call was made and Felicity appeared, carrying a doctor's bag

"No," I said. "No needles, no pills, no drugs."

"You're wearing yourself out," she said.

"Sleep would be infinitely more tiring at this point."

She looked over my shoulder, to Charlie, who had come up behind me. "Do it," he said.

"No!"

"Sorry, love," he said through clenched teeth as he held me despite my struggling, "but I have to go out and I want to make very certain you'll be here when I get back." He nodded to Felicity. "Do it now. A dead weight will be easier to carry upstairs."

I watched her open the bag and take out the hypodermic syringe. Her hands were shaking a little, but the needle went in smoothly, and everything else swiftly began to fade.

When I opened my eyes, Roger was draped casually over the end of the bed, on his side. His right hand propped up his head, and in his left, he twirled a gold cuff link.

"You never were very good at holding up under stress," he said, suppressing a yawn. "I've been waiting for hours."

"You're dead." I was dreaming, I thought, or worse.

He laughed with easy insolence. "Brilliant observation, my dear. Yes, I'm dead. Dead, but not powerless."

I watched with a fascination born of horror as he rose from the bed in one fluid motion and pulled a chair from the darkness into the circle of light that the small bedside lamp cast. "What do you want from me?" I asked.

"You know what I want, Valerie. And when you get the chance, you'll do it. But in the meantime, I thought I'd drop by for a little chat, to pass the time. It's been such a long time since we've talked."

"Go to hell."

He laughed again. "Where did all this spirit come from? As if I didn't know. Where is your little tin soldier now, little Valerie? Why isn't he here to save you?"

"It wouldn't help if he were," I said. "You're not real. You're only inside my head, and he can't get inside my head."

Roger leaned forward, leering. "Well, he certainly has gotten into other parts of you, hasn't he? Did you really think that was going to save you?"

"No. I did it because I wanted to. I wanted him."

"You wanted to?" His eyes were cold, and I shivered under the blanket. "You have no will of your own, Valerie. You never have and you never will. You do what you're told."

"No," I said stubbornly. "I wanted him. He loves me."

"Love? What a fool you've been! You aren't the kind of woman men love. You're the kind of little girl men *use*. Why can't you accept that? You're no more to him than you were to me."

"Nooooooo . . . " My cry was high and thin, and it echoed in the distant darkness of the room.

"Oh, yes. All the queen's horses and all the queen's men won't be able to put you back together again. The only way you can save yourself is to follow the plan. Go where you've been told to go." He stood up and looked down on me with chilling cruelty. "Finish the game, Valerie. It's the only way you can get rid of me."

I couldn't open my eyes, but I was able to hear movement in the room, feet shuffling across the floor and the sound of small objects being moved.

"She's asleep," a man's voice said in irritation. "After the dose you gave her, a cow would be asleep. There's nothing more we can do."

"But she moved her lips," Felicity insisted. "She's dreaming. Something's happening. If we lose her now . . ."

"What's happening is your imagination. You've been on this case too long." He laughed, reminding me of Roger's taunts. "The case is blown, anyway. Your precious Captain is in the fire this time."

"Chiswick's always in the fire."

"But this time he won't be coming back. Don't look

so shocked. It's been coming. He doesn't even have a file anymore, did you know that? It's been pulled, sent to God knows where. Nobody knows what his *real* rank is, or who pays him. He's become the invisible man. They're phasing him out; he's not coming back. You'd better get used to taking orders from Charlie, old girl." There was a short pause and then the man laughed again, but the sound was softer, now. "I don't like him, either. Nobody else would have him, except Chiswick. I'll say this for the Captain: he knew how to keep the wild dogs on a leash. But getting involved with an informant is intolerable. He's finished."

"He'll be back."

The man went on as if he hadn't heard her. "He should never have been in this work, you know. I had lunch, a couple of months ago, with the fellow who assisted in Chiswick's workup when he was pulled from the rank and file for special duty. He said Chiswick was the toughest man he'd ever met, impervious to pain and absolutely unbreakable under interrogation. The officers drove him to the limits, and he would go until his body couldn't perform anymore with hardly a ripple in resolve. That's the sort of person they want for this work. But my friend said that someday Chiswick would fall in love, and that would be the end of him. And that's what's happened, isn't it?"

"It's happened before, and it didn't stop him."

"A man takes a mistress for many reasons," the man responded knowingly, "besides love. When she was killed, he spent more time catching the kidnappers than he did actually grieving for her. It was business to him. He's finished. He won't be back."

"He will!" Felicity whispered fiercely.

I tried to speak, to offer her support, but I couldn't move.

"You're on your own now," Roger said from the darkness. "You'll do what you're told to do when the time comes. You always have. You've always been such an accommodating victim. You've always wanted it that way, haven't you?"

I felt a cool touch on my forehead, and was surprised how easily my eyes opened in response. Dorrie smiled down at me, wiping my cheeks with a wet washcloth.

"You look better," she said. "How do you feel?"

"Scared. I've been talking to Roger." Her eyes widened a little, and I regretted saying it. There was, after all, nothing she could do. "How did you find me?" I asked.

"I got a phone call from Ian. He gave me the address and told me to look after you until he got back."

"Is he coming back?"

She looked genuinely surprised. "Of course."

Had I only dreamed I had heard Felicity and the man talking? Had that, too, been a hallucination? I said, "Did you know Ian's mistress, the one who died?"

She turned away abruptly, stood, and walked to the window. "She was a friend of mine," she said softly, staring out at the night.

So I had heard them. "I'm sorry. I didn't know."

"Well, he wouldn't have told you that, would he?"

"He wouldn't tell me anything I . . . overheard some people talking."

"It's common knowledge to this lot, I'm sure." The anger slipped away from her voice with a sigh. "He sent you a message. He said to tell you, 'But the lion just smiled to himself, and waited.' "

I sat up and reached for the water glass beside the bed, drinking and thinking.

"Does it mean anything to you?" Dorrie asked.

"Maybe. It's a line from a book I wrote, called *The Dandy Lion*." I hesitated, not wanting to oversimplify a book I had worked hard to shade with humor and whimsy, and then almost laughed at myself. Pride no longer mattered. "The lion had a beautiful, glossy coat and all the other animals were jealous. They all got together and decided to taunt the lion until he got so angry he would chase them in the tall, dusty grass. But the lion refused to be bothered, and in trying to outdo each other, the animals fell to fighting amongst themselves and wound up dusty and dirty. And the lion, of course, was as handsome as ever."

Dorrie frowned. "Oh."

It fitted with what Felicity and the doctor had said. Maybe Chiswick intended to let the bosses fight amongst themselves until they saw that the only reasonable alternative was to let him finish what he had begun. To let me finish. I rubbed my eyes. I was still groggy from the sedative, and already the restlessness was returning.

Charlie announced himself at the door with a short knock, but didn't wait for an answer. "On your feet, sunshine," he said to me, picking up my shoes from the floor and putting them beside me on the bed. I hadn't noticed before then that I was still fully dressed.

I looked at the shoes and then at Charlie. Even though my body was demanding to go, I wasn't sure I wanted to leave with him. He shrugged, and pulling back the blanket that had covered me, sat down on the bed and began loosening the laces of my jogging shoes.

"Where are you taking her?" Dorrie demanded.

"You're not cleared for that information," Charlie said, without looking up. He worked my right foot into the shoe.

"Where's Ian?" she pressed "I want to talk to him."

"He's unavailable." Charlie made no effort to conceal his irritation. He tied the laces and pulled me to my feet, but the rise was too quick for me. I swayed uncertainly.

"You can't take her out like that!"

"She'll be all right. She'll be sitting, most of the time."

I wondered if I would be able to find my way in the dark. Still, Charlie knew London, and if I could describe the landmarks I needed to pass, it should work.

We took a few steps toward the bedroom door before Dorrie crossed in front of us, barring the way. "You're not taking her anywhere until I talk to Ian."

"Get out of my way." Charlie's voice was quiet, but the sharp edge was plainly audible.

"It's all right, Dorrie," I said, but she didn't move. I could feel Charlie tensing beside me. "It's all been by my choice. Even my refusal to acknowledge what was happening was a choice. And so is this."

243

Her eyes burned through me for a brief second, and then she stepped aside and allowed us to pass. And when, after helping me on with my coat, Charlie handcuffed my hands behind my back, I made no objection, and that was a choice, too.

Chapter 17

I didn't speak to Charlie, even after he slipped into the seat beside me and started the car's engine, even though I desperately wanted to know where we were going. It was uncomfortable sitting with my hands cuffed behind me; my shoulder had started a steady ache in protest. But Charlie wouldn't have been moved by that, not pain or logic or tears.

I supposed, watching him, that that made him a better man for this job than Chiswick, but I couldn't have trusted him in those final hours, not since I had seen the underside of the rock.

"What will they do to him?" I asked.

"Eh? Do to who?"

"The Captain."

"Nothing, if they're smart. The more you *do* to him, the more stubborn he gets."

"The doctor with Felicity said he wouldn't be back."

He half smiled to himself. "He'll be back. It'll be too late for you, but he'll be back."

"And what about you?"

"I'm just doing my job." He shrugged, cocky. "It's a simple trade we're making. You, and the information you have, for a politician, someone sufficiently powerful to make this an offer we can't refuse."

"It was always going to be this way, wasn't it?" I asked dully. "It was always going to come to this in the end."

He was silent while he pulled the car off the side of the road and parked. "I don't know what the Captain's plan would have been, but this situation has always been a possibility, and he knew that. I'm surprised it hasn't occurred to you."

I sighed and shifted for the hundredth time in the seat, trying to get comfortable. "Maybe it has, how would I know? I've been more or less stoned ever since I woke up in the hospital, haven't I? Would you expect that much rational thought from a junkie?"

"It will be over soon," he said, looking ahead into the blackness. I saw the headlights of an oncoming car.

"Has it all been for nothing?" The words spilled out suddenly, loudly in the quiet car. "Has this whole charade been for nothing? Am I going to die for nothing?"

He turned to look at me, and in the approaching headlights he looked as though he wasn't sure whether he should answer. Finally he said, "It will not be for nothing. And your death isn't a certainty."

Someone was getting out of the car. "What does that mean? Please! Help me!"

He leaned over to button the top button of my coat and said, softly, "When you get to the inner sanctum, where all of the important players are wearing masks, do what you're told, without hesitation."

I watched him get out of the car, and I remembered what Chiswick's message had been. I didn't really understand it, and I didn't have enough faith in Charlie's motives to really believe the glimmer of hope he'd offered me, but I felt calmed. Was this what death would be like? When the barrel of the gun touched my temple, would I be able to wait for the end with quiet dignity, content that I had done what I could to stop the destruction that Roger had put in motion?

"It will not be for nothing," Charlie had said. It was a grudging admission and he hadn't wanted to say it, but to me it was proof that I had, at least in some part, redeemed myself. It occurred to me that although for most of my life I'd been content to let others live it for me, in the last few days I'd lived a lifetime: I had loved and lost and in a very small way, conquered.

When Charlie opened the door and pulled me out, I stood up straight and faced Brendan Fierlan without flinching. Charlie offered him the key to the handcuffs, but Fierlan responded, curtly, "Take them off."

I rubbed my wrists, appreciating the gesture I had seen so many times in movies. The metal had been cold. Then Charlie laid a hand on my shoulder and turned me gently, surprising me.

"Goodbye," he said. "Good luck. And mind what I told you."

"I will. Would you give Chiswick a message for me? Tell him I said, 'Thank you.' "

"Thank you?"

"For what he did and what he tried to do, and the time we had." It seemed inadequate, in view of what the doctor had said. If I was the end of Chiswick's career, he would need something more. He had given up his future for me, and my simple gratitude seemed paltry payment. "No. Just tell him I love him."

The light wasn't good enough to see what passed over his face, but when he spoke there was a note of respect in his voice. "I'll tell him."

I turned so that I wouldn't see him walk back to his car, and said to Fierlan, "Let's go."

He led me across the blinding path of headlights and settled me into the car with a courtliness that seemed out of place with his villainy. But that was his way, I remembered. His was the genteel side of terrorism. It wasn't until you woke up, afterward, that the pain began. I crossed my arms and stuck my hands inside my coat, under my arms, in an attempt to bring some life back to them.

"Would you like something to eat?" he asked.

"So I could throw it up later? No thanks." I thought for a moment. "But I would like to go to the bathroom."

He nodded, and a short time later, stopped at a gas station. Outside the door marked "Ladies" I turned and asked him, "Are you going to come in with me?"

It hadn't been an innocent question, but if he caught the sarcasm, he ignored it. "That might seem a bit peculiar to the other customers," he said, smiling. "And you'll come back to me. You'd come back even if I'd chosen to stay in the car, because I'm taking you where you have to go, and you know that. It isn't where your feet want to go at this moment, but it's the place where the key will be spoken and the numbers repeated by you, and that will release you."

"Will they kill me, afterward?"

His smile faded. "Finish your business here. We can talk in the car."

I finished my business, and, washing my hands (would someone remember to tell my mother that I had died in good underwear, with clean hands?), I looked into the mirror. The face that I saw there was drawn and haggard, with dark circles around the eyes. It looked more like Chiswick's face than mine. Chiswick, the strong one, who could walk through the doors of hell and bargain with the devil himself. I was glad they hadn't made him deliver me.

A soft knock on the door brought me back to the present, and Fierlan, ever the pretense of a gentleman, escorted me back to the car and held the door open for me. "Do you want a drink?" he asked, producing a flask before turning the key in the ignition.

"From you?"

He opened the flask and took a sip himself. "I knew that you consider me a monster, but I am disappointed to learn that you also think me a fool." He offered me the bottle again. "It will warm you up."

The liquid burned in my throat, and I coughed.

"Not a whiskey drinker, are you?" he asked, weaving in and out of the evening traffic.

"No," I managed to wheeze.

"Have another swallow. That should be enough, on an empty stomach." He took back the flask without taking his eyes from the road. "I don't suppose it would change your opinion of me, to tell you why I'm doing this. For the motherland and home, et cetera."

I looked across at him in surprise. "Why should you care? You've won and I've lost. What difference does it make what I think of you? I'll be dead before morning."

"Is that what Charlie told you?" he asked sharply.

"No, it isn't what Charlie told me. I wouldn't have believed him, even if he had. Charlie would sell his grandmother into prostitution if the powers that be ordered it."

"Yes," he agreed, quietly. "If that weren't true, he wouldn't have been selected for his profession. What did he tell you?"

"Go to hell."

"Oh, come, now. As you said, what difference does it make?"

But I hesitated, still. "He said not to put up a fight. To do what I was told."

"Good advice. I think you'll walk away from this, too, Mrs. Douglas. You don't actually know anything, do you? Aside from the numbers of the bank accounts. By surrendering you, Charlie has effectively given up his claim on you as a witness, even if you were to recognize a face. And you must be aware that the principal players in this farce are well known to the authorities already.... You didn't know that?"

I closed my jaw, which had dropped. "But why, then?"

"I asked you that, the last time we met. You couldn't answer the question, and neither can I." He sighed. "That's what makes Chiswick such a formidable opponent. The logic behind his actions is always obscure. The people we are about to meet are much more predictable. They're after money, not blood. Ah, well, not *your* blood, anyway."

"And what are you after?"

"Money. It's a straightforward arrangement: I pick you up from Enders and deliver you to—Mr. X, and I get paid for my trouble."

I didn't answer him. It had Roger's touch, all very simple, with money as the lowest common denominator.

The car slowed, and in the darkness, I couldn't make out the surroundings, although we were obviously in the suburbs. Fierlan braked the car and turned the engine off.

"It's early, still," he said. "We don't want to look too eager."

I crossed and uncrossed my legs. I felt eager, but I knew I wasn't.

"The waiting is always the worst part, isn't it?" he asked. "Even dying is better than waiting for death."

"If Stone had killed me, this wouldn't be happening," I said. The words came out quickly, drawn by my nervousness. "I wish he had. You know, when I came here, I wasn't really sure I wanted to live. But then the more uncertain life became, the more I wanted it. I was willing to fight for it. But now . . ." I couldn't blot out the memories of Penning and Stone and the people in the pub. We were all so fragile, and yet I hadn't been fragile enough. "But now the price seems too high, and my life seems already too long."

"Why reproach yourself, Mrs. Douglas? You can't stop the war by yourself. None of us can. You did your best, but in the end, we do what we have to do."

"We have a choice," I answered bitterly. "We all have a choice."

"Do we? On a small scale, perhaps. You could have chosen not to marry Roger, not to be dominated by him. But that wouldn't have stopped him. He would have found someone else, someone more manageable, perhaps. At least you gave the authorities a chance. You won't want to believe it," the disembodied voice continued, its Irish accent growing thicker, "but in my own way, I have no choice, either. From the day of my birth I had no choice, for I was programmed to be here just as you were."

"Programmed how?"

"Not like you. Not with drugs. With life. Simple, day-to-day life. I have always lived with this war; I was born into it. I grew up with the explosions and gunfire and police raids. And if I got scared or I cried, I was told to be brave, like 'the brave boys fighting for our country.' At night I used to sit and listen to my older brothers talk about joining the army, like my father." He hesitated, and his next words were soft and sad. "They did, and they died, just like he had died. Fighting for the homeland."

"But you joined anyway."

"Oh, yes, I joined. What else could I do?"

The suddenness of my anger surprised me. "Damn the wars! Damn all of them. What about the babies being born today—what are you programming *them* to do? What are you fighting for, Mr. Fierlan? Whom do you expect to inherit your victory? If you win, who will live in that Ireland, in peace and without bitterness? You're destroying the children, and the children are the future. What's the point of these goddamn wars, if they destroy the people they claim to want to save?"

There was a long moment of silence. "Yes," he said finally, "what am I fighting for? It's a question I've asked myself before, many times. More frequently as I get older." He did sound old now, and tired. "Maybe I'm getting too old for this game. Maybe the money I receive tonight won't be used to kill anyone."

I wished that I could see him, to have even a moment of visual evidence. Lies were so easy in the dark. And then I thought that truth was probably easier in the dark, too, if the truth was deep enough, and dangerous enough for the professor.

"Who killed Roger?" I asked.

"I don't know," he said, and I believed him.

Ahead of us, a light shone briefly, twice, and then was swallowed up by the night. "They're coming for us," he said. "We'll be blindfolded and searched for weapons or transmitters — it'll be done electronically, so all you'll notice is a slight delay — and then they'll take us to the meeting place. Stay calm and do what you're told, and don't ask unnecessary questions. They've probably been instructed not to talk to you, and they won't appreciate your talking to them."

I took a deep breath.

"And please, Mrs. Douglas, don't do anything foolish. They won't kill you if you try to escape, but they can be rough if you provoke them."

Shadows appeared beside the car doors. "I'm scared," I whispered.

He reached over to squeeze my hand. "So am I. You see, I *do* know what it feels like to be helpless in the company of killers. But I'll be with you. Even if you can't see me, I'll be there."

The door opened and I looked up into a face that was covered with a ski mask. When the head jerked to motion me out of the car, I opened the door and climbed out. I understood that much about what Charlie and Fierlan had told me.

I stood quietly while I was blindfolded. There was a delay, but as Fierlan had promised, it wasn't long, and soon we were herded into what I thought must be the back of a delivery van, fitted with benches. Unseen hands lifted and pulled me up, and I could hear the hollow thud of my footsteps echoing in the metal chamber. Then I was gently pushed backward until the backs of my legs touched the edge of the bench, and I sat down. I could hear other people coming in, and then the back doors closed and there were two loud raps on one of the walls, probably to signal the driver. No one spoke.

It was a long ride, full of twists and turns and stops and starts. I inferred from that that Fierlan wasn't that well trusted by these people. They were making sure we wouldn't be followed. Could Chiswick have followed us, I wondered, even if he had discovered my absence in time? Charlie's route had been fairly direct, and Fierlan's had seemed so. Did they trust each other?

But of course there was always the threat of death for the nameless man for whom I was being traded. I wondered who he was. I didn't expect to be worth the Prime Minister; even if the accounts contained two million dollars, that was surely only a small portion of these people's annual income. Maybe I had merited a Secretary of something. Maybe it would make the news. If the American Embassy discovered that I had been handed over to terrorists, maybe they would try to help me. Maybe the help would be too little and too late.

Whoever had been kidnapped, Charlie's bosses, the ultimate British defense against terrorism, had decided he was worth the money and the deaths that would be caused by it. I frowned underneath the blindfold. I hadn't been given that choice. And I hadn't really been given the choice of whether or not to help in the investigation. The only choice I had been offered had come such a long time ago, and in such a clever disguise that it had seemed more like a duty than a decision. Fierlan was right. Why was I reproaching myself?

I let out a long breath, and Brendan asked, "Are you all right?"

"I'm fine," I said. "I'm going to be okay."

I was surprised by the proximity of the voice. He was right beside me, just as he had said he would be. Thinking about it, I had to admit that he hadn't ever lied to me. He hadn't told me the whole truth, but whatever he'd told me had been essentially true. That was more than I could say for Chiswick.

Chapter 18

The car finally left the smooth surface of a road and bumped down what I presumed to be an unpaved driveway before coming to a stop. The driver turned off the engine and I felt doors opening and people getting out, so when a hand pulled my arm, I followed it. The air was misty and cold, and the only sound that I could hear was the soft thump of our feet on the damp earth. Chiswick could probably have guessed the size of our party from that information, but I couldn't.

The ground evened out, and I knew there would likely be a step eventually, but when it came I was unprepared for it, and stumbled. My foot twisted beneath me, and the hand that still had my arm firmly in its grip brought me upright again with a jerk. I hadn't hurt my foot—a small blessing, I thought, considering the circumstances—but when I tried to move forward again, hand restrained me.

I shivered in the night breeze. "Brendan?" I called uncertainly.

"Be still, I'm coming," came his answer. He hadn't been behind me, as I had thought, but a fair distance in front of me, walking faster, probably no longer wearing a blindfold. "What happened?"

"I tripped over something." There was a tremor in my voice.

One hand released me and another took hold — Fierlan's, I supposed. "Stay calm," he said, trying to soothe me with his voice. "No one's going to shoot you for tripping over a rock. Did you hurt yourself? Can you still walk?"

"I can walk, but if there are rocks here . . ."

"It's a broken flagstone path," he said, encircling my waist with an arm. "I'll help you. It won't be much farther now."

"Can you see?"

"Sssh."

I didn't need to be warned twice. It was a foolish question; I didn't want to see. I didn't want to be a witness to anything that made me more expendable than I already was.

We traversed the path and I heard the sound of a door creaking in protest. "Step," Fierlan warned when we came to the threshold, and then we were inside. He dropped his arm but he didn't move away, and taking his cue, I waited quietly beside him.

The building wasn't heated, but it had a floor. Footsteps echoed in the stillness, stopping before us.

"Is this the woman?" a man's voice asked. I recognized the Irish brogue. It might have been one of Fierlan's brothers, they sounded so alike. But I remembered that Brendan's brothers were dead.

"Yes," Fierlan answered.

There was a long silence. Nervousness accented my need to be moving. I bit my tongue, hoping the pain would distract me, but I still found myself shifting and swaying.

"What's the matter with her?" the man growled.

"She can't help it," Brendan answered evenly. "This wasn't where the meeting was supposed to take place. She's been programmed to go somewhere else."

The man grunted. "Keep her still."

A hand on my shoulder propelled me forward and then stopped me and pressed downward. "There's a box behind you," Brendan said quietly. "Sit down."

I lowered myself onto the wooden crate and waited.

"Is this the woman?" the man's voice asked again.

This time there was no spoken answer, only the sound that Chiswick had made when I hit him, louder this time, indicating a more forceful punch, and followed by a moan. I tensed, and then jumped as my blindfold was jerked down. The pressure of Fierlan's hand on my shoulder kept me seated as I blinked and tried to bring the surroundings into rapid focus.

We were in the center of a building roughly the size and shape of my two-car garage at home, and the large, double door at one end could easily have accommodated the tractor that was probably ordinarily stored here. The long walls on either side of us each had an identical door and a small, grimy window, and against the short wall parallel to the double doors was a jumble of what I assumed to be farm equipment. Dead grass, or hay, and dirt clods littered the floor.

"Is this the woman?" the man asked again, louder. He was standing in the center of the small pool of light, a gray-haired man with a steely face, wearing a cheap blue nylon parka and worn brown pants. He didn't look like a colleague of Fierlan's. I had to look hard at the man slumped in the chair opposite me to recognize Mosby. His face was bruised and swollen, and a trickle of blood oozed from one side of his mouth.

The man nodded to a guard who stood beside Mosby's chair, and the guard hit his prisoner again. Mosby fell out of the chair sideways, and the guard reached down and hauled him back into the chair.

There were other guards, too, on the outer perimeter of the light, with rifles slung over their shoulders. Two of them could have been anyone's sons, ready to start college, but the other . . . I leaned forward, only to be pulled back by the warning pressure of Fierlan's hand. The other guard was the one I had seen peering out of the upstairs window of the house where I had met the Black Knight.

"Perhaps you need a little more motivation," the man said, and gestured to a guard I hadn't identified. He stepped out of one of the side doors and returned dragging a small child. Mosby recognized Penelope before I did and let out a moan of anguish. Fierlan's fingers tightened on my shoulder.

The man seemed pleased with this. "We aren't as stupid as you thought, are we? Didn't you think we would ever figure it out? Didn't you think we were smart enough to realize you were stealing from us? You, and your good friend Mr. Douglas." He laughed without amusement. "You fool! Douglas planned for you to meet the woman alone, didn't he? And it never occurred to you that he could simply have killed the both of you and walked away with the money. And he might have, without worrying about us, because to him we were nothing more than simple country boys, dangerous but stupid. Did you figure that out, Mosby? Is that why you killed him?"

Mosby shook his head, croaking out his answer. "I didn't kill him."

"No?" the man said. "Then who did?"

"I don't know."

The man turned, facing me now, his back to Mosby. "It won't make any difference after tonight, anyway. Is this the woman?"

Mosby's guard raised his pistol and pointed it at Penelope, who was frozen in fright.

"Is this the woman?" the man shouted.

"Yes!" I cried, managing to rise to my feet but not escaping Fierlan's grasp. I reached inside my shirt for the necklace with the golden key charm and pulled it over my head, holding it out to him. "I am the woman!"

He took the necklace and regarded me with a cold, appraising stare. "Yes, you are. Mosby is fortunate that you, at least, care about the welfare of his daughter." He took a fat envelope out of his pocket and tossed it to Fierlan, who caught it deftly with his free hand. "All right. You can go."

"Wait!" The sound of my own voice startled me.

The man had started to walk across the room to Mosby, but now he turned.

"Send the child out with Fierlan," I said. Fierlan's hand relaxed and then squeezed once.

"I'm afraid I can't do that," the man said quietly. He reached out to pat Penelope on the head, causing her to jump and then cringe as his hand slid down the brown curls. "I might . . . need her."

"You need the numbers," I told him with a good deal more firmness than I felt. "And you're not going to get them unless you release the girl."

"You can't even stand still," he reminded me. "You can't withhold the numbers."

I remembered Chiswick's message, and tried to imagine myself as the implacable lion. I gave the man as calm and unblinking a stare as I could deliver. "I can if the motivation is strong enough. I can die on my own terms."

"I hadn't planned to kill you, but if you insist . . . it could be a very painful experience." The words were soft, but I heard the menace in them.

I swallowed against the rising fear. "I'm not in very good shape," I said. "It won't take much to kill me. And the pain will make it easier for me, not harder. You have neither the expertise nor the equipment to even keep me conscious for long under torture." I stopped and realized that I'd almost overlooked the most obvious argument. "You want to be gone before sunrise, don't you?"

He was before me in two steps, and raised his hand and slapped me so quickly that all three things seemed to have happened at once. Brendan caught me and kept me upright on my seat.

"You don't know anything about pain," the man growled.

I met his eyes. "You don't know anything about me."

He hit me again, harder this time, knocking me off of the crate and out of Brendan's grasp. I tasted blood at the corner of my mouth as Brendan bent over me.

"Don't provoke them," he said, almost pleading.

"I won't let them have Penelope," I said, wiping the blood on my hand. "They've already destroyed too many children for their war." Fear was hardening into resolve inside me. Was that the way it had happened to Fierlan?

I stared up at the man, towering over me, pleased with the result of his work. "Beat me, then," I said in defiance. "But you won't get the numbers." He turned away, abruptly, and Brendan helped me back onto the crate.

"If I let the child go," the man asked, his back still to me, "how will I get the key word from Mosby?"

Across from me, Mosby's face was working, trying to seize on an expression and hold it. "Let Fierlan and the child stand by the door," I told him. "Mosby can give you the key word, and I won't answer until they're gone."

"And after they're gone?" the man asked. I couldn't tell if he was really considering going along with the plan. And, of course, I wasn't sure that I would be able to fulfill my part of the bargain. Perhaps I wouldn't be able to hold back the numbers once I'd heard the trigger word. I looked at Penelope, small and frightened, somebody else's child. I would never know the pain of bearing a child of my own, I thought. To give this child her life would be the closest I would ever come.

"After they're gone, I'll give you the numbers," I said. "I was betrayed by the people I trusted to protect me. I don't owe them anything."

He stood in the center of our little circle and thought about it while I prayed.

"Well?" he said to Mosby.

Mosby raised his head with difficulty. "It's a chance," I said to him, pleading. "We have to try."

He nodded.

"All right," the man said. "Give her to Fierlan," he said to the guard holding Penelope.

She fought the transfer, but it succeeded. Fierlan gave my shoulder one last squeeze before releasing me to accept the wiggling girl.

The guard stepped back, looking to the man. "Move over by the door," the man ordered Fierlan.

Before he could move, there were simultaneous explosions at either of the side doors. I turned to look, already on my way to the floor, having been pushed squarely in the back by Fierlan.

A body, clothed entirely in black and wearing a black ski mask, hurled itself into the building and threw a small metal object into the room. I heard the clink of metal on cement, and then the room was full of noise, smoke, flashing lights and gunfire. It seemed that several more black figures entered over the body of their prone comrade, but the stinging smoke made it impossible to see clearly.

Suddenly a weight fell on top of me, knocking the air out of me with a whoosh that sent the dust flying off the floor. My breath came back in shallow pants, to accommodate my compressed lungs and pounding heartbeat. The noise and gunfire had stopped in the room, and I could see the survivors stirring, but I remained still. I knew that it was a dead weight on top of me, and I didn't want to look into those sightless eyes. It was probably the guard who had been holding Penelope. One child had lived and another had died.

The men in black that I had seen before had disappeared as suddenly as they arrived, leaving behind only two. One stood just inside one of the small doorways, and the other was moving methodically around the room, checking the bodies for signs of life. When he got to me, he rolled the body off of me, satisfied himself that it was really dead, and asked gruffly, "You all right, miss?"

I saw the blood dribbled on the sleeve of my coat and glanced quickly at the red-spattered heap that only a few seconds before had been a living, breathing thing, knowing there were at least two more like it in the room, and probably several more outside. I had prayed for deliverance without awareness of the form it would take.

And yet, to the soldier who stood above me, this was a normal consequence of the situation. He knelt beside me on one knee, resting the butt of his rifle on the ground. There was a flashlight taped to the end of the barrel. "Miss?" he asked.

Only his eyes and lips were visible, but they bore no evidence of the wrinkles that come with age. Did his mother know what he did, I wondered, or had he told her some plausible half-truth? I said, "I'm okay."

He moved on in the rapidly clearing smoke, gathering weapons as he went. When he had completed the circuit, he passed the weapons to someone outside, stepped back into the building, and returned to the other shadowy figure's side, still poised with his weapon ready. "Three dead, no hostages wounded, sir," he reported to the man who was obviously his senior officer.

The officer nodded, and then crossed to Mosby and squatted beside him for a brief conference as the rest of us sat up. I noticed that the leader of the terrorists was still alive, as well as Fierlan, Penelope, and the guard I had recognized.

The officer signaled to Fierlan, who released Penelope. She flew to her father's waiting arms, and after reaching her sanctuary, began to sob quietly. He rose to his feet and picked her up, but before he left the room, he turned back to me.

"Mrs. Douglas," he said, "I . . ." He stopped, reconsidering, and then said, simply, "Thank you," and left.

The junior officer hauled the terrorist leader to his feet and pushed him into the chair that Mosby had lately occupied. The man's face was beginning to look a little ashen, but I had no sympathy for him. I hoped his interrogation would be long and brutal.

The officer drew out a large manila envelope from underneath his black sweater and tossed it to Fierlan, who was on his feet. "I hope everything works out for you," he said, looking down at me. On impulse, he leaned over and kissed me on top of the head. "Thank you," he said softly.

On his way out of the building, as he passed the man in the chair, the man said angrily, "You're finished."

"Yes," Fierlan replied. "I am. I am finally finished." He motioned to the guard and they left together.

Was it just my imagination, I wondered, or was I the only one in the room who hadn't studied a script beforehand? The extras had died, the secondary characters had made their graceful exits, and only the aging terrorist, the black-suited officer and the rescued damsel remained in the spotlight, with a soldier in the wings. Who would cue me for my lines?

As if aware that the scene needed impetus, the officer reached up and pulled off his ski mask. I gave a little gasp of surprise when I saw Chiswick's face appear.

He had taken a breath to speak when he was interrupted by a hiccup of static from a walkie-talkie that hung from his belt.

"All clear," it barked.

Chiswick smiled and lifted the radio to his lips. "Thanks," he said. "I owe you."

"Like hell! We weren't here tonight. We don't even *know* you, old son."

The man started in his chair. "I don't believe it," he said.

Chiswick replaced the radio, shaking his head. "Every man has his price, Tom," he said. "That's a lecture you've delivered often enough."

"They'll come after you. They won't let you keep the money."

"Won't they?" Chiswick smiled. "They've got you and the return of your hostage. And they won't have to pay me a pension. They ve paid out more and gotten less. They'll grumble, but they won't come after me." He nodded to the other soldier. "Cuff him to one of the bodies. We don't want him wandering off before the police get here."

I watched him saunter over to me, a casual and easy gait, but too jaunty to be his normal walk. "You were magnificent," he said, his eyes shining.

"Guinevere has never been played better. Give me your hand, it's time to go."

He held out his hand to me and I watched mine reach for it with the sickening realization that it wasn't by my volition. This couldn't be part of Roger's plan. Who was controlling the puppet now?

He pulled me up and caught me around the waist. I tried to gargle out a protest, but he smiled and pulled my arm across his shoulders. "Lean on me, love. It's been a bit of a jolt, I know, but it's over now."

But as we passed the handcuffed man, and I saw the murderous look on his face, I wondered if it really was.

Outside, Chiswick dropped his assumed persona and caught me up in a bear hug. "Did you mean it?" he asked. "Do you really love me?"

This caught me off guard as much as the performance I had witnessed inside the building. I drew back. "Well, yes . . ."

"She loves me!" he told the soldier walking beside us. His voice was quiet enough not to carry, but joyous.

The soldier took Chiswick's rifle. "Congratulations, sir," he said respectfully. I had turned enough to see him step back and melt into the darkness.

I was torn for a moment. In a way, Chiswick had made an admission of his own, and this one wasn't playacting for someone else's benefit. But I hadn't *meant* to take his hand so readily inside the building. He had produced that response by Roger's methods, and I was angry about that.

The anger won out. "Now, just a minute," I hissed

at him. "We have some things to talk about before we start planning the future." He urged me forward down the uneven driveway, and I found my legs were wobbly enough to make it necessary to cling to him for support. "I should have seen it coming. I should have realized you'd done it when you yelled at me and I almost fainted. What else have you programmed into the human robot? Did I sleep with you of my own free will?" I stopped suddenly. I hadn't planned to go that far.

He pulled me closer, still moving me along, not slowing the pace. "If you didn't, you're a hell of an actress," he said mildly. "No, there was only the one response. I couldn't predict exactly what would happen, Valerie. I had to plan for every possibility, every extremity. If things had gone wrong, your life might have depended on that word 'Guinevere.' I hadn't planned to use it just now, but when you didn't answer my associate right away, I was afraid your performance wouldn't be convincing enough for Tom. And this was a command performance in a dangerous theater."

I looked across at him so suddenly I almost stumbled, and then caught myself. You are tired, I told myself. "If I had had a chance to study the script, you might have gotten better results, but I have to admit I can see the danger in that, too. Anyway, I don't think Tom was totally convinced. What were you trying to convince him *of?*"

He mumbled something I didn't quite hear. "What?" I asked.

"That you and I were going to take the money and disappear," he repeated, a little louder. "I take it *you* weren't convinced."

"No. You may have your price, but it wouldn't be money. You worship the greater good, the sacrifice of the few for the benefit of the many."

He was silent for a few steps. "I suppose that's a fair description. Hostages are always shaken by the rescue assault. It's overwhelming when you haven't been prepared for it, and especially for you, being bandied about like Helen of Troy. I should have found an opportunity to talk to you about it before it happened."

My knees buckled and the sudden rush of tears to my eyes made it impossible for me to go on, and he picked me up and cradled me in his arms. "It was so quick, and so vicious. There wasn't even an attempt to take prisoners, except for Tom. You just killed them. And my God, they were so young."

"They're always young," he said. The words were so soft they were almost inaudible. "And they're always unpredictable, and therefore doubly dangerous. The trial is over before we get there. The child becomes a man and the death sentence is passed when he picks up the gun and points it at a hostage. Can you understand that?"

I closed my eyes and saw again Penelope's terrified face. My arms tightened around his neck. "Yes," I whispered.

He let out a long breath, relieved that a crisis point had been passed. I could imagine, in a country where most of the police force didn't routinely carry guns, that the violence aspect could be a sore point with the general public. How many rejections had he endured because of it? It couldn't have been easy, calling Dorrie and asking her to stay with me. She had surely had some choice observations, and she wasn't the type to hold them back.

The tears washed away something inside me. "It's over, isn't it?" I asked. "I can feel it. I've told you the bank account numbers."

"Yes. I gave you the code phrases and you gave me the numbers."

We had come to the end of the drive, back to a deserted but paved road. A dark sedan waited for us, parked well off of the road, but visible when Chiswick pointed it out. He put me down and we walked across the street together, but when he opened the door for me, I hesitated.

"I don't feel any better," I said. "Part of it is gone, but . . ."

"Get in the car, Valerie. We don't want to be here when the police arrive."

I put one foot inside the car. "Will you stay with me tonight?"

"This morning," he corrected me. "Yes. I'll be with you."

Chapter 19

I ate in those predawn hours, and I bathed, but sleep was harder to come by. Chiswick had reserved us a room in a country inn, and the bed was comfortable enough, but in my dreams the scene involving Penelope was replayed countless times, usually ending with her death. In one nightmare, the terrorist Tom shot her, in another it was Chiswick, and in a third it was Roger wearing Chiswick's clothing and mask.

Once, in the early dawn, I awoke to find myself sitting bolt upright staring at the door to the room.

"What is it?" Chiswick asked quietly.

"I don't know."

"Are you expecting someone?" It was a serious question.

"No, of course not." I made myself lie back down. "It was just another nightmare. I've even forgotten now what I was dreaming."

"Would you like something to help you sleep?"

I snuggled closer to his warmth. "You know better than that. I'm okay. Just a little scared, still, and probably missing the tapes a little."

"The tapes are here if you want them."

"I don't. I'm all right. Go back to sleep."

But he wouldn't, I knew, until I did, so I closed my eyes and forced myself to relax, gradually dozing again. I awoke only once more, this time without a nightmare or sudden movement, and looked across at Chiswick's face. The morning light had begun to filter through the drawn curtains, and I could see clearly the peaceful expression he wore. There was no cherubic innocence along the stubble on his cheeks and chin, or among the wrinkles around his eyes, but it was the face of a satisfied man. As if to emphasize his point, he rolled over on his side and stretched an arm across me, warm, familiar and possessive. I went back to sleep shortly afterward, and this time I really slept, not the sleep of innocence, but of redemption.

He was gone when I woke up, but I could hear the water running in the bathroom. The remains of the cold roast chicken and salad we had eaten last night were on a tray before the single, curtained window, but I wasn't hungry yet, even though my watch said it was half past noon. I turned on the television.

I didn't really expect to find the plethora of channels that cable had produced in America, and I wasn't disappointed. But there were no obvious soap operas, and I considered that a mark of a media culture more advanced than America could claim. I skipped past a cricket match, and settled on a play involving two middle-aged men meeting for lunch at an athletic club.

The accents made it difficult for me to follow the dialogue, but one of the men seemed quite agitated. It might have been something to do with his wife, because he was wearing a wedding ring which he twisted from time to time. The other man nodded knowingly and mumbled replies that were totally unintelligible. The two made their way from the lobby of the club to the empty locker room, dressed, and played an active game of squash punctuated by enigmatic grunts. I was developing a great deal of sympathy for the man's wife. It was obvious to me why she didn't understand him. He muttered in obscure dialects.

The squash game finally ended, with neither man seeming particularly happy about the outcome, and the men shuffled back to the locker room, which was no longer empty.

Suddenly I sat straight up. "Good God!"

My eyes had been glued to the television screen, but I heard the bathroom door crash open and turned to see Chiswick standing there in a half crouch, gun pointed at the room in general. He was shirtless, and patches of shaving cream still dotted his face.

"No, no, it isn't that," I hastened to calm him, "it was the television. Look! There it is again. A naked man on TV. Jesus! A *totally* naked man on national television in the middle of the day."

He looked at the screen, unimpressed. Thunderclouds were forming in his eyes, and I could see that he wasn't going to find any humor in the situation. He lowered his gun and cupped his left hand under my chin, tilting it upward. "Don't *ever* do that again." His voice could have chipped rock.

"Never," I promised.

He let me fry a few more seconds under his glare

and then released me. I turned off the television and followed him back into the bathroom, watching him wash away the flecks of shaving cream. He was angry with me, but I wasn't frightened by that this time. It was the implications of his fury that scared me.

"How many more are there?" I asked. "How many more do we have to draw out and capture, or kill? Will it ever be over?" I was surprised by the steadiness of my voice. I wanted to scream the words.

He dried his face. "What do you really want to know?" he asked, without turning to face me.

"I want to know how many."

"One," he answered. "Just one more, and then it will be over."

I sighed heavily. "I don't see how you can prolong the plot any further. We've used up all the characters, except Bromley. I can't believe he's caught up in this."

"He isn't."

"But there isn't anyone left, except . . ." The words froze in my throat. Except Nickie. I didn't want to think about that. "Will it be over then? Really, truly over?"

"I promise."

I wrapped my arms around his middle, wanting him to be as much my prisoner as I was his. When it was over, would we be over, too? When had I stopped doing this for myself and started doing it for him? "Please, don't tell me any more. Give me today," I pleaded. "Give me this one afternoon and evening with you."

He turned in my embrace and took me by the

shoulders, trying to pry me away enough to see my face, but I held my head against his chest until he abandoned the effort. "Valerie, are you all right?" he asked with real concern.

"I don't know whether I am or not, but I know that I have to be. Give me this day. Please."

"All right," he said gently. "This day is yours."

I saw when we stepped out of the room that we were still in the countryside. Rolling green hills rose gently behind low stone fences, and trees shaded almost every inch of the walk from our hotel to the public house down the road.

"This is beautiful," I kept saying. "This is fabulous."

Chiswick looked around as though seeing it for the first time. "Yes. It is beautiful, isn't it? It's been a long time since I've seen it. Donkeys' years."

The main buildings of the town were built along the curves of a winding, narrow road, cream-colored stone walls almost on the edge of the pavement. I glanced at a tiny but immaculately kept churchyard as we passed.

"You've been here before?"

"Not here, but someplace like it."

"With someone like me?"

He didn't answer, and I added, "Or perhaps someone I know."

I could see Nickie walking down this street, her hair ruffled by a slight breeze, holding Chiswick's hand and laughing. She would be gay and beautiful and all the men would turn to look at her as they passed. And Chiswick would be spellbound by her feminine magic. Was that the way it had happened for Roger? Had I always been fighting two ghosts?

We were across the street from the pub. It was of a darker stone than the other buildings, accented by massive black beams. The door was open and bits of conversations and laughter carried to us. Chiswick stopped and put both hands on my shoulders.

"It's a fair question," I pointed out. "You know everything about me."

"Maybe not everything." Chiswick's answer was the sound of a door closing inside of him. A door that closed so often it no longer even squeaked.

I had a quick sense of déjà vu. It was happening again; I was losing Chiswick just as I had lost Roger. Or more accurately, I thought, I was realizing that I had never really had them. I had given my body and soul and it hadn't been as much as Nickie's smile.

I broke away angrily and started across the street. "Definitely not everything."

"Valerie, wait." He pulled me back.

I struggled even though I knew I couldn't get away.

"Please, Valerie. Stop."

"Let me go," I growled at him, "or I'll hit you. I swear to God I'll hit you and break a rib."

He caught my hands and crossed them behind my back. The movements were swift and practiced. "Now stop it," he said firmly, and when I stopped he added, "I'm always going to win these fights. Couldn't we find a more civilized solution?"

"A more civilized solution would be to talk about it. But you don't. You *won't*."

A group of men exited the pub and stared at us

with open curiosity. Chiswick let go of my wrists but continued to hold me.

"I'm sorry. It's the job, Valerie."

"I'm not asking for government secrets."

"I know that." He hesitated, and I rested my forehead against his chest.

"Fuck it," I whispered, beaten. "It doesn't matter, anyway. Let's have some lunch."

"Never with Nickie," he said. "With other women, yes, but never her. And never anyone like you."

It was the tenderness of his voice that drew my face upward. I knew that he wouldn't give any more than that. We were both soldiers now. And a soldier, I had learned, slept only when he found a safe haven, and he couldn't let the brevity of that security keep him awake. I closed my eyes, and tilting my head back, I smiled at the sun shining on my day.

"I *really* don't want to see Nickie," I protested as the car stopped in front of her building the next morning.

"She only wanted to help you," Chiswick said.

"You may be convinced of that, but I'm not."

"Why not?"

"Because!" I said with irritation I didn't understand.

He frowned. "Valerie, what's wrong?"

"Nothing is wrong. I'm just tired."

"Of course you're *tired*. You've hardly slept the last two nights."

I ran restless fingers through my hair. "It's just knowing someone is out there."

"He isn't the only one out there."

"I know. You've explained it. It's all part of the plan and we're not really alone. I want it to be over, that's all."

He studied me for a moment, unconvinced. I couldn't blame him. I wasn't sure I'd convinced myself. Maybe the stress was finally getting to me, I thought. Maybe I was cracking up and Chiswick was wondering if the pieces would hold together long enough to finish what we'd started. I shouldn't be fighting him.

"All right, I'll be good," I promised. "What should I tell Nickie?"

"Tell her the same thing I told Tom."

"That we're running away with the money? Do you think she'll believe it?"

He shrugged. "It doesn't really matter, but do your best."

"It doesn't matter? No, don't explain that. I don't want to know this time." I looked up at the building. "Nickie is going to send the message to someone, isn't she?"

"Yes."

"Will it be dangerous for her?"

He chose his words carefully. "For her, silence would be the greater danger at the moment."

"Isn't there any other way?"

"A moment ago, you didn't even want to see her," he reminded me.

"I still don't. I don't want her to be hurt and I don't want to talk to her. What will I say when she opens the door?"

"What do you feel like saying?"

I frowned at him in annoyance. "I *feel* like not

seeing her."

"Why don't you tell her that, then? Tell her you didn't want to come."

"Because she'll ask why I did come and I'll still be stuck for an opening line."

"No, she won't." Chiswick's voice was quiet and reassuring, the Captain coaching his undercover team. "She cares about you, and she won't be belligerent. She wants to hear the story you're going to tell her. She's going to make it easy for you. In fact, the hardest thing about this visit isn't going to be the beginning. It's going to be the ending."

I sighed. "That's probably true. I don't know how to manage that, either."

"You will, when the time comes."

We rode the elevator up in silence, but as I raised my hand to the buzzer, I hesitated long enough for one last look at his face. He was relaxed, a study in confidence. Nickie might believe he had seized the pot of gold at the end of the rainbow. But would she believe me?

I rested my finger lightly on the button. "Did you sleep with her?" I asked.

"No." He covered my finger with his hand and pressed.

The sight of my face in the mirror that morning had shocked me, and Chiswick looked little better, but Nickie's face, when she opened the door, almost made me recoil. Skin that had once been translucent and glowing had dulled to a light gray, and her eyes, devoid of makeup, seemed to have sunk deep into cavernous sockets.

My planned speech was instantly forgotten. "Oh,

Nickie," I said. "I didn't know."

The tears that had been brimming in her eyes spilled onto her cheeks and she flung her arms around me.

"Vallie!" she sobbed. "I thought you were dead. They came and took your things but they wouldn't tell me anything, and then when I called the number, they said Ian was 'unavailable' and they couldn't release any information about you." She began to sag in my arms and Chiswick helped me get her inside the apartment and lowered onto the sofa.

"I'm all right, Nickie," I told her. "Look at me. I'm all right. It's over. It's okay."

I cradled her head in my arms while she cried herself out. Chiswick sat in one of the overstuffed chairs and watched us, and I couldn't help remembering the night he'd told me Fierlan had been freed. I didn't want to tell Nickie what I'd been told to say, and yet I accepted that there was no other way for any of us. I wiped away my own tears with the back of a hand before I saw the box of tissues on the table by the sofa, taking one for myself and giving one to Nickie. It had even come to that, I told myself. I was following in Chiswick's footsteps right down to a need for a supply of handkerchiefs.

When Nickie had enough of a grip on herself to sit up, I let go of her and propped her up with some cushions.

"Well, I'm still alive, obviously," I said. "In better shape than you, so you can stop worrying about that."

"But what happened? Where did you go?"

I was still holding her hand, and I squeezed it

gently and tried to smile. "I've been busy. Kidnapped, threatened, drugged. You know, the usual tourist routine. It doesn't matter anymore, because it's over. It's over, Nickie. We found the money."

She looked from me to Chiswick and then back again. " 'We'?"

"You had your chance with him." My smile became more genuine. He hadn't slept with her. And Nickie wasn't an easy woman for men to pass by. "You wanted me to find a man, didn't you? I did."

Her face registered disbelief first, and then softened. "I'm glad. I'm happy for you, Vallie. But what about the money?"

"The money. Yes, the money. We earned it, to make a long story short. The government—yours, I mean—decided to trade it, *and* me, for some political bigwig who'd been taken hostage. And then Lancelot over there came riding in full armor and rescued me. He had to pay out a fair amount of money in bribes, of course, to pull it off. Sort of an investment." I smiled again at him, but what had really pleased me was the cleverness of the lie. It would impress Nickie, I knew, to hear that Chiswick had invested personal funds in the scheme.

Chiswick was smiling, too, his eyes half closed. He was thinking about sex, I thought, and almost laughed aloud. That was a fox's trick. Lust was always believable.

Nickie saw the look that passed between us, but her doubts hadn't quite been satisfied. "They won't let you get away with it."

"Who is 'they'?" Chiswick asked. "The IRA has already risked and lost too much in their attempts to recover it. Fierlan's collected bonuses from us and his old mates and been allowed to retire quietly; he won't be looking for trouble. And the Home Office have their politician back and Tom O'Neill besides. There is no 'they.' We're free to go as we please."

She let out a deep sigh, and I would have liked to do the same, but I didn't. I let go of her hand and smoothed back my hair instead. Maybe it was over.

"You just came back to say goodbye," she said quietly, mostly to herself.

So I wasn't going to be spared after all. Still, it was a better beginning than what I'd feared, I told myself. I wasn't overcome by the desire to strangle her. Chiswick's words rolled easily off my tongue. "I guess so. I didn't really want to come."

"I don't blame you." Her voice was trembling a little. "I'm so sorry, Vallie. I know how it must seem. If I hadn't helped him, none of this would have happened. If I'd just said no at the beginning, if I hadn't gotten involved . . ."

The speech sounded uncomfortably familiar. "No, Nickie, no," I whispered.

"If I'd tried a little harder to stop him when it started . . ."

I was no longer sure whether she was talking about Chiswick or Roger. "Nickie . . ."

"It seemed like such a little thing, though, when it began. Not even illegal, really. Just a little chancy." She seemed not to be aware of Chiswick and me anymore. "He just laughed about it. You know how he was, Vallie. You remember. 'Don't be such a prude, Nickie,' he'd say. 'It's just business, and business is amoral.' "

"I remember," I said, getting the words past the constriction in my throat with difficulty.

"But it got to be bigger and bigger and then I didn't know how to stop it. I was involved. I would have lost my job. I would have lost everything. Can you see that?"

I had ceased to see her as she was then. I was seeing her as she had been in the years between, happy, laughing, confident, successful. I couldn't find a single image in my memory of a woman haunted by fear and recrimination. She had known about Roger, and about Mosby. She had known about me.

"He wasn't really hurting you." She was pleading with me. "He said he was just using your memory, like a computer, and you wouldn't really know anything, you wouldn't remember, so you couldn't be hurt. Oh, God, Vallie, I'm so sorry. I'm so sorry."

It struck me, then, that I had never really understood Nickie. I had always been puzzled by her solicitous attention and her kindness to me, her interest in me when I wasn't the sort of person she would ordinarily have found interesting. I had gratefully accepted her help when Roger had died, thinking it had been given out of pure, inexplicable friendship, not wanting to recognize the baser motivation. The guilt had always been there. Not in an overt way, but it had been there, and I had refused to see it.

I drew her close to me again, laid her head against my chest and stroked the fine, soft hair. "It's over now," I whispered over and over. "It's all right."

Finally the sobbing slowed and then stopped, and her breathing became even again. I felt something pull her away, and I was surprised to look up and see

Chiswick bending over us. His face was blurred, and I realized that I had been crying, too, even though I couldn't feel the wetness on my cheeks.

"I'm all right," I told him, but when he lifted me to my feet, I found I couldn't stand on them, and he had to carry me back to the flowered bedroom. He deposited me very gently on the bed, as if I were a flower, too, dried and fragile.

"Close your eyes," he said softly. He took off my shoes and then his, and stretched out beside me. "You don't have to sleep. Just close your eyes for a little while."

"But what about Nickie?"

"Nickie will do what she has to do."

Chapter 20

It was almost dusk when I woke up. Chiswick was no longer beside me, but I dimly remembered rolling over, half awake, and finding him there during my sleep, so I supposed he had slept, too. His jacket was crumpled at the foot of the bed, but his gun and its shoulder holster were gone, as well as his shoes.

I toyed briefly with the idea that it was all over at last, and he was off somewhere interrogating his captive, or else delivering a body to the morgue, but I couldn't bring myself to hope that, if it meant he'd left without even saying goodbye. And I didn't want to be left alone in this apartment with Nickie.

I sat up and threw back the blanket, appreciating the reviving coolness. The room had changed while I slept. The wallpaper seemed faded in the dimming light, as though the unrelenting brightness of a lifetime of sunny days had robbed it of its gaiety. Even the chaise that sat in front of the window no longer seemed quaint and inviting. It just looked old. I felt old.

I didn't bother to put on my shoes when I got up. I'd been wearing my jogging shoes, and I still had on the terry socks. I stood up and stretched and had to admit that in spite of everything, I was beginning to feel better. I didn't know whether it was the sleep or finally confronting Nickie, but I felt a little better. I wondered how Nickie was feeling.

I didn't hate her. I didn't even feel betrayed anymore. Roger had simply claimed another victim, and if she'd been a willing accomplice, she had loved him. And Roger had come closer to loving her than anyone else in his life, I thought. I knew from my experience with Chiswick that love was a potent force, more powerful, perhaps, than even the drugs that I had taken. I knew how to end this visit, how to finally free myself.

The mirror over the bureau beyond the foot of the bed showed a face with a good deal more color in the cheeks, but hair that wouldn't have looked out of place in a Texas hurricane. I looked around for my purse and dug inside for a comb. What I found was larger and heavier. I drew my hand out and stared down at a gun.

"What's this doing here?" I muttered to myself.

It wasn't that I didn't recognize it. Even with the silencer screwed into the end of the barrel, I knew it instantly by the pearl inlay on the butt. It was my gun; Roger had given it to me not long after we were married.

"Everyone in Texas owns a gun," he'd explained breezily.

I had accepted the gun and his statement at face value. At that point Texas had seemed like another world, in which anything might be considered normal. But I hadn't fired the gun in over six years, and I certainly hadn't brought it to England with me. It should have been in the attic of the Houston house, packed away years ago.

I put it back in my handbag and then tried to decide if the extra weight could have been added before I got to Nickie's. I didn't think so. I didn't think Chiswick would be likely to entrust a gun to a woman likely to tumble off the edge of sanity at a moment's notice.

But it wasn't any easier to accept that someone had put it in my purse after I got to Nickie's. Chiswick was a mortal and therefore not perfect, but a quiet sigh could rouse him from a deep sleep. No one had snuck into the apartment while we'd slept.

Nickie could have done it. Even in my spirit of forgiveness, I was willing to admit that she could have come back into the room after Chiswick had gotten up and left the gun. But why?

I put the pistol on the bureau and brushed my hair, and when I was finished, I picked it up and started to tuck it into the waistband of my pants, beneath my shirt and sweater. Then I thought I'd better check to see if it was loaded. It was, but the safety catch was on, so I tucked it away close to my side. The metal was cold, and the bulge felt unnatural. It wasn't going to be there for long, I assured myself. I was going to find Chiswick and give it to him at the first opportunity.

The first thing that struck me, as I opened the door to the bedroom, was the unnatural stillness of the apartment. Even the normal muted noises of the traffic outside seemed missing. I hesitated for a moment in the doorway and then crept back to the window and looked down at the street below. Chiswick's car was still parked in front of the building. I shivered involuntarily and went back to the bed. It seemed that my feet were going to be cold, after all.

I put my shoes on slowly and deliberately, taking more time than I needed, but even so, the task was soon finished. There was nothing now to hold me in the room except an unsubstantiated fear. I remembered what Fierlan had told me. "Even dying is better than waiting for death."

When I'd sat down on the edge of the bed, I had removed the gun and set it beside me. Reaching for it, I discovered I'd laid it on top of Chiswick's jacket, and my fingers brushed against the worn leather as they closed around the weapon. Without really thinking about it, I moved the gun and put the jacket on. It wasn't armor, I knew, and it wouldn't make me invincible, but it was warm, as if some of Chiswick's body heat had been stored there.

I went out of the door and down the short hallway to the sitting room, hoping desperately to find Chiswick and Nickie sitting on the sofa, sharing a quiet conversation, oblivious of the nightmare I had imagined. They were there, sitting side by side as if they were waiting for something, but I wasn't really relieved to see them. Nickie looked a little better and Chiswick looked a little worse, and they both looked up in surprise when they saw me. I realized that I was still holding my gun. I looked down at it, still surprised myself.

"I found it in my purse," I said.

Whatever answer anyone might have made was forestalled by an electronic beep, or more accurately, a series of beeps. They were quiet but clearly audible, like the beeping of an alarm on a watch.

I could feel it happening, the loss of control, the encroaching remoteness, the distancing. I was turning into a robot again, and I couldn't stop it. I raised my right hand, knowing I was pointing the gun, but not watching it. I was watching Chiswick's face, my eyes pleading. He wasn't wearing his gun, but there were books on the coffee table he could have thrown. He could easily have cleared the table and grabbed my hand before I took aim. But he didn't.

He didn't speak, but Nickie gave a small cry and raised a hand to her mouth. He grabbed the other one to keep her from running. I looked into his eyes, cool and confident and silent, as I released the safety and my fingers tightened on the trigger.

"Stop me!" I wanted to scream, but all I could say was a soft and breathy, "No!" Still, he refused to speak, holding the fighting Nickie and looking at me as though I were simply about to say something that might be important, or at the least interesting. It was the expression that I knew best.

I aimed and fired two shots.

Nickie collapsed immediately, but Chiswick shook his head at me reprovingly. "Next time, I'd appreciate a wider margin of error," he said mildly. "That last shot barely missed some of my best qualities." He pointed at the two bullet holes inches to the left of his left buttock.

"I could have killed you," I whispered, unsteady on my feet.

He got up and put his arms around me, and I put the gun in the jacket pocket to return the hug. "No, you couldn't. I didn't exactly anticipate this situation, but I knew you wouldn't shoot me. I think you had Nickie fooled, though."

"Nickie—"

"Fainted. She's all right. It's better than she deserves."

"It's hard to believe that she actually did it," I said. "I've always thought she was so much stronger than I am."

"You were always the stronger one, Val," Roger's voice said.

Chiswick and I both turned toward the sound. It had come from the hallway behind me, rather than from the front door. Roger was leaning against the wall, casual and pleased with himself. In one hand he held a large manila envelope, in the other a gun only generally aimed. He'd changed in the last two years: his hair and eyes were brown now, he was a little heavier, and the shape of his nose seemed different. But it was Roger. I knew that voice.

I should be surprised, I thought, but I wasn't. He was just something else I'd ignored because I hadn't wanted to face it. No one had killed Roger because Roger wasn't dead.

"Nickie could never have done what you did," he went on. "Not that you didn't screw up on a major scale. Jesus, Val, how could you have managed to get into so much trouble in so short a time?"

"You should know," I said, my voice shaky at first, but rapidly gaining strength from my anger. "You started it. You planned it and programmed it and then sent the letter."

He shook his head. "O'Neill sent the letter. Or maybe your boyfriend. I had only intended to use you as a backup, darling. Then when I got here, I decided to go with the original plan, to fake my death and just disappear. I was surprised when I found out you were coming; I never expected the programming to last that long." He shook his head again, amazed. "Honest to God, Valerie, I never expected for you to hold onto it that long. Or that tenaciously. Right up until this moment, I really expected you to stop. Although I guess you did. You didn't kill these two. But I tried, I really *tried* to keep things from coming to this." He was starting to whine. "I had somebody shoot you, bomb you—I even killed Penning. Damn it, Val, the technique didn't work that well in Vietnam!"

"Well, it worked here," I said.

"Except for the part about staying away from the police. I screwed that up. It should have been stronger. But then, I didn't want you to break into a panic every time you saw a policeman on the street." He leveled the gun at Chiswick. "You didn't exactly panic with him, did you?"

"Not exactly," I said. "But it wasn't the only time you screwed up. You came here. And that was a big mistake."

Roger laughed. "Are you going to arrest me? Do you really believe there's an army outside, waiting to haul me off to justice? There's nobody out there."

"I don't believe you," I said stubbornly.

He tossed the envelope onto the low table in front of the sofa. "I figured as much. Take a look at those."

I chose to sit in one of the overstuffed chairs rather than on the sofa, and Roger motioned to Chiswick to sit beside Nickie, who was beginning to show signs of life.

The pictures weren't really incriminating. They showed Chiswick meeting with the faces that had become familiar during my stay in London: Mosby, Fierlan, Tom and Mr. Striped Tie, and several I didn't recognize. One of them may have been the Black Knight. The only thing even slightly strange about the photos was the lack of guards, but they could have been excluded by the angle of the shot, or edited out.

"What is this supposed to prove?" I asked. "That they know each other? That they talked? So what?"

Roger shook his head, for what seemed like the millionth time. "Valerie, Valerie. You are hopelessly naïve. This man has offered you no proof of his identity. Have you ever seen an office? A *real* office. The SAS has offices, you know. Christ, the Home Office has an *office*. Didn't you ask for any identification?"

Of course Roger would have an answer for the very question that had so haunted me, but I wasn't going to ask to be insulted.

"There were never even any *police*," he continued, seeming not to notice my silence.

"There were police," I said.

"How many?"

He had a point. There hadn't been a lot of police. I could only remember two. But there hadn't been any need for more. Chiswick had employees and friends who were more efficient, anyway. I said, "His identity was convincing enough for Fierlan."

"Of course it was. They're old friends."

"And Tom?" I asked.

"Not exactly friends," Chiswick answered dryly. "Just longstanding acquaintances."

"But there were SAS men. I saw them."

Roger's laughter was colder than I remembered. "You wouldn't know an SAS man from an ice-cream vendor."

I felt the anger rising up in me, and fought it back. "Get to the point, Roger," I snapped. "If he isn't SAS, who is he?"

But Roger wouldn't be rushed past his enjoyment of a full disclosure of my shortcomings. "The SAS is controlled by politicians, Valerie. They're tied to public opinion and political pressure. They wouldn't stage an assault on British soil just to rescue *you*."

"Somebody did," I said softly, remembering the gun in my pocket. "And it wasn't you."

It startled him a little, but it didn't stop him. "He's a mercenary, you little fool. A hired killer, hired to find and kill me. And he almost succeeded, thanks to you. Jesus, you made it so easy for him."

I turned to look at Chiswick, my face no longer totally visible to Roger. Chiswick sat with both feet on the floor, his left hand resting lightly on his thigh, and his right on the sofa, over the space between the cushions. He wasn't an ice-cream vendor. Ice-cream vendors didn't coil to strike.

And maybe he wasn't SAS, either, but the organization did exist, and I'd heard enough about it, even in a casual way, to be sure of its ability. SAS knew I was in London, and they knew I'd been spending time with Chiswick. They probably knew everything we'd been doing, and they hadn't interfered.

But in the end, it came down to faces. Chiswick's

face in Duncan's bathroom when he grabbed me out of the tub and when he'd walked over to me after the rescue in the barn, Dorrie's face when Charlie had taken me from the house in Surrey, Mosby's and Penelope's faces when death seemed certain, Nickie's face when she admitted she'd helped Roger. And Roger's face, changed somewhat but eternally the same.

I slipped my hand into the pocket of Chiswick's jacket. It was a small gesture and Roger didn't see it, but Chiswick did.

"No, Valerie," he said quietly.

I was looking at Roger again. "And what about Nickie?" I asked. "Are you going to kill her, too?"

His eyes flicked over to her, briefly. She had recovered herself enough to sit up, but she wasn't making any unnecessary movements.

"I suppose I'll have to," he said, sighing, "since you didn't. It's a waste of a beautiful woman, but women are easy to find when you've got money. Yes, I suppose I'll have to kill all of you."

My hand found the gun and closed around the gun's butt.

"No," Chiswick said again.

"You screwed up," I told him.

"I wasn't sent to kill him," Chiswick said. "I was sent to take him alive. It was never the money. We knew the money wasn't there, even though we couldn't prove it. We knew Roger had faked his own death and taken the money. It's the information we want, the names, the companies, the transfer methods. That's how you cripple a business, isn't it? You stop the cash flow. If we can do that, we can save lives. Think, Val. *Lives.*"

"I am thinking about lives," I said. "Dennis Penning, the people in the pub, the kids who were killed in the barn." I had maneuvered the gun slowly in my pocket until it was pointed roughly at Roger's stomach.

"You're blown," Chiswick told Roger. "Can't you see that? If you leave here on your own, you won't make it across the street."

"Shut up," Roger said.

"I'm not stupid," Chiswick pressed. "I have associates. They know I'm here, and they know why."

"They know you're here," Roger said, "but they don't know I'm here. I've been here since last night, waiting for you. I knew Valerie wouldn't leave the country without saying goodbye to her very best friend." He bared his teeth at Nickie, in a gruesome imitation of a smile. "And I've planned an escape. It's all been planned. I always plan."

My eyes widened as I stared at him. Behind him, in the lengthening shadows of the hall, a figure crept forward on silent feet. I couldn't see its face, but I knew it was Charlie.

"You're a bastard, Roger," I said. "You're a monstrous, egotistical bastard, and I guess I've always known that. But up until this moment I never really understood that you're also insane."

"Valerie!" Chiswick's voice was almost pleading.

"It won't be like killing a person," I said. "He's not a human being. He's an animal."

"It won't change anything."

"The hell it won't!" I said it loudly, surprising and momentarily confusing Roger. Charlie stopped in the hall, still several feet behind him. I pulled the gun out of my pocket and Roger's jaw dropped. In that moment of confusion, Charlie leaped forward and caught Roger with an arm under his neck, and probably a gun at his back. Roger let his own weapon drop to the floor. My aim was steady.

"Put the gun down," Chiswick said. "It's all over. It's finished."

"It's finished for you, but it isn't finished for me. Not while he's alive. Not while there's a chance he could make a deal and go free."

Chiswick made a slow and cautious shift, but I jerked my head in acknowledgment and he relaxed again, backing off. Charlie's attention seemed torn between Chiswick and me.

"He won't go free," Chiswick said, low and quiet, coaxing.

"You know how to lie."

"Yes," he said. "I do. We talked about that once, don't you remember? I said I would use you if I had to, but I wouldn't betray you. I had to use you, but I didn't betray you, did I?"

"Not yet." But there had been so much betrayal. Roger's.

"Valerie. Listen to me. I trusted you with my life today. There's a gun here, beside me, stuffed between the cushions. When you came down that hallway and pointed your gun at me, I could have shot you. I could have shot that gun out of your hand before you pulled the trigger. Do you believe that?"

I remembered the assault at the barn. The blood on my sleeve. The death of children. "Yes."

"But I didn't. I trusted you. I took that chance

because I couldn't lose you. And if you pull that trigger now, I'll lose you. I won't be able to save you if you kill him. I don't have the power to do that."

He had leaned forward a little. "Don't let him do it, Valerie. Don't let him win. I love you. Don't let him destroy that."

I had so wanted to hear him say that. I had wanted it more than anything in the world, but I wanted it to be true, not just a tactic in a tight situation. I couldn't see Chiswick's face. I couldn't *know*. I was in the dark again, in a car driving down the road, in a warehouse, blindfolded, walking up a bumpy flagstone path. "I can't see you," I said.

His movement was deliberately slow. "There will always be a degree of uncertainty," he said, rising to his feet. "There will always be times when you can't prove the truth. If you want to love you have to learn to trust." He crossed in front of Nickie, placing himself within my line of vision, although I didn't take my eyes from Roger. "I love you and I trusted you." He moved closer and closer toward Roger, and my line of fire. "If you love me, Valerie, you'll trust me." Then, with a single step, Roger's body was shielded behind his, and I let the gun fall from my fingers.

Epilogue

Chiswick closed the manuscript and let it rest on his chest, tilting his head back to get the full benefit of the sun.

"So what do you think?" I asked. I was resting with my arms on the tiled edge of the pool, my feet dangling in the cool water.

"I think there should have been a sex scene with Brendan on the way to meet Tom."

"There wasn't."

"There *could* have been," he grinned. "Brendan would have been willing. Anyway, this is a work of fiction, isn't it? The public likes a little extra slap-and-tickle."

"Well, you're too late. The final copy has gone to press. I'm due to hit the road in two months for the promotional circuit." I pulled myself out of the pool and sat down in the chair beside him. "How is Brendan? Did you see him last week?"

His eyes, behind the sunglasses, were probably annoyed. "I'm not going to discuss business with you. The less you know, the safer you are."

"I know, I know. I'm not asking you to discuss business. I'm asking how Brendan is."

"He's fine."

"Would anyone blow up the villa if you asked him

here for Christmas? Would armies march at the thought of the two of you under the same roof?" I held a wet arm over his bronzed stomach and watched the water drip off my fingers. I could tell by the tightness of his lips that he didn't like the idea.

"Brendan blew his cover for me," I reminded him.

"It wasn't his decision. He was just following orders."

"But it was his life. It was his home, and now he can't go back."

"Now he has a new life and a new home, and he's doing very well for himself."

"I know that. I know you've worked together since London. And no, I haven't been snooping. I just know. I know you're friends. I know if you asked him, he'd come." There was a long pause, and I knew I was getting closer. Felicity and Roger had simply disappeared from my life, and Nickie was isolated in prison. I had accepted that I would never see them again, but I was determined to keep contact with Fierlan.

"Brendan likes snow for Christmas."

"We could go to Switzerland. Switzerland has lots of snow."

"I'll talk to him about it. *If* neither one of us is working."

"Darling, you're not on active duty, you're in the reserve. You could say no. Even to the SAS, you could say no." I got no response from this, as I knew I wouldn't. He would say no for a number of reasons, if the job were too risky, or unnecessary, or not in the basic interests of the free world. He would even say no if the pay wasn't high enough, unless it was the SAS who were contracting. But if all of those conditions were met, I knew from experience that he wouldn't say no because the date on the calendar read December 25. I had found a tender and passionate lover and an interesting and loving companion, but I hadn't acquired a homebody. "Anyway," I continued, "why should Brendan give up his skiing just because you're working?"

A muscle twitched along his jaw and I knew I had him. "Aha!" I cried. "You're jealous. You're jealous of Brendan. You macho types are all alike. Tough on the outside, with a heart made of jello."

He rose just enough to grab me and pull me on top of him, a move I hadn't anticipated and wasn't fast enough to have avoided even if I'd wanted to. The lounge chair creaked beneath us. "You are a bloody irritating woman," he said.

I took off his sunglasses and kissed him. "But extraordinarily faithful. I just don't want to be alone at Christmas. Please."

"Well, hell," he relented. "If we're going to have a party, we might as well have Duncan and Dorrie, too."

I hugged him, and thanked him and then got up and started for the house. "It's all set then," I said happily. "Switzerland for Christmas." I turned, as if in afterthought. "Unless, of course, you want your child to be born in Britain."

I didn't manage to outrun him to the house, but it didn't bother me. I would never be a match for him, physically, but I would have my power, nevertheless. It had always been there.

THE ULTIMATE IN SPINE-TINGLING TERROR FROM ZEBRA BOOKS!

TOY CEMETERY (2228, $3.95)
by William W. Johnstone

A young man is the inheritor of a magnificent doll collection. But an ancient, unspeakable evil lurks behind the vacant eyes and painted-on smiles of his deadly toys!

SMOKE (2255, $3.95)
by Ruby Jean Jensen

Seven-year-old Ellen was sure it was Aladdin's lamp that she had found at the local garage sale. And no power on earth would be able to stop the hideous terror unleashed when she rubbed the magic lamp to make the genie appear!

WITCH CHILD (2230, $3.95)
by Elizabeth Lloyd

The gruesome spectacle of Goody Glover's witch trial and hanging haunted the dreams of young Rachel Gray. But the dawn brought Rachel no relief when the terrified girl discovered that her innocent soul had been taken over by the malevolent sorceress' vengeful spirit!

HORROR MANSION (2210, $3.95)
by J.N. Williamson

It was a deadly roller coaster ride through a carnival of terror when a group of unsuspecting souls crossed the threshold into the old Minnifield place. For all those who entered its grisly chamber of horrors would never again be allowed to leave—not even in death!

NIGHT WHISPER (2092, $3.95)
by Patricia Wallace

Twenty-six years have passed since Paige Brown lost her parents in the bizarre Tranquility Murders. Now Paige has returned to her home town to discover that the bloody nightmare is far from over . . . it has only just begun!

SLEEP TIGHT (2121, $3.95)
by Matthew J. Costello

A rash of mysterious disappearances terrorized the citizens of Harley, New York. But the worst was yet to come. For the Tall Man had entered young Noah's dreams—to steal the little boy's soul and feed on his innocence!

Available wherever paperbacks are sold, or order direct from the Publisher. Send cover price plus 50¢ per copy for mailing and handling to Zebra Books, Dept. 2708, 475 Park Avenue South, New York, N.Y. 10016. Residents of New York, New Jersey and Pennsylvania must include sales tax. DO NOT SEND CASH.

MYSTERIES TO KEEP YOU GUESSING
by John Dickson Carr

CASTLE SKULL (1974, $3.50)
The hand may be quicker than the eye, but ghost stories didn't hoodwink Henri Bencolin. A very real murderer was afoot in Castle Skull—a murderer who must be found before he strikes again.

IT WALKS BY NIGHT (1931, $3.50)
The police burst in and found the Duc's severed head staring at them from the center of the room. Both the doors had been guarded, yet the murderer had gone in and out *without having been seen*!

THE EIGHT OF SWORDS (1881, $3.50)
The evidence showed that while waiting to kill Mr. Depping, the murderer had calmly eaten his victim's dinner. But before famed crime-solver Dr. Gideon Fell could serve up the killer to Scotland Yard, there would be another course of murder.

THE MAN WHO COULD NOT SHUDDER (1703, $3.50)
Three guests at Martin Clarke's weekend party swore they saw the pistol lifted from the wall, levelled, and shot. *Yet no hand held it*. It couldn't have happened—but there was a dead body on the floor to prove that it had.

Available wherever paperbacks are sold, or order direct from the Publisher. Send cover price plus 50¢ per copy for mailing and handling to Zebra Books, Dept. 2708, 475 Park Avenue South, New York, N.Y. 10016. Residents of New York, New Jersey and Pennsylvania must include sales tax. DO NOT SEND CASH.

THE FINEST IN FICTION
FROM ZEBRA BOOKS!

HEART OF THE COUNTRY (2299, $4.50)
by Greg Matthews
Winner of the 26th annual WESTERN HERITAGE AWARD for Outstanding Novel of 1986! Critically acclaimed from coast to coast! A grand and glorious epic saga of the American West that *NEWSWEEK* Magazine called, "a stunning mesmerizing performance," by the bestselling author of THE FURTHER ADVENTURES OF HUCKLEBERRY FINN!
"A TRIUMPHANT AND CAPTIVATING NOVEL!"
— *KANSAS CITY STAR*

CARIBBEE (2400, $4.50)
by Thomas Hoover
From the author of THE MOGHUL! The flames of revolution erupt in 17th Century Barbados. A magnificent epic novel of bold adventure, political intrigue, and passionate romance, in the blockbuster tradition of James Clavell!
"ACTION-PACKED... A ROUSING READ"
— *PUBLISHERS WEEKLY*

MACAU (1940, $4.50)
by Daniel Carney
A breathtaking thriller of epic scope and power set against a background of Oriental squalor and splendor! A sweeping saga of passion, power, and betrayal in a dark and deadly Far Eastern breeding ground of racketeers, pimps, thieves and murderers!
"A RIP-ROARER"
— *LOS ANGELES TIMES*

Available wherever paperbacks are sold, or order direct from the Publisher. Send cover price plus 50¢ per copy for mailing and handling to Zebra Books, Dept. 2708, 475 Park Avenue South, New York, N.Y. 10016. Residents of New York, New Jersey and Pennsylvania must include sales tax. DO NOT SEND CASH.

TERROR LIVES!

THE SHADOW MAN (1946, $3.95)
by Stephen Gresham
The Shadow Man could hide anywhere—under the bed, in the closet, behind the mirror . . . even in the sophisticated circuitry of little Joey's computer. And the Shadow Man could make Joey do things that no little boy should ever do!

SIGHT UNSEEN (2038, $3.95)
by Andrew Neiderman
David was always right. Always. But now that he was growing up, his gift was turning into a power. The power to know things—terrible things—that he didn't want to know. Like who would live . . . and who would die!

MIDNIGHT BOY (2065, $3.95)
by Stephen Gresham
Something horrible is stalking the town's children. For one of its most trusted citizens possesses the twisted need and cunning of a psychopathic killer. Now Town Creek's only hope lies in the horrific, blood-soaked visions of the MIDNIGHT BOY!

TEACHER'S PET (1927, $3.95)
by Andrew Neiderman
All the children loved their teacher Mr. Lucy. It was astonishing to see how they all seemed to begin to resemble Mr. Lucy. And act like Mr. Lucy. And kill like Mr. Lucy!

DEW CLAWS (1808, $3.50)
by Stephen Gresham
Jonathan's terrifying memories of watching his three brothers and their uncle sucked into the fetid mud at Night Horse Swamp were just beginning to fade. But the dank odor of decay all around him reminded Jonathan that the nightmare wasn't over yet. The horror had taken everything Jonathan loved. And now it had come back for him!

Available wherever paperbacks are sold, or order direct from the Publisher. Send cover price plus 50¢ per copy for mailing and handling to Zebra Books, Dept. 2708, 475 Park Avenue South, New York, N.Y. 10016. Residents of New York, New Jersey and Pennsylvania must include sales tax. DO NOT SEND CASH.